IN THE DESERT

IN THE DESERT

a novel

Barbara Byar

Cowboy Jamboree Press
good grit lit.

First Edition
ISBN: 979-8-90271-700-3

This is a creative work. Any similarities to persons living or dead is coincidence.

No A.I. was used in the creation of this novel.

Cover Design: Ashling Lynch
Cover Photo: Keith Bernstein
Interior Design: Adam Van Winkle

Cowboy Jamboree Press
www.cowboyjamboreemagazine.com

Praise for Barbara Byar and **In the Desert**

"A propulsive, original and startling read. If the likes of Ford and Wolff had 'dirty realism', Byar — with her collection of misfits, dreamers and lost souls — is pioneering a path in 'dirty cosmic realism'. A striking debut."

–Noel O'Regan, author of *Though the Bodies Fall*, shortlisted for the James Tait Black Fiction Prize

"*In the Desert* is a wildly imaginative, all-encompassing, barn burner of a book! Byar knows the language of the desert, the harsh, sun-drenched days, as endless and mysterious as the universe itself, where anything is possible, even carnivals or a wish-granting phone booth materializing into thin air, ready to challenge the friendship of five young teenagers as they make their way through life. I am in awe of Byar's inventive, nonlinear narrative that pulls the reader in with rich, unsentimental prose, weaving a gripping tale of love, friendship, and betrayal in a dying world. It felt as if I were looking up at the night sky, witnessing the overlap of the multiverse, watching the death and rebirth of stars, contemplating the cost of a wish that may take your soul or grant you a soulmate. At once tender and hopeful, brutal and unforgiving, *In the Desert* is ultimately about never losing sight of what universally draws us together."

–Sabrina Hicks, author of *Coyote Girl*

"*In the Desert* evokes the danger and magic that lies in the parched landscape and in the restless hearts of those who live there. Barbara Byar's cinematic writing creates an electric portrait of lives spinning on their edge."

–Rónán Hession, author of *Leonard & Hungry Paul*, shortlisted for the Kerry Group Irish Novel of the Year

"*In the Desert* is the most wildly original and compelling novel that I've read in the last few years. Fans of Emily St. John Mandel, David Lynch, and Wim Wenders will find themselves right at home in this character-driven speculative adventure like no other. But be warned. Your heart will break. You will definitely shed a few tears. You'll be on the edge of your seat. And—most of all—your faith in love and the human spirit will be renewed."

–Casey Stegman, author of *Kill Current*

"*In the Desert* is like watching *Paris, Texas* and *Blood Simple* in 3D, on acid, at a blisteringly hot drive-in movie theatre. This is the American Dream turned bad and mean, the death of naive and youthful fantasy on tortured desert highways, the agony of lost love. It is dark, and so darned beautiful you will want to read it again and again. I swear, you will never forget this novel. It will haunt you, reinvigorate you, and make you believe that even at the end of all things cherished, true love can endure. Read it, love it, tell everyone about it. *In the Desert* is a true classic!"

–Jennifer McMahon, author of *Queen of Cork City*

"*In the Desert* is a wild fucking ride, man! Barbara Byar writes without fear and leaves nothing untouched: form, memory, time, love, death, and secrets. So many secrets. This novel invites you into a fever dream, one that will stay in your bones long after you wake up."

–Stephanie Austin, author of *Burn*

"A fever dream of dust-blown horizons, carnivals, quantum transporters, Hollywood ambition, and backroom abortions, *In the Desert* peels back the mysteries of its characters layer by layer, with one revelation giving way to another buried beneath. In her debut novel, Barbara Byar tells a story of shifting landscapes—geographic, temporal, and personal—where each turn of the page feels like dunes reshaping in the arid desert wind."

–Jonathan Danielson, author of *The Lowest Basin: Arizona Stories,* longlisted for the PEN America Robert W. Bingham Prize for Debut Short Story Collection

"With *In the Desert,* Barbara Byar blends raw, unsparing grit lit with the shimmer of the surreal, where a galactic carnival, complete with a two-headed dog, collides with the dust and heat of a southwest desert. But at its core *In the Desert* is a love story–of dreams chased, passions rekindled, a mother's fierce devotion, and a kind of cosmic, unexpected love that defies all earthly rules."

–Andrew K. Clark, author of *Where Dark Things Grow,* shortlisted for the North Carolina Book Awards Sir Walter Raleigh Award for Fiction

"Barbara Byar's *In the Desert* takes readers deep into the cold, dry night of an unnamed southwestern community, through time and space, and back again. Byar entwines so many threads for her group of friends and acquaintances and is masterful at tying them together by the end of the novel. Her storytelling and inventive twists defy genres and will keep you reading late into the night, when magical phone booths and whimsical carnivals are most likely to appear to offer a wish—for a price."

–Melissa Flores Anderson, author of *All and Then None of You.*

"Inventive, dark, and transcendently disorienting, *In the Desert* delivers a relentless narrative of love and loss. Wielding time and space with inventive force, Byar's voice is a knife: sharp, precise and cuts straight through to the heart of the matter. She brings us on a gritty, surreal journey of hope, examining what remains when everything else unravels."

–Charleen Hurtubise, author of *Saoirse*

"Compelling genre-bending tale of love, violence and hope at the end of the world."

–Claire Hennessey, author of *In the Movie of Her Life*

In the desert
I saw a creature, naked, bestial,
Who, squatting upon the ground,
Held his heart in his hands,
And ate of it.
I said, "Is it good, friend?"
"It is bitter—bitter," he answered;

"But I like it
"Because it is bitter,
"And because it is my heart."

Stephen Crane, 1895

PART ONE

An End

He runs, heavy breath puffing ghosts into the misty, desert air. They haven't found him yet, but they will. He must find her first. If nothing else, that.

Milky Way splashed like God's outcast children across the sky, moonlight glazes a milky cataract over dust and dirt, shrub and stones. Where is it? Where's the damn phone booth?

Eyes darting, head turning, he doesn't see the rock jutting from brittlebush. Trips. Ground meets him, cold and hard as he rolls from the landmine hiss of a disturbed rattler. No Jessie to save him this time—he gets bitten, he's a goner, and they won't have to shoot him, just watch him die.

He curls into an armadillo ball, cuffs his ears against the demon cackle of coyotes, the rumble of rolling thunder. Give up, you're no hero. It's hopeless, and if he's learned anything in his long, short life, it's that hope is what you cling to when you don't have the guts to pull the trigger.

You need to believe now, Raphael.

He never was much of a believer in anything except himself and look where that got him. Still, he's lived in the desert long enough to know strange comes and goes and magic proffers its wares whether you believe or not.

Fuck it. He gets up. Keeps going.

Shouts. Searchlights scour the sand, licking his heels. Dogs bark. A nightmare screech as drones drag race down from the mountains. Minutes. Only minutes before they reach him. Faster, now. Move. He's seen what they do, what they'll do to him, to them.

There! A silhouette on the horizon. He's found it. Finally.

The phone booth is cactus-clustered on three sides. Door open. Light off. She's leaning hard, head on top of the phone. She could be resting… or not.

Cold metal bites his palms as he grabs the edges of the open door. She falls into his arms—eyes ablaze, searchlights closing in, hounds rabid at their scent.

"Jessie." His voice is sand-blasted hoarse. Heart ragged. He gasps. Might puke.

"You found me."

"I will always find you."

He kisses her. World closing in, and all he wants is this kiss, and it can end. Right here. Right now. Sky fall or bullet rain, he won't feel a thing, only her dry lips warm against his, her skin hot under his desperate hands.

"Raphael. Raphael." She brushes his tears away with her thumbs.

Breath mists and glass fogs. He strokes her hair while sand blows in the open doorway, dunes at their feet. Her breath smells of stale smokes and pints of resignation, eyes star bright as she looks up at him on this desperate night. Eyes full of hope. Cause hope is always the last thing to die.

More shouts. Light slashes the booth.

He holds her. Will shield her from the future mere minutes away. He pulls her close, so close, not even death can come between them.

She pushes him away. "Close the door. Close it, now."

It won't budge. Door old and desert-dry, the hinges creak and groan, but it won't move, only rattle. He two-hands it, and the handle snaps off. Jessie falls to her knees. Digs out the rock crammed in the metal runner, dirty fingernails fracturing, breath panting.

"Now, Raphael."

He forces the accordion door closed. The light goes on overhead, a beacon for their bullets. They wheeze as they pass, ricochet off nearby rocks and send shale shards flying.

"Ain't no escape. Come out with your hands up." It's not his voice, but sure as shit, he's there behind them, darker than their past and just as relentless.

Jessie pulls Raphael up with one hand, picks up the receiver with the other. Doesn't drop it.

Dials.

And someplace,
somewhere,
in a dream,
as bullets rain like falling stars upon them,
someone answers.
And the wind begins to howl.

The Future

An Essay on the End of the World by Ryan Williams, aged 9 and three-quarters.

The end of the world will be full of surprises. There're all sorts of predictions—water all gone and the crops turned to dust, nuclear bombs, disease, dangerous people doing desperate things—something new every day, always the same story only told a different way.

This world is going to die.

Carl, the cook at the diner, has the talk radio station on every day and half the night. Mom tells him to turn it off cause Apocalypse Alex scares the customers, but Carl only turns it down. Apocalypse Alex has theories, what mom calls *conspiracies,* about how the world will end, but I reckon we won't know how we're gonna die until we do.

I'm only nine and three-quarters, but even I remember when things were better. When the sage and brittlebush bloomed, and the desert turned purple and yellow. All kinds of birds chittered and chattered, not just the vultures, and the howling of coyotes wasn't the only song you heard.

These days, there's not much water. Even Aunt Dakota has trouble finding any now. I can't remember the last time it rained. Maybe a year ago? Mom has a picture of me dancing in a puddle which I've attached. So much water all at once, I could splash. Couldn't truly believe it. Rain is good, but too much, too fast is bad. Causes flash floods nobody or nothing can escape. A roaring ocean appears all at once and washes the face of the earth away.

Aunt Dakota tells me not to be afraid of the apocalypse because if our world ends, another will begin. That in the death of civilization, magic can be reborn. Seems a load of Bible nonsense, but Aunt Dakota ain't no believer, so maybe what she says is true. Most of what Aunt Dakota says is.

I'd like to see some magic. I reckon magic is believing in what you can't see and seeing what you can't believe. Some nights when mom's asleep, I stand outside the front door of our place and watch the sky. Late, when even Carl, who lives in Number 10, is snoring in his rocking chair on the porch. I call it the magic time. The stars are so bright, the world so quiet. Time seems to stop, and I don't see constellations blinking, but doorways opening and closing.

The scientist down at the observatory—Mom says he's called an astrophysicist—comes into the diner. He has one coffee and a steak, no potatoes. Every single time. I keep trying to work up the nerve to talk to him, maybe see if he'll let me look through one of the giant telescopes, but Mom says he's from a place called Korea and can't understand our language. Not well, anyway, even with a translator app. But I've seen Aunt Dakota talking to him a time or two. They don't say much but seems to me they have an understanding.

Maybe I'll learn Korean. Maybe then, I can ask him about magic doorways that lead to other worlds. Worlds we can escape to when this one dies. Scientists don't believe in magic though, so maybe we're stuck here until time stops for good.

*

Jessie removes her bare feet from the plastic lawn chair and motions for Ryan to sit. It's hot on the landing but still cooler than inside. Better to broil than boil, she supposes.

"All done?"

He nods. Bites the cap off and hands his pen to her. "Can you please sign my homework journal?"

Jessie flips through his notebooks. Her kid is nothing if not smart. Soon, he'll be smarter than her. Who'll check his homework then?

"What's this?"

Ryan cranes his neck as she reads. "It's my essay. Miss Renard asked us to write about the future."

Miss Renard. The one who accused her son of using artificial intelligence to write his papers. Jessie had told her a few things about that.

"And you think the world is going to end?"

"That's what Aunt Dakota says. She's seen the signs; says we need to get ready."

Dakota and her damn portents. Jessie doesn't want to know what the future holds; she's got enough problems with the present. She puts a finger under Ryan's chin. Raises it till his big green eyes meet hers. If she could stop time right now, while he still believes anything she tells him, even when he knows it's a lie, she would.

"This world ain't ending any time soon, least not if I can help it. You hear me?"

He nods and smiles up at her. "Don't worry, Mom, anything happens, I'll protect you."

Jessie blinks back tears and scoops him into a tight hug. His hair is dirty, but the sweet baby smell lingers, same as his innocence. Won't be long before both are gone completely.

A car approaches down the main road, its shadow stretching in the late afternoon sun. A long, black sedan. Jessie rises, gathers Ryan's books and holds open the door to their apartment.

"Let's go inside, honey."

She locks the door. Heads to the window. The car is slow as it can be without stopping, but Jessie's not afraid. Not a chance.

"You okay, Mom?" Ryan's eyes are huge in the gloom.

She lets the curtains fall. Limp with dust, they smell of nicotine and polyester. A miracle they don't spontaneously combust. They do little to obscure the truck stop and diner across the street, which Jessie has been running for the past ten years along with the motel.

"I'm fine, honey." It isn't really a lie; you get used to anything given enough time and shortage of options.

The car stops. Jessie lights a cigarette and continues to watch it through the threadbare curtains. It's been a while, a week, maybe. She tries to forget, but it always returns to remind her. She's never seen the driver—he's not visible behind the tinted glass—but that sure as hell isn't the point. She stubs out her cigarette in the overflowing ashtray. Cheaper than food, though only barely, they take her appetite away, same as the heat and his drive-bys.

"Mom?" Ryan calls from the couch. It's covered by a blanket to hide the stains. She keeps meaning to replace it, same as the curtains. Neither is gonna happen any time soon.

Ryan doesn't complain. Ever. Not about living in the caretaker's apartment of a dying motel. Nor about wearing the same clothes to school, the cheap sneakers, or his long hair. The one time she tried to cut it; she only made it worse. He doesn't even complain about the sweltering heat cause the AC is broken, the fan is shit, and the curtains filter some of the sun but none of the heat.

"Hmm?" Jessie says.

"I'm thirsty."

It must be bad for him to even ask. She fishes through the past-due notices on the dinette table, finds the water card. Prays there's something on it, knows there isn't. Which is worse? Seeing his hope, or crushing it?

She's not due into the diner for a few hours yet. There's water there and food, but it's also low on supplies and high on debt. Soon, the black sedan won't be the only problem at her door.

"It's okay, Mom. I can wait." There's no sadness in his voice, no disappointment on his face, only acceptance.

The car drives off, but it will return. Tomorrow, next week, next month. It will sit outside her door long enough for her to wonder if this is the day the driver gets out. If it's the day she finally kills him.

Out of nowhere, a cloud appears in the vast blue sky and covers the sun near completely. She could use a fucking break, and rain would do nicely, thank you very much.

"Is it going to rain?" Ryan asks excitedly. But there's no thunder or air crackling, only a faint whiff of ozone.

"Don't think so, honey." Jessie brushes sweat-damp hair from her face. Heat builds till it bursts but that doesn't always mean rain. "Listen, I have to go see Dakota. I want you to stay up at the diner with Aunt Alice. She'll make you something to eat and give you some water. You can read your astronomy book at the counter."

There's no trucks at the stop, and only two cars in the lot. Business is slower and slower every day in this small oasis of something in the middle of nothing. Things will hopefully pick up later when passing truckers pull in for their dinner. After, like clockwork, the working girls down the short L of the motel will open their doors. Pa didn't used to allow such carry-on; Jessie has no choice. How anyone else chooses to survive is none of her business. She takes no cut from the girls, only the rent, and truckers pay fifty bucks for overnight parking. It gets business through the door. Sometimes, it's enough to keep everything going. Sometimes, not.

It's cooler at the diner but not much. The AC units have been on low for months, and the ceiling fans only push warmish air around. A cowboy eats a burger and fries at the counter, and a handful of teenagers are giving Maria their order. Two townies sit in a corner booth.

Alice catches sight of her from the kitchen hatch and wheels herself out. Her apron is speckled with blood and the arms of her chair with grease splatters. Sweaty, hair in a bun under a cap, sleeves rolled, her shoulders are as straight as her legs are bent. Everyone calls Jessie the pretty one, but Alice glows despite the grease.

"Hey, kiddo." Alice tucks Ryan's long hair back behind his ears. Frowns as her eyes crinkle. "Don't know why you insist on keeping this mop of hair." She winks and looks up at Jessie.

"You mind?" Jessie says, "I gotta catch Dakota before I come on shift."

Alice inclines her head towards the counter; Ryan scootches up onto one of the stools and pulls his books from his backpack.

"Can I please have a glass of water?" he says.

Maria returns and clips the teenagers' order on the ticket wheel for Carl, puts her pencil behind her ear and her ticket book in her apron before pouring Ryan a glass of cool water. He tries hard not to gulp it all down at once; Jessie's told him a thousand times it would give him stomach cramps.

Maria lifts the glass dome off the cake stand. "Saved the last piece of pie specially for you, young man."

Alice shakes her head. "Dinner first."

Jessie kisses Ryan on the cheek. "Mind your aunt. Love you."

He blushes and side-eyes the teens in their booth.

Back outside, the cloud has vanished, and the sun has begun its long descent. The truck stop, diner, and motel all sit on the edge of town, right off the last highway ramp and before the railway tracks. Further on, there's some empty grain silos, Dakota's place and eventually, the observatory. After that, nothing but miles and miles and miles of desert with only highway or train to get you through.

Jessie hears the trains at night. The hobos and illegals try to hop the long line of freight, but the cars are patrolled by armed drones that warn once, then shoot. Jessie's seen the bodies. Sometimes, they're collected, most times they're left for the vultures, the sun-dried bones in their floppy clothes, a warning.

Cheap sunglasses and a straw hat are better than nothing against heat and glare, but not much. Although Dakota's place is only a few minutes up the road, she really shouldn't walk, not in this heat, but why waste the gas. Sneakers sticking to steaming road tar, Jessie moves to the shoulder. Kicks up dust.

Dakota is home, but not in; she's around the back, fussing with her plants. She has more water than anyone else in town. Bought the land and drilled the well before even building the house. A mini oasis, there's even a tiny pond for the local wildlife. No fence, no wall to keep anyone in or out—how the critters gonna get through? —but at least Jessie convinced her to get a couple of guns to protect herself against any type of predator.

"It's hotter than hell on a Sunday." Dakota straightens from the purple sage she's been pruning, tosses her gloves on the table and gestures to Jessie to sit while she goes inside.

It may be hot, but it's always cooler here. Cool and calm. Crickets chirp on damp pebbles while desert hares drink from the pond. Dakota returns with some lemonade and a spliff dangling from coarse lips. Offers both. Jessie takes the lemonade. A long silence follows, which isn't like Dakota at all.

Dakota cracks her knuckles, then her back, and finally says, "Been a while."

Yes, it has. With good reason. Dakota is her father's stepsister, but she's also a reminder. A reminder of things Jessie keeps forgetting to forget.

"I'm sorry." And Jessie is. Nothing is Dakota's fault.

"I'm sure you got plenty to be sorry for, but none of it to me." She looks about to say more but doesn't, just reaches into her back pocket, pulls out a thick envelope and pushes it across the table.

It's not the first envelope Dakota's given her and will contain water vouchers, money or both. Sheltered under a gazebo, fan blowing cool, Jessie wishes she could close her eyes and ignore both the envelope and her need for it

"Can't I just visit?"

"Sure, you can. Any time, you know that." Dakota sits back and takes a long soft look at her. "Things have been tough, but they're getting tougher, aren't they?

Jessie nods. Thirst and hunger make desperate people do desperate things. "You sure you're safe out here?"

"Safe as anywhere. When my time comes, I'll have plenty of warning, so don't you worry about me."

They are quiet for a few minutes, maybe ten. The envelope loud between them. Jessie takes her time with the lemonade—sweet and tangy but, oh, so cold—it trickles down her throat. A warbling rock wren fills the silence.

"You used to sing pretty like that," Dakota says.

Jessie shrugs. "Yeah, well, I lost my song a long time ago."

Dakota stretches her long arms overhead. Pockets of flesh swing from her upper arms, and her jowls waggle as she shakes her head. She's not a big woman, only sun-worn and life-hardened.

"How's Ryan?"

"Good. Great. He's so smart. Smarter than I'll ever be. The principal says he'll definitely get into a top college. He wants to be a scientist. Lately, he's fascinated with the stars."

Dakota nods as if this is no news to her.

"He misses you. Why don't you come to the diner again soon? Have a meal with him."

The hares at the watering hole freeze. Jessie takes no notice—hares are afraid of their own shadow—but Dakota freezes as well, cocks an ear as if listening to the wind, but there is no wind. The air is stiller than still and eye-of-a-hurricane heavy with all hell about to break loose.

Dakota glances at the hairs standing up on Jessie's arms. "Do you feel it?"

Afraid to speak, Jessie merely nods as the windchimes begin to tinkle without the slightest breeze.

"We need to get to the diner."

Jessie has never seen Dakota run in her entire life, but she's running now. She's in her car, engine on, and passenger door open before Jessie has a chance to open her mouth.

It's bad. Whatever it is, it's bad.

Jessie climbs in and turns on the radio. There ain't much in the way of airwaves. The one local station plays mostly country and western and blues, but there's no music, only an announcement:

...madman on the loose. If seen, do not approach. The suspect is armed and extremely dangerous. Lock your windows and doors and contact law enforcement...

"Ryan." Jessie gasps and Dakota floors it, dust and gravel flying. "Please tell me it's not Ryan."

But Dakota says nothing, only drives faster.

All's quiet at the diner. Jessie forces herself to walk calmly across the parking lot. Six o'clock. The door should be slapping open, truckers hoisting their jeans under full bellies and belching, teenagers giggling over their phones and sneaking a smoke. Six o'clock when Matty and his wife, Ethel come in for their daily coffee and pie.

It's quiet. Too quiet.

"THE SONG!"

It isn't a voice so much as a sonic boom. Loud but not nearly as loud as the subsequent shattering of the window and cascade of glass when a table jukebox comes crashing through. It skitters across the parking lot, selection reels flipping and flapping.

"The song! Play the song!"

They see him through the broken glass—tall, broad, and demented. He stamps up and down the aisle, clutching his head, roaring. Jessie doesn't hesitate, but Dakota holds her back, grasping her bare, sweaty arm and pulling her close.

"Wait, Jessie."

"I ain't waiting. Ryan's in there. Alice... Maria... Carl..." Chest tight, heart frantic, she shrugs Dakota off and runs.

Inside, the diner is still except for the tornado of a man spinning in the aisle with a .50 cal. Kids in two booths, Matty and Ethel in another. No one moves, not even the truckers at the counter, heads bent over their soup bowls; they'll be carrying, for sure. Maria's got her hands in her apron behind the counter. No sign of Carl or Ryan.

Alice is at the condiment station filling ketchup bottles, eyes wide when she spots Jessie. The man sees Jessie next and grabs her with one hand, Desert Eagle in the other. He's big as fuck, dressed in dusty blue coveralls with BARTHOLOMEW stitched in red thread on his breast pocket. Eyes spinning, breath rancid, he's either high as a kite, a complete lunatic, or both.

"The song. Play the song."

No one has moved, but a song starts playing on one of the smashed-up table jukeboxes. He shoots it three times before it falls silent. That booth is empty, but either side of it are the schoolkids. They'd run if they could. Hide. They would know that much, but there's no room to move in the aisle, only die.

The law pulls up outside with a slow crunch of gravel. Joshua Thomas emerges, pushes back his cowboy hat, and spits before Dakota approaches him. All in five minutes, but it seems five years.

Jessie smiles, speaks slow as a brake squeal before a crash, though inside she's screaming. "Bartholomew..."

He freezes at the sound of his name. Pulls her closer. He's all sweat and slick, his breathing short and shallow as if he's run a long distance or is about to cry.

"Tell me the song, and I'll sing it for you."

He lets her go, and the raised gun falls limply to his side. Behind him is Ryan, her not yet ten-year-old son. He holds the diner gun, which is kept under the butcher block in the kitchen. He can barely lift it even with both trembling hands.

Jessie tries not to react. Fails. Grabs at Bartholomew's gun as he turns towards her son. Holds it just long enough for Carl to appear, shielding Ryan and taking his gun.

Shots ring out. Two bodies fall.

Jessie screams and screams and screams.

"The song. Will you sing it?" What's left of Bartholomew's face is mere inches from her own. Blood spurts from between his remaining teeth as Jessie's screams become gasps. The pain in her side is immense, somehow worse than childbirth. Worse even than him leaving. *Where are you, Raphael? Where are you now that I'm leaving too?*

She knows nothing but his name as she screams it one last time, and as her eyes close, slowly but inexorably, all she hears is his voice, and all she sees is that one perfect day...

One Perfect Day

It was one of those days when the sky gathered, and the air crackled in warning. Raphael drummed his fingers on the steering wheel along to the radio, but there was only one Stairway to Heaven, and it was between Jessie's thighs. He only hoped to God he'd finally climb it soon.

He turned the radio off and listened to the music of the desert blowing through the open window. "You hear that?" he said. Over road rumble and under her steady breathing, there was the faint trill of carnival music.

Jessie stuck her head out the window. Wind whipped her long hair, and she gasped from the thrust and thrum of it. Waved her hands and hooted. She laughed and settled back in her seat. Her chest hummed, rising and falling as it did when they kissed, and the wind was knocked out of both of them.

"I hear nothing but the wind," she said.

Should he tell her? Probably not. Best to change the subject, but he couldn't help himself. "Remember the phone booth Dakota told us about when we were kids? Near the carnival? The one at the end of the world? Where dreams come true?"

Jessie picked at a dirty hangnail. Bit it off. Grimaced at the short, sharp sting of torn flesh. "Yeah, but nightmares are dreams too."

"That's the challenge," he said, chest hairs glistening through his wifebeater. "It's like roulette, we just gotta dial the right number."

Bare feet on the dashboard, sundress surfing her hips, Jessie smoked a Marlboro Red to get his taste from her mouth. Raphael hit the indicator for Exit 33, but Jessie flicked it off with her big toe.

"Let's keep going and never stop. Not till we find it," she said.

Raphael nodded, eyes on the road, mind on her. He rubbed the chin stubble that had sandpapered her neck, while she scratched at mosquito bites on her ankles. When they were younger, they searched for years for that phone booth and never found it, but their belief persisted because in the middle of nothing, you had to believe there was something.

Jessie startled cat stiffened. "I hear it." She looked at him through a haze of honey-blonde hair, one eye meeting his in excitement. "The song."

The music was wonder and, in the wonder, warning and beyond the warning, welcome. Jessie squeezed his thigh and grinned. Raphael brushed the hair from her face, kissed her quick and put his foot down on the accelerator.

Steered towards the storm.

Back in Time

Raphael is lost but doesn't want to be found. It will be his last night at the Hollywood motel. Out of options, out of time, he needs to get out of town. Doesn't want to do this shit anymore. Once did, but no more. Gonna check out and check out for good.

The cab drops him on the corner, and he stumbles the rest of the way. Streets slow, air thick, the homeless camped under the fire escape are quiet except for snores, hiccups, and coughs. He makes it as far as the building, then slumps with his back against the motel wall. Once his head stops spinning, he'll summon the strength to get to his room. In the meantime, he'll pretend the sidewalk mist is dream dust and hope he never wakes.

"Good night?"

Despite his proximity, the speaker is dark in the darkness. The only thing clear about him are the whites of his eyes and the smell.

"Had worse," Raphael replies, which is no lie.

The man holds out a street-mottled hand and in it, a pack of crisp, white smokes. American Spirit—homeless fella with organic smokes—LA, go figure. He shakes one out, and Raphael takes it, cupping his hands around the man's lighter from habit more than need, for the air is still and muggy. The man's breath is not liquor-laced and fetid, but surprisingly sweet, as if he'd eaten a bag of Skittles or drank a Slurpee.

Raphael nearly vomits at the smell, but there's nothing left in his guts. He takes a drag, head back against the wall, legs splayed in front of him.

"You been out here long, man?" he says, but the homeless fella's eyes are closed, his smoke burnt to ash between singed fingers.

For a moment, he thinks the man is dead—he certainly looks dead—but his breath keeps locomoting sugar-sweet tang in slow, measured exhalations as his head lolls onto Raphael's shoulder, and he begins to snore.

Few cars pass and even fewer people. Raphael has no idea what time it is, only that it's late. It's very fucking too late. His pickup is in the parking lot with a tank full of gas, but there's no going back, no going forward. Only down. How low you gonna go, Raphael boy? How low? There's still sinking to be done, but he'll check out before then. Tonight, maybe.

The moon is high and bright. He remembers a moon, their moon. A million years ago, it seems, and it might as well be. If only he could go back in time, back to then, back to her.

He flicks the cigarette butt into the gutter, reaches in his pocket for his wad of cash, peels off two hundreds and shoves them in the bum's inner coat pocket then closes his eyes. Finds no comfort there. He fades, trying to remember the last time he was happy, not Hollywood happy, but truly happy—back before he'd ever thought of leaving her—when the scream bolts him to consciousness. It carries over the valley, loud and clear and chilling.

"Hey." He shakes the bum awake.

The guy stirs. Grumbles.

"You hear that?"

The guy cocks his head, scratches his ear. "Hear nothing, man."

"You can't hear that?" It is no longer a scream but screaming and somewhere in the shrill despair of the sound, Raphael hears his name.

And then, it stops.

He scrambles to his feet. Somehow, makes it to his room. Steps over the designer clothes moldering in piles, the half-empty to-go boxes and empty bottles. He strips and showers, ears ringing while hot water pelts him. It's been ten years, but he'd recognize Jessie's voice anywhere.

There's some credit left on his burner phone. Enough. He spends what's left of the night making phone calls which go unanswered. He leaves no messages. Types no texts. There's only one plan and that is go.

The mattress sags as he sits on the edge of the bed, and the springs groan. Maybe just a quick nap, and he'll set out in the morning. The night, the week, the ten years finally catch up with him, and he passes out on the bed as the world spins towards day and blankets him in light.

*

Air full of portents even an unbeliever can't deny, Raphael drives the deserted highway. He doesn't believe in Gods or hell's myriad demons, but there's plenty of both in the desert. Maybe they'll commune with the ones he's brought with him; leave him the fuck alone.

Low sun so bright, his seaside eyes burn even behind Ray-Bans. He's been driving four hours and will be driving three more. Nothing to see, nothing to do, he turns on some tunes to drown out the memories threatening to burst through his unfortunate state of sobriety. He's alone in the car except for one suitcase and a gun with two bullets. Not enough ammo to do much good, not out here—there's always a cop, a killer or a trucker on the road—but enough to do the job that might need done.

He floors it; he's about ten years late, but better than never. He'd left cause he had to. Would have shriveled like shed snakeskin. Blown away. It was a mistake, he knows that now, but there's no undoing, only done.

Heat seeps heavy through open windows, road rumble drumbeat to a thready eight-track. He left with this pickup, and now he's returning in it. If she's still there, she'll recognize it. If not, he'll find her, and they'll find *it*.

Everything will be okay then. Nothing undone but everything fixed.

Time passes, but the scenery remains consistently bleak until the sun goes down, and the moon comes up, and the vast empty provokes imaginings. Tired as a washed-up movie star with no more skin to tighten, his eyes wander, see things. Flashes. Some might be real, some not. All are dangerous. There're phantoms out here, and if you stare long enough, they solidify. Race you to the end of nowhere, pull you into the rising fog.

There's no radio signal, only coyote cackle. No passengers to keep him awake. No light in the endless stretch of darkness, only passing trucks lit up like Christmas trees. White lines. Broken, solid. He drives so far, so fast, so straight, it's all the same.

He splashes water from a crumbled bottle onto his face. Slaps himself to come around. A freight train keeps him company for a while, rumbling alongside the interstate until finally, when there's more demons than ghosts closing in—riding the windscreen, clinging to the roof and howling—Exit 33 gleams in his high beams. That last hope before the end-of-his-world rises in anticipation. Tears pool in his mind, but the map to his eyes was lost long ago.

The slow slide of the ramp takes him to the heel of town. There's not much left. The desert has claimed most, time, the rest. Paint sun-faded, roofs dust-blown, fences leaning, water towers toppled. He passes the motel on one side—flickering neon sign a siren to a plague of kamikaze bugs—and the truck stop/diner on the other, dark and boarded up.

What happened?

He keeps on, too unnerved to stop and investigate. No other lights except at Tom's. Tom is still behind the bar, the regulars around. No one seems surprised to see him. No one happy either. It's the same as he remembers it, back when the four friends—Raphael and Jessie, Travis and Sarah—sat in a corner booth and ordered white Russians with tequila backs, cause it sounded exotic. Travis always the one to eat the worm to impress the girls but mostly grossing them out.

Sarah. Gone, what? Ten years now?

He decides to have one drink. Just one. Prepare himself mentally to find what is to be found. Tom is already pouring it, a white Russian. What kind of life is it to remember someone's drink from ten years ago? Impressive or sad?

Raphael takes it, shakes Tom's offered hand. "Still remember, huh?"

"What else I got to think about?" Tom slaps the bar towel over his shoulder. All the hair on his head seems to have migrated to his eyebrows and ears. His teeth are tobacco-tarred, and his smile is still more grim than grin.

There's a ball game on the one TV. Their team is losing. Some things never change, not the losing nor the shitty ceiling fans which blow more warm air than cool, not the dusty top-shelf bottles, nor the worn elbow whorls on the bar. Even Tom looks the same, only leaner and balder. The only new thing is the unframed and unsigned poster hanging pride of place on the wall leading to the toilets.

"Well, well, well, look what the dust blew in."

Raphael doesn't need to see him to identify the voice. He turns on his stool nonetheless, fast enough to make his aching head spin once more.

Travis strides over to him, slow but intent. "Christ, you look like shit."

Woozy, dizzy and probably dying, Raphael slides from his stool. Luckily, Travis catches him before he hits the ground.

"Man, what the fuck?"

Travis drags him to a dark booth and splashes some water on his face. Ice cubes catch at his shirt collar, slide down his back, cool him quicker than the nicotine-lacquered fan rotating slowly overhead.

"Got a smoke?"

The table wobbles as Travis reaches in his pocket and pulls out a pack and a silver lighter. Lights two, offers one. Raphael takes a long pull. Inhales. Coughs up half a lung.

Instantly feels better.

"How's Hollywood?"

Raphael shrugs.

Travis points to the movie poster. "All anyone's seen of you since you left."

The poster is simple: a phone booth in the middle of the desert. In it, a couple cling to each other as if their lives depend on it, and they do. The movie made him a star. For a hot minute.

Tom puts two beers and a shot of whiskey in front of Travis and retreats to the bar. Travis mauls the neck of one of the beers with a big hand while he waits for an explanation.

"Thought it best to make a clean break," Raphael says finally. That's right, you coward, lie.

Travis meets his eyes and holds them. Never would have done that before. "Clean, huh? Well, you left some mess behind."

He knows it's not what Travis means, but he's never done drugs. Not on purpose. Only the mickie they slipped him that horrible night.

Travis finishes his smoke and grinds it out in the ashtray. Straightens. He appears inclined to leave, pretend he never saw Raphael, but something's itching its way out of his chest, and he'll probably never sleep again if it doesn't come out. "The movie…your idea?"

It's really Dakota who deserves the credit, she told them the story, but Raphael took it all for himself. She's funny that Dakota, can find a drop of water on a rolled dirt plain with nothing more than a couple of sticks. Weren't many drops back then, fewer these days. She was old when he left and must be ancient now. Old enough to have lived every strange story she ever told, including the one about the phone booth.

And the carnival…

Once Upon a Time

"The desert is full of danger but also magic and the more magic there is, the greater the danger. Some enchantments are worth the risk, others not, because no matter how clever you think you are, you are not clever enough. No one is."

Dakota settled upon her low stool and adjusted her long red skirt with its dust-laced hem, frill cuff unravelling. The children gathered round. They sat on fruit-market crates, feet bare or sandaled. There were five. Always had been, always would be, that's the blood oath they swore—a needle prick, a tower of hands, three shakes and the bond was born. Eyes eager, they sipped fresh lemonade from jam-jar glasses.

Dakota sipped her own lemonade, which may or may not have also contained tequila. She looked at each of them, one by one: Raphael, Jessie, Travis, Sarah, and Alice. All but Alice born under the same moon. The children loved her stories, and she loved the children for she had none of her own.

"The desert is a place of magic and mystery, because the fewer steps man has taken upon the land, the more magic can grow. But magic, you must understand, is neither good nor bad, only possible. It's how you use it that counts."

It was the spring the four eldest turned ten and 'possible' stretched before them limitless as their imagination. Dakota's gaze settled on Raphael first as most eyes did. He was a quiet child who read more than spoke, but when he did speak, strange notions came forth: how he could hear the song of the scorpions or talk to the man on the moon. Raphael was a beautiful child, his green eyes as wide as his wonder, but he was not without his faults.

"Tell me, Raphael," Dakota said, "what do you want more than anything else?"

Most would have answered straight away, because everyone, child or adult, harbors a dream—that one thing they want more than anything—but know only a miracle or magic will make it come true. Like bringing your parents back to life.

Raphael straightened his hunched shoulders, closed his heavy lids and looked deep inside before answering.

"I want to be remembered," he said at last, "I want to be famous."

Dakota made no comment, only moved onto Jessie who sat next to him as usual.

"I don't want to be poor," she said. Not rich, just not poor. "Have enough to take care of my family…" She looked around at the others, "and my friends."

Sarah would save all the animals, and Travis would be a boss so no one would ever tell him what to do again.

"What about you, Alice?" Dakota said.

Alice was Jessie's younger sister and tagged along everywhere Jessie went. She was tolerated but not encouraged and always felt an afterthought to the main group.

"I want to be loved," she said, crossing her heart and blowing the words up and out into the sky.

Dakota nodded while she fingered the lapis lazuli beads hanging around her neck. They'd all answered much as she expected. Each desire feasible without magic, but an impossibility in their childish minds and circumstances. "All worthy aspirations. Now, what if I told you there is a place where your dreams can come true?"

The children stopped fidgeting and leaned in close.

"A place you can only find in the desert."

"Where, Dakota? Where?" they asked as one.

"Settle down, and I will tell you."

She began…

"Once upon a time, a time long ago, a phone booth appeared in the desert. It had a proper phone with a dial tone and everything, and if you dialed the right number, your dreams would come true."

Travis scoffed. "In the desert? Ain't no phone booth in the desert." He had been sitting at the edge of his crate, eyes aglow, sweat beading a trail through the dirt on his face.

"Some say it's a myth, but I've seen it with my own eyes. Once. It comes and goes and will only materialize for those in the most desperate need."

"What's the right number?" Raphael said.

"Ah, now that's the million-dollar question…"

Alice spoke up. "How do we find it, Dakota? How?"

"It will only be found when it wants to be found... it might never come again, but if it does, and you're lucky enough to find it, you must be careful, because the phone booth is never on its own."

Dakota told lots of stories, most of them just that: stories, legends and myths, and other imaginings. The children—even Travis, despite his protestations, believed most of them because that's what children do. Though it seemed unlikely there was an actual magical phone booth which came and went, the possibility was a powerful lure, and each child was already plotting how to find it.

"It only appears near the carnival," Dakota said.

"A carnival? With rides and games and stuff? In the desert?" Sarah had been quiet for some time now, but she was fond of adventure—what most adults called mischief—and discovering a carnival in the middle of the desert would be the best adventure. Ever.

"Yes. With all that, but more. And the more of it is this: the carnival is bright and shiny and gleeful, but if you ever hear the Ferris wheel music, you must plug your ears immediately and run away, fast and far. For while the phone booth is all possible good… the carnival is all possible bad."

The Second Time He Almost Died

"She's gone." Travis downs his whiskey and puts on his cowboy hat. "Ain't nothing or nobody here for you now, Raphael."

"Wait."

Travis looks down at Raphael's desperate hand on his arm. Removes it. "Don't do what you or anyone else tells me anymore. Those days are over."

Raphael's face flushes.

"You only ever thought of yourself, you know that? Even now, you're worried cause you need her, not whether she's okay."

That stings. The truth always does.

"How's your brother?" Raphael's low voice is calm in the certainty of retaliation.

Silence. If Raphael wasn't already intent on dying, he might have been afraid.

Eyes hard and lips curled, Travis stares at him for some time before he smiles just wide enough to show the tips of his teeth. "He's gone too."

Once Travis leaves, Raphael returns to the bar. Orders another whiskey which he downs in one gulp.

"That right, Tom? Everyone gone?"

He doesn't expect an answer but gets one.

"Alice is over at the motel. She's running things best she can on her own, not that there's much business, what with the diner and all."

"What happened?"

Tom pours him another, then one for himself.

"Some lunatic shot the place up a few months back."

A few months? The heat in the bar stifles, but a chill frosts Raphael's neck. "Jessie?"

"She was hurt pretty bad, was in the hospital a good while, took every cent they had and then some. Nothing left to put the place back together. So, she went off to find some."

"I had no idea."

Tom looks over to the movie poster. It's not old but already the edges are curling, the white bits yellowing. "Sure. You've been busy."

Raphael doesn't try to explain how his head got caught up in the cloud climb. The questionable things he did to get to the top, the unforgivable things he did to try and stay there. His spectacular fall.

"Yeah," is all he says.

Tom sets the bottle before him, fills his glass every time it's empty. When the game is over, so is the night. He pours a last one for the road.

"On me."

When Raphael wakes some hours/days/weeks later, he finds himself face down on a paisley bed cover, puke congealing in his hair. He lays there awhile, listening to the slow pace of passing cars and the low hum of the ceiling fan. His head has felt worse but not much. How he got here, or even where here is, are not questions he knows the answers to.

Eventually, the stink of vomit is enough motivation to overcome the pain in his head, and he rolls over. Gets up. Immediately pukes again. This time he makes it to the trash can.

Sun seeps through threadbare curtains. Late morning? Who cares. He's sorry he woke. Sorry he didn't choke to death on his own puke like the movie star has-been he is.

Now, he'll finish the job.

He'd taken his shot, shot his load, but it was time to face facts, the music, a barrel. No hope or even rumor of it. Only the constant refrain of regret: coulda, shoulda, woulda.

Didn't.

The gun is still in his satchel. Whoever moved him didn't move it. Everything's still there—money, pills, knife—all the fucking options.

He hoped to see her one last time but that's not going to happen, and it's probably for the best. His shoulders sag and the bedsprings creak under him. All motel rooms are basically the same, but this one is oddly familiar. He checks the number on the door, sun atom bomb blasting when he opens it. There're people about. Their voices are wordless warbles, real life a cartoon on crack, as he stares at the room number.

I love you, Jessie.

Her laugh is windchimes in a sudden breeze.

Are you sure, Jessie?

She takes his hand and pulls him into Room 33. Closes the door and opens her arms.

Raphael slams the door. Takes in the room: the faded painting of the mountains, the bed massage coin box, the bedspread, the carpet brown as wet dirt, worn and torn in places, threadbare in others. Christ, was it all still the same?

Yes. Here. It was here.

He pulls out the gun. Gotta finish the job before memories finish him. He cocks it. Puts it to his head. Closes his eyes.

Is darkness the last thing you're gonna see, you miserable bastard, the last?

He opens his eyes. There's a drawer. Half open. *Who opened the drawer?* He didn't. His finger twitches on the trigger. Who the fuck cares? Do it. Now. *What's in the damn drawer?*

He puts the gun down.

A bible? A motherfucking bible? He tosses it on the bed. The pages flutter. Settle. Not gonna look. There's no sign at the end of his world. No sir. No way. No how.

He looks.

It's open to the beginning, a blank page filled with a familiar scrawl:

Dear Raphael,

I reckon you'll never see this. How could you? You've moved on to bigger and better things. I went up to Tucson when your movie came out. You were so good. So handsome. You did it. I'm so proud of you, baby. All of us are.

It hasn't been so good here. Hard times rolled into town, squatted in my life and haven't left. I thought about checking out. Thought about it long and hard, but I've too many people depending on me, and I can't. I want to, but I can't. Ain't that the sorriest thing you ever heard?

I told you to never come back, and I hope you never do. You're bigger than this small place, bigger than the desert and all its horizons. You don't belong here. You never did.

When I said I didn't love you anymore, that was a lie. I'll love you till the day I die. But I couldn't go with you, and I didn't want to hold you back. I was right, even though I never felt right without you.

I gotta go now, too. I'm scared. More scared than I've ever been, but I gotta do what I gotta do. If ever we meet again, I'm gonna hold you so close. Tell you, I love you, always and forever.

And remember, no matter where you are in the world, we will always have this room.

Jessie

PART TWO

The Start of it All

In the desert, back when things still grew, they drove out to the old ship boneyard. Jessie and Raphael in front, Travis, Sarah, and Alice on the bed of the pickup. It was March, the month between cold and hot and either snow or sunburn likely.

There was once a lake of some sort or another out about ten miles northeast of town. It had dried up same as everything else in that part of the world and left a bunch of boats high and dry. There were hazard warnings posted all around, but the sun had bleached those white, same as the wooden hulls whose planks sprang like the bones of beached whales. Not that the local kids paid any attention to the warnings anyway.

Each generation captained a ship, and Raphael and Travis had picked the biggest one, not because of its size or fiberglass hull, but for the fact it had settled on an even keel. There were two bunks, Raphael called dibs on one, Travis the other. Once they checked for snakes and scorpions, repaired loose boards and brought some old blankets and couch pillows, they had themselves a glorified sand yacht.

They'd never stayed overnight, not once. Mostly due to Dakota's warnings about Átahsaia, Dzoavits, and other old creeps who ate young souls. Not to mention the skinwalkers. The older they got, the less inclined they were to actually believe in such things, but better safe than soul meat.

"This is how every teen horror movie starts, you know that, right?" Sarah glanced first at Jessie, who shrugged, then steadily at Raphael, who laughed, until her eyes settled on Travis. "Right?"

Travis took her hand. "I promise we'll be gone before dark."

Raphael and Jessie winked at each other.

They spent the better part of the morning on deck sipping soft drinks and eating packed sandwiches, Travis and Sarah sat on one blanket, Jessie and Raphael on another, with Alice alone on a third.

It was that spring morning Alice first noticed how close the others sat. How they looked at each other and no one else. Spoke in whispers and side-looks. She lay back and closed her eyes against it.

Alice's mind drifted. As the sound of their laughter faded, a yearning so strong came upon her, amplified by the empty half of her blanket. She thought not of any particular boy, certainly none from school, but of an imaginary hero come to rescue her from this dull existence where nothing ever happened unless you made it up in your head.

And what she made up in her head, what she dreamed of behind closed but not sleeping eyes, was this…

She stands on a cliff perched over a vast sea. There is a breeze, but it is not windy. Summer dress and bare feet in tall meadow grass, it is warm without being hot. Everything is alive or being born. Hand shielding against sun, there, on the horizon, a ship. Not a new ship, but old, with sails unfurled and bow protruding and upon it, a young man. Not just a young man but one tall and fair with gentle eyes and strong arms. He's searched all seven seas and as their eyes impossibly meet from across the water, he's found her.

He dives from the ship for he cannot wait another second after searching all his life, and she rushes down the hillside steps for she cannot wait another second after yearning all of hers. They stare at each other a thousand years, him soaking wet, her eyes full of tears. He touches her face, and her tears drop from the tenderness of it, as he scoops her in his arms, and they fall together to the sand.

Alice opened her eyes though she didn't want to. She wanted to cling to her daydream as long as she could, but an unexpected cloud had veiled the sun, and she was startled awake by a sudden chill.

"Guys?" She was alone on the deck, the air thick with ozone menace. Her watch said four; it wasn't late-dark, but storm dark.

She scrambled below, nearly smacking her head on the companionway hatch. Called her sister, Sarah, the boys, to warn them. Flung open a door and there was Jessie half-undressed, boobs popping from her bra, Raphael hard in her hand as he kneaded her breasts. Both moaning.

Eyes glued to each other, they took no notice of Alice until she screamed.

"Oh, shit." Raphael fumbled with his pants, struggling to pull them over his erect penis.

"Fucking hell." Jessie pulled down her shirt, tits bouncing.

Alice didn't wait as they scrambled to sort themselves out, cursing and mumbling. Couldn't. Wouldn't. She ran.

The sky was furious overhead when she emerged from the berth. She'd never be able to look at either of them again, let alone get back in the truck with them. No way. She'd rather die. She pulled out her phone to call Pa. Prayed for a signal she wouldn't find.

"Alice!"

Alice ran.

*

"Oh shit, shit. Shit." Jessie was out the cabin door before Raphael could even get his dick back in his pants. "Hurry, Raphael."

He sighed and raised his hands in exasperation: "What the actual hell do you expect me to do here?"

Sarah poked her head out from the other cabin looking every bit as disheveled as Jessie still felt. "What's the commotion?"

"Alice… shit… Alice opened the door on us."

Sarah's eyes widened. She quickly buttoned her shirt and slipped on her sneakers.

"What's the big deal?" Travis said as he tried to pull Sarah back into their cabin. "I told you not to bring the kid. All she does is cause trouble."

Both girls ignored him.

"She ran off. I'm going after her," Jessie said over her shoulder as she climbed above deck.

Raphael finally emerged, fully clothed but tent-poled. Sarah and Travis laughed.

Raphael rolled his eyes. "Grow up."

Travis looked down. "Seems you've done enough growing for all of us," he said, and even Raphael laughed.

"I'm going after Jessie."

"Seriously? Where is Alice going to go? There's nothing out here for miles."

"Exactly. Either of them gets lost, we'll never find them once it gets dark. Now, if you don't want to spend the night out here, get in the truck."

Soon as the words left his mouth, the truck's engine roared to life.

"Fuck." Raphael scrambled to deck only to catch Jessie peeling away, hand waving out the window. He sat with a thump on an over-turned fruit crate.

When Travis and Sarah emerged, bits of sunlight clutched the hills under an angry sky. Either darkness or storm was about to fuck up everyone's day completely.

"Look, there." Sarah had the best eyesight of all of them and pointed out a cloud of dust. "Must be the truck."

The sound of a horn echoed across the flatlands and reverberated in the distant hills.

"Let's go," Raphael said.

*

Alice was the first to see the lights. The minute the sun went down, they popped up—ping, ping, ping—in the distance, all the colors neon bright and twinkling.

She'd run so fast and far she couldn't get her bearings. Hands on thighs and breathing hard, one thing was certain, it wasn't town. Town had no spinning, swirling structures, no fancy lights except the motel sign and a string of old Christmas lights they never took down at Lincoln's Supermarket.

She was hopelessly lost. Dead tired, thirsty and dressed only in jeans and a bright orange T-shirt, she'd freeze if she didn't find shelter. There were no stars to navigate in the sky full of clouds, no signposts or traffic, only the bright lights and the faint trill of carnival music.

*

"Fuck. Fuck. Fuck." Jessie smashed the horn with each expletive. What had she been thinking? Even with a 4x4, going off-track was dangerous at best, deadly, at worst, and here she was, alone in the middle of who knew where, wheels spinning in sand.

No phone signal. No sign of Alice or the others. She'd never shift Raphael's truck on her own, certainly not before dawn. She leaned on the horn so the others could find her and hoped with all her might nothing else did.

It was while she was smoking her third cigarette that she saw the lights. Despite appearances to the contrary and the opinion of her teachers, Jessie was not stupid. Not at all. She was mostly just disinterested in schoolish things: algebra, science, Spanish—though she spoke it frequently—all of it bored her. All except history. There was something about studying the past and its endless repetitious cycle of war and evolution that fascinated her. Here in the desert, life was a constant battle, and those lights meant only one thing—she was going to have to fight.

Night fallen; stars obscured. She tried her phone again. Nothing. No signal. No sign of the others.

No choice.

*

Travis kicked one of the half-buried tires. "You've got to be kidding me."

Sarah was already shivering at that point. Raphael pulled a blanket from the flatbed and wrapped it over her shoulders. She'd always been thin but lately her cheeks and collarbones jutted.

"Hey. Hey." Travis squeezed between the two of them. "I'll do that, thanks very much." He tightened the blanket around Sarah and kissed her on the forehead. "You want to wait in the cab while we have a look around?"

"What's that?" Raphael said, pointing to the lights.

*

The lights weren't as far as Alice thought. In fact, they seemed to be moving closer to her rather than her to them. There were many optical illusions in the desert, and this was probably just another, but the spinning Ferris wheel, whirling teacups, musical merry-go-round and thunderous roller coaster were a bit too loud and elaborate to be mere illusion. She pinched herself. Gave herself a couple of hard slaps. No, she wasn't dreaming.

Alice was foolish but she wasn't a fool; she remembered Dakota's warnings about the mysterious desert carnival, and she reckoned this was it. She should get far away quickly as she could, run as if her life, or at least her mind, depended on it. But… what if there was a phone?

She looked back on the way she'd come. Back into darkness. Where were Jessie and the others? With both her bearings and her nerve lost, Alice teetered in indecision until the sound of a horn propelled her forward. She'd chance anything rather than face her sister.

Decision made, courage kicked in, and it didn't take long to reach the entrance, which was all balloons and banners and flashing lights.

"Tickets please."

A smiling fat man appeared from behind a banner proclaiming: "BEST GAMES IN TWENTY-FIVE GALAXIES! FISH FOR A WISH! LUCKY DIP! SHOOT TO KILL! STAR THRILL! HALL OF MIRRORS! MARLENA THE FORTUNE TELLER! Alice assumed he was the carny Showman. He was dressed in a three-piece suit and had a red rose boutonniere in his buttonhole. His belly bulged under his waistcoat, and the cuffs and collar of his white shirt appeared gray. His skin was flawless except for his nose, which was red but that could have been the cast of the neon. His twinkling eyes settled on Alice as he held out his hand.

"I've no ticket, sir," Alice said.

At that, a long wand sprung from the Showman's sleeve, which he pointed at a booth Alice swore hadn't been there a second before.

TICKETS

The woman in the booth couldn't have been much older than Jessie. She blew bubbles with her gum and smacked them till they burst. Alice fished in the pockets of her jeans but didn't even find a dime.

"I'm sorry. I have no money."

The Showman's wand retracted up his sleeve like a snake deciding not to strike. "No money? No matter. We offer credit."

Alice didn't like the sound of that. Credit on what? An organ? An arm or leg? The carnival lights brightened, the rides spun faster, the music crescendoed, and Alice took a step backward.

"Could I please borrow a phone to call my dad?" She didn't mention being hopelessly lost because if it wasn't obvious already, she didn't want to put herself at an even further disadvantage.

"A phone? A phone? Do we have a phone?" The Showman stuck a pudgy finger in the air to test the wind, then cocked an ear to listen. He tugged at his lapels, which gleamed and glittered as if all the missing stars had aligned upon them. "Sorry. No phone."

Alice's face fell. Probably for the best, anyway; the Showman gave her the creeps. She shrugged and turned away. If she kept walking, she'd end up somewhere eventually, even if it was just dead. There were worse things than death. She was still young enough to remember that.

"But..." the Showman called after her, "we do have wishes. Those might suit your need."

Alice paused. Wishes? Seriously? A wind picked up behind her, howling across the plain, though it could have been coyotes. She shivered as heat lightning blanketed the sky. Don't turn. Keep going. You've faced lightning, coyotes, and desert night before.

All at once?

"What do you take me for? No one can grant wishes."

The Showman was crafty, for sure. He had her the moment she turned back. She would enter; it was only a question of the cost.

"You would be incorrect. The game for you is Fish for a Wish. Straight through the Hall of Mirrors, take a left at the Snake Charmer, then a right at the Fortune Teller. You can't miss it."

Alice kicked a pile of stones in a last-ditch attempt to convince herself she had options. "Sure is quiet here. Not much business," she said.

"The night is young, my dear. Now, off you go." He bowed deeply, then waved her in with a flourish.

Alice took two steps under the flash-bling-whizz entranceway, then turned back. "Wait. How will I pay?"

But the Showman was gone.

The Bargain of the Century

Jessie saw the whole thing. She ran. Screamed. "Alice!" Begged heaven, earth, and the devil himself for her sister to stop. Alice did not stop. Either deaf from howling wind or ignoring her completely, her sister entered the carnival.

Lightning flashed, thunder rumbled, tents flapped, signs swayed, lights blinked, and Jessie panicked. By the time she reached the entrance, Alice was gone.

"Alice!"

The place was deserted. No Alice. No carnies. There was only the tin-tin tone of tinkling Ferris wheel music from a late-night horror movie soundtrack. Jessie hesitated. Did fear hold her back? Damn straight, it did.

"Alice?"

Fuck it to hell, she was going to have to go in.

"Jessie!" Raphael grabbed her by the arm, hunched over and breathing hard. "Couldn't you hear us?"

Sarah and Travis followed quickly, all gasping for breath and caked in dust.

"How can I hear anything in this wind?"

"You're not thinking of going in there, are you? This storm's going to hit any minute; we need to find shelter." Sarah's voice was no more than a hoarse whisper as her eyes darted here, there, and everywhere before settling on the deserted entranceway. Like the others, she knew what this place was, and what they might gain or more likely, lose if they entered.

Travis sat on the ground, fished in his pockets and lit a smoke. "Throats raw from all the shouting."

Jessie gestured to Travis, and he tossed the pack to her. "I've no choice, I have to go in and get Alice. You guys wait here and if I don't come out, well…"

She took a long drag and exhaled a thick mist. If it rained, the whole place could be washed away in a flash. Danger ahead, danger above… "Never mind that. Shelter in the truck till morning, then get help."

"You're not going without me." Raphael looked hard at the other two. "You guys can wait in the truck. Stay warm. Hopefully, we won't be long."

Or forever. Jessie tried hard not to let on how scared she was. The longer she procrastinated, the harder it would be to find her sister or her courage. Now or never. She ground out her smoke with her heel.

"I'm going."

Sarah pulled Travis up. "We'll come with you."

He knew he had no choice, but Travis protested anyway. "This will end in disaster or at least one of us, probably me, chained to a sideshow platform."

They crept forward, eyes darting and hearts hopping, anticipating anything and sure of nothing. Once they passed through the entrance, a massive gate crashed down behind them, blocking their exit.

Travis grunted. "What the hell?"

They all looked at the gate. At each other.

"Guess we got no choice now," Raphael said.

The girls shivered and the boys shrugged as they moved forward.

"Where is everyone?" Sarah's voice trembled as her eyes darted. Other than the four of them, there was not a living soul to be seen.

They hunched together, nearly tripping over each other. The boys jostled each other to be brave, but Jessie took the lead, with Raphael one step behind.

"I don't like this. Let's get out of here and get help." He whispered in her ear.

"Alice!" Jessie shouted.

A flash of orange vanished into a large, mirrored building signposted:

HALL OF MIRRORS

Jessie tried to find the door which Alice had gone through, but by the time they reached it, the Hall of Mirrors had become less a hall and more a wall. A wall of mirrored glass that stretched in either direction further than seemed possible, vanishing into the distance where the carnival lights eventually extinguished.

Travis knocked on the glass and shouted, "Hello?"

A window opened above them, and a woman poked her head out. The carny was young and beautiful with long blonde hair and eyes too blue to be real.

"Enter the Hall of Mirrors and see your true self! Find your destiny before it finds you!"

Raphael leaned his head back and shouted up to her. "How do we get in?"

The carny smiled, "Admittance is one year."

Travis rolled his eyes. "One year of what? My Playboy subscription?"

"One year of your life," the carny replied.

"I've had enough of this crap." He banged on the mirror with his fists, but it didn't crack, only reverberated with a high-pitched hum. Everyone covered their ears until the cacophony ceased.

Raphael was the first to straighten. "Shit, Travis. Don't do that again."

Jessie stepped forward. She was tired. Tired and fed up. "A second," she said, "I'll pay a second."

The negotiating commenced and continued until they were hovering around one day.

"One *random* day," the carny said. "Each."

Jessie looked at the others, all with wide eyes and shuffling feet. Raphael and Sarah nodded, while Travis rolled his eyes before agreeing.

"All a bunch of bullshit, anyway."

Jessie squinted up at the carny. She really was breathtaking. So much so, you'd almost, no *would,* do anything she asked. Jessie blinked but did not avert her gaze even when an itch of sweat ran down her back, and her hands began to involuntarily clench and unclench.

Don't ever enter the carnival, and if you're ever so unfortunate to find yourself there, never, ever, ever negotiate with a carny. You will never get the better of any bargain.

"Same day for each of us," she said.

The carny's eyes narrowed, bluer than blue and just as true. "Same *random* day each... including your sister who owes a debt."

Alice? A debt?

Intent on hard bargaining, Jessie was unaware that the Hall of Mirrors had curved until it surrounded them completely.

Sarah saw. She tugged on Travis' sleeve, and they spun, mouths wide as mirror became screen where scenes from their lives flickered in a late-night TV static: past, present, and presumably, future.

"Erm, guys…" Travis pulled Sarah close. "You might want to hurry it along."

A scream from behind the wall. Alice!

"Done!" Jessie shouted.

The carny smiled, teeth whiter than white and straighter than straight. "Done."

The wall became hall once more and slowly, inexorably, a door creaked open to the darkness beyond.

Somewhere in Time

Alice stood before the mirror. Instead of her reflection, she saw mist. A mist thick as rain-heavy clouds. Rain? There were worse fates in the desert. She trailed her index finger along the surface, and it hummed to her touch. Strange images appeared and disappeared: figures, creatures. She was mesmerized. Entranced.

Until a hand emerged from the surface directly in front of her.

It was a human hand with five fingers, covered by a thin layer of pale hair. So far, so normal, but the skin… the skin glowed like the mood ring she'd stolen from Jessie a few years back, and the colors swirled and swayed to the pounding of her heart.

Alice was no longer a child but enough of her childish inquisitiveness remained for her to be fascinated instead of fearful. She stepped forward. Took the hand.

Froze.

It was not flesh but frost. A cold infested her palm where their skin touched and crept up her forearm, sprouting crystals as it went. She poked at one, and it melted, pooled, and dripped to the hard ground.

She shook her hand free but the stranger's remained, palm up, fingers together. Waiting. Well, they could wait forever. She took a deep breath, turned her back and continued walking, and as she walked, the mirror became mirrors became mirrored walls. Above, below, all around.

She was trapped. The mist evaporated and, in its place, the walls projected a memory…

"Mom! Bobby! Stop!"

It was spring when the desert attempted to come alive before summer taught it a lesson: brittlebushes in bloom with their yellow flowers, bees and butterflies hovering, cacti sprouting a riot of red, orange, and pink blooms. Bobby had an interview for a job in town, and Mom needed to buy groceries.

"Get in the car, Chipmunk," Bobby tousled Alice's hair and opened the back door for her.

Mom bustled out of the motel office adjusting her pocketbook strap and jangling car and office keys. "Gotta hurry," she said, "Bobby can't be late."

Alice dug her heels in and crossed her arms. "I don't wanna go."

Bobby picked her up. Alice squirmed as he tried to shove her into the back seat. "I can stay with Pa. Pa, I wanna stay with Pa."

Mom's smile faded, and the tired shadows under her eyes darkened. Alice would keep going until she got her way, which she nearly always did.

What hell was this? Alice's lips quivered and tears burned as the memory played out in slow-motion across the mirrored screens.

Bobby waved his hand out the window, then flipped her the finger. Mom tooted the horn goodbye as they approached the last lights at the last intersection in that last town. Happy as a lark, Alice skipped away towards home.

There was a squeal of brakes and a cataclysmic crunch of steel as a truck ran the light and went straight into Mom's car.

"Mom! Bobby!"

A hubcap rolled down the road, spun, then stilled. Still as her brother. Her mother.

"Stop!" She had to get out. The exit. Where was the exit?

EXIT

The sign appeared above a fire door similar to one at school. She ran fast as she could to reach it before it disappeared. Pressed the bar and was back on the midway where lights flashed, rides spun, and the air crackled.

A phone. A phone was all she needed.

The game for you is Fish for a Wish. Left at the snake charmer, then a right at the fortune teller.

She kept walking down the deserted midway. Flags billowed and puckered, and metal concession signs clanged in an eerie chill breeze. No sign of the Snake Charmer, Fortune Teller, or Fish for a Wish.

The blanket of human silence under carnival din was oppressive. Frightening. Needling pricks marched between her shoulder blades, and all her hairs stood on end. Someone or something was watching her.

Stalking her.

Her eyes darted for closeted monsters, but nothing stirred behind the haunted house curtains, no horses snorted on the carousel. She braved a glance over her shoulder. The Hall of Mirrors had accordion-folded and was no bigger than any of the other side-show stalls. Nothing to fear, except the misty trail of ground fog which billowed down the midway after her.

She hurried. Prickles turned to sweat and apprehension to conviction at the sound of footsteps behind her. She paused to listen. Did not turn. Was she imagining things? No. There was no mistaking the tap of boots on hard ground. She walked faster, took sudden, unpredictable twists and turns, then ran as if her life depended on it.

For it surely did.

Alice screamed at a gasp of cold breath on the nape of her neck and didn't stop screaming. She screamed for her dead mother and brother, her living father, sister, and aunt. Her screams merged with the music of the amusements, her heartbeat with gathering storm, her fear with the fog.

Tap. Tap. Tap. The footsteps approached. Closer. Louder.

Alice kept running.

The mist caught up with her and the world became obscured, as if she'd run so fast and far, she'd run into a dream. Finally, there were people. Carnies gathered around barrels warming their hands over a fire, their teeth shiny. Gleaming. She tripped over tent posts. Teetered. Tottered. Nearly fell. Scrambled past dark caravans and glowing eyes. The fog thickened. Settled. Cold. So cold.

She'd never been more afraid.

Jessie. Raphael. So what? Who cared? Why had she run away? Why? She was stuck in a nightmare with no way out.

"Help me," she whimpered.

And through the chaos of her fear, a voice: *Don't stop. Don't stop.*

She kept going. Ran and ran till she could run no more. Ran until the fog parted, music silenced, world stilled, and clouds lifted. And there, in the middle of nowhere, in the middle of the desert, under a sky splashed with stars, was a phone booth.

It wasn't far but like the end of a nightmare hallway, she struggled to reach it.

Don't stop.

But she wanted to stop. Wanted to sink to her knees, sink in quicksand, sink to China, scale the Great Wall and vanish.

Keep going.

Alice gathered her last bit of energy and determination and just as the fog trail licked at her heels, she made it.

An OUT OF ORDER sign was taped to the phone booth but somehow, the light inside was working. Alice pushed open the hinged door and shut it behind her. The fog curled around the booth. Crept up the glass.

No coins in her pockets. Nor in the change slot. Not a cent. She picked up the receiver to place a collect call to Pa. If anyone could find her in this god-forsaken place, it was him.

No dial tone.

Alice tapped the receiver. Once. Twice. Hello? Three times. Four. BANG. BANG. BANG. Pooling tears began to spill. She sank to the ground, knees to her chest, dangling receiver about to bottle her, looked up at the ceiling and saw the sign.

DIAL 777 for DESTINY

Oh hell, what did she have to lose? She scrambled back up and dialed. There was no ringing, no answer.

"Hello? Hello, please help me. I'm lost."

It wasn't long before he coalesced from the mist. Eyes blue, hair sandy blonde, he was not yet a man but no longer a boy. Dressed in blue jeans and leather, his face was angelic, his skin iridescent.

She palmed the closed door, torn between keeping him out and letting him in. "Why are you following me? Do you want to hurt me? Go ahead, everyone else does. Why not take your turn?"

Fear turning to frustration to anger to capitulation, Alice opened the door and stepped out into cool mist. Tilted her chin.

He studied her for a time, time all eternal, his eyes the deepest blue.

Do your worst, her eyes challenged.

But there was no worst in him, if he existed at all. He seemed human, looked human—was human—but when he moved towards her, lifted a hand to brush away her tears, caught and held one in his palm, the air shimmered ghost-like around him and in his eyes so blue, there were multitudes of light.

Stars, they were stars.

"I will never harm you." He brushed desert-dusted and sweaty hair from her face. His fingers solid and warm as they cupped her chin. "Sleep," he said, "sleep, and you will find me."

When Alice woke some minutes, hours, eons later, she was in her bed. Jessie was in her own bed snoring gently. Had it all been a dream? Something bit into her palm. She opened her clenched fist slowly, afraid of what she would find, expecting anything but the large diamond faceted with endless, eternal cuts glittering in her hand.

The First Time They Almost Died

"Right. So, we all had the same dream? Is that what you're trying to tell me?" Jessie was having none of it.

Sarah and Raphael shrugged. Stranger things were known to happen.

"So, where's your damn truck then?"

That was the question. They'd all awoken in their beds—fully-dressed, clothes cruddy, minds foggy—all from the same exact dream: ship, carnival, hall of mirrors and that crazy fortune teller hag. They all knew it was no dream but not one of them wanted to admit what that meant.

"Where's Alice?" Raphael ran his long fingers through his long hair and squinted against the sun. He'd somehow lost his designer shades and was pissed the hell off about it.

"Still asleep."

Travis returned with four coffees from the diner. "Your Pa is none too impressed with your skipping, Jessie, and he advises you to get your damn ass to school this instant."

They sat in lounge chairs around the pool. The filter hum and sun warmth were powerful sedatives, but Jessie couldn't settle. She took one of the coffees and sipped it slow as her mind seemed to be operating. "We're going back out, right?"

"Hell, no." Sarah nearly spluttered her coffee all over the rest of them. "Dream or not, the fortune teller gave me the creeps."

No one else said a word, but everyone knew the conversation wasn't over.

Raphael downed his coffee in one gulp, crushed the cup in his fist and fired it at the trash can. "Later, then. I gotta get my damn truck."

Jessie sighed. "You two might as well go into school." She headed after Raphael.

Travis laughed and took Sarah's hand. "Yeah, right. We're going back to my place."

Travis' father owned half the town and his older brother, Cal, most of the rest. Their house wasn't so much a home as a ranch. Travis had his own apartment and mostly minded his own business long as he got his weekly allowance.

Sarah shook her hand loose and crossed her arms. One look at her face and, "Oh, come on," was all Travis could say, for sure as shit, he was going to have to drive them out.

It wasn't a long drive—twenty minutes max—but it was still the middle of nowhere no matter which direction you came from. Raphael's truck wasn't in sight at the ship graveyard and wind had erased any tracks. There was no sign of any carnival.

Jessie and Raphael headed out on foot while Travis and Sarah remained on their ship.

"You don't reckon Travis spiked our drinks yesterday, do you?" Raphael had his arm around Jessie as they trudged in the general direction they remembered going the night before.

"He wouldn't dare. Not after the last time."

"Maybe."

It was late morning, and the heat was already high noon. The air palpitated. It hurt to breathe, to see, to think. Raphael had the foresight to bring a pair of binoculars and kept scanning. Found nothing.

"What the fuck am I gonna do?" he said.

"Walk."

"Fuck that." He kicked a small tower of rocks someone had piled.

There was no time to even draw breath, let alone scream, before the rattler got him. Jaws clamped on his leg and fangs sliced through his jeans and seized flesh. Raphael paled while Jessie scrambled for a rock and tried to beat the snake lose. By the time it let go and slithered away into some sage brush, Raphael was down.

"Fuck. Fuck. Fuck." He rolled away from the rocks, clutching his leg to his chest.

They'd lived in the desert all their lives and knew what to do, but "Shit. Shit. Shit," was all Jessie could say as she fumbled for her phone.

No signal, and they were too far from the ship for Travis and Sarah to hear given they were probably busy making plenty of their own noise. Jessie screamed for them anyway.

No response.

Stay calm. Whatever you do, stay calm, she told herself. "Stop moving. Whatever you do, don't panic," she told Raphael.

"Easy for you to say."

They had no anti-venom. It was in the truck. No truck. No fucking luck. She pulled him up best she could, but when she let go to retrieve her pocketknife from her back pocket, his leg gave out, and he went back down.

"That's no good, Jessie. You know it."

Jessie cut up his pant leg and grimaced at the wound. "You got any better ideas right now?" She sliced the punctures, sucked and spit.

He was right; it did no good. His leg was already starting to swell and his body to sweat. She helped him back to his feet. He began to drool as he limped along, dragging his bad leg behind him. Jessie was a tall girl, slim and strong, but Raphael was taller and broader and leaned on her more and more with each step.

She took the binoculars from his neck and scanned for the ships.

"Raphael?"

"Hmm?"

She looked again. There was no mistake; it was a phone booth, and it was closer than the ship graveyard. She could call someone for help.

But it wasn't that kind of phone booth, was it?

If you dial the right number, your dreams will come true.

Jessie had dreams. Big dreams. Lots of em. Dreams of escaping this hellscape and living by the sea. Swimming in water so cold her nipples hardened, and her breath caught. Crashing waves big enough to wash away eons of dust. Of drinking in bars and flirting with stars. Of singing in a band and touring the world and by her side, Raphael, a famous actor, and everyone would want to know them, be them—Queen and King of it all—and, love, love was all that mattered, and it was there, a solid foundation like the earth beneath their feet, the endless sky full of possibility, each star a dream to cling to, and they could have it all. It all… it all.

This was her only chance, wasn't it? She'd never have another.

"Oh hell, Jessie, it hurts like a motherfucker." Raphael moaned and the spell was broken. "I can't walk. Leave me here and go get Travis."

The wound was swollen, the skin red and purple. His face was twisted in pain. *Don't leave him. If you do, he will die. All those dreams are only wishes which will never come true, and you know it.*

"Raphael, you must. Come on." With a strength Jessie didn't know she had, she half-dragged him another hundred feet, phone booth a mirage of regret on the horizon. "Travis," she screamed without hope he'd hear. "Goddamit, Travis. Help!"

The only answer was the screech of a golden eagle overhead. Looking up, Jessie tripped over her own feet, and they both tumbled. Face in dust, Raphael heavy on top of her, Jessie nearly started to cry, but she was a Williams and made of stronger stuff than that. She'd lost her mother and her brother; she wasn't about to lose Raphael too. She scrambled from under him and roared again for Travis and Sarah.

A glint of sunlight caught her eye a few feet ahead. An old road sign. She didn't know or care what it was doing there, only that it might work. She kicked it first to make sure there were no surprises, then dragged it over to Raphael and somehow rolled him onto it. She jerry-rigged the binocular cables through two holes and wrapped her shirt around them to have something to hold onto. Not pretty and barely functional but she managed to drag the sign and Raphael along with it.

It was slow going and by the sound of Raphael's breathing, too slow. She kept screaming until she could scream no more, moved till she could move no more. He wasn't going to die, not here, not like this. Raphael was gonna be a big star and so was she. They'd be right beside each other, together, forever. Jessie sank to her knees, then her hands, bent and panting hard. She'd never been this thirsty, not ever. What she'd give to swim in the sea—all that water, without a drop to drink—but she'd rather drown in that water than in this sea of dust, a nobody in the middle of nowhere.

The last thing she heard before she was swallowed by despair was the crunch of gravel and the squeal of brakes when Travis and Sarah arrived after finally hearing her call.

Night of the Falling Stars

Raphael lay on the sun lounger by the motel pool. Filter off, there was only the slow plop, plop of bugs as they landed on the water and struggled not to drown. The pool was a luxury these days and people from all over town paid to swim in it but not tonight. Tonight, all was quiet.

It was late. The neon MOTEL sign hummed, the red VACANCY sign flickered and hissed. Carl had needed to replace the transformer for some time, but money was tight and only getting tighter. They weren't alone. Hard times were evident everywhere, not only at the motel and diner but in the slow, inexorable evacuation of the town itself.

Hands under head, lounger's plastic ribs sticking to his skin like the heat of the day to night, Raphael stared at the sky. Even diffused by neon, it glittered. Was there life somewhere out there? He reckoned there was. How could there not be?

As he stared at the stars, a nascent feeling bloomed in his chest. Expanded. A star about to supernova. The yearnings of his heart were too big for this endless nothing. He wanted to be something. Shine brighter than the neon sign, bright as the stars above. He couldn't do that here, could do nothing but shrivel up and tumbleweed away, even with Jessie by his side. What good would he be to her then? To himself? To anyone?

"She is so beautiful. So kind. So strong. I don't want to leave her, but I will, if I must."

Jessie came out with two cold ones. She wore a light summer dress with nothing on underneath. A nervous Raphael drank nearly half of his in one go. Nothing tasted better than a cold beer on a hot night.

Except Jessie.

Raphael cleared his throat and set his bottle on a rickety plastic table. "I was telling the stars about you," he said.

"Hmm. What did you say?"

He didn't reply at first, and she remained silent, waiting, and in the silence, what he wanted to say was this…

Come with me, Jessie. We'll flee this hellscape together. I'll act, you'll sing. Together, we can do anything. Be anything. Go anywhere. I can't live without you, but I will only die with you here.

What he did say was this:

"I said you were the prettiest star of them all." And she was. She stretched out her long legs, summer dress riding her thighs, bare toes twiddling. Looked at him. Didn't matter her long, blond hair stuck to beads of sweat which glitter-bombed her slender neck, the tired circles under her eyes, or the chipped finger polish and lack of makeup, in Jessie's eyes, universes unfurled.

He could tell by the tick-tock of her eyes there was something she wanted to say but wouldn't.

What she did say was this:

"I love you, Raphael but you're meant for bigger and better things. You're gonna be a star. The biggest. I know I promised to be there by your side, but I can't go with you. Not yet. Pa's ticker is dodgy; I gotta help him round here long as he's around. And Alice, well, you know Alice."

He knew that's what she would say and the saying of it somehow made it easier.

She took his hand; it was time. They'd played around long enough. Done everything but the deed. She rose, brushed his long, brown hair from his forehead and kissed it. "Room 33," she whispered in his ear.

Raphael watched her walk away, soft cotton dress sashaying over slender hips. He downed the rest of his beer and followed her up the stairs.

He found her naked on top of the bedspread, not nervous at all, not like him—suddenly tongue-tied and teary as he stared. He'd seen every bit of her naked but never all at once. He felt unable to speak. Unable to move.

He sank to his knees and rested his head on her flat stomach. She ran her fingers through his hair once more. Silent. Serene. Slow. Until his breath evened to the slow ebb and tide of her own, and his heart stopped racing.

"Raphael?"

He'd always loved the way she said his name in quiet moments, as if he were an actual angel and not just named after one.

"Hmm?"

"I'm cold."

The chill of night had crept into the room, and her flesh was goose-pimpled. He pulled his clothes off quickly but stopped at his underwear. Instead of taking them off, he traced a slow finger down her neck and over her breasts, settled in the hinterland between her belly button and clit. He'd played with her a hundred times, but this night wasn't about playing, no matter how much he loved to hear her beg. He'd only ever known her body and his own. There had never been another, and he wanted this moment to last forever knowing it would be over too soon. He moved himself between her bent legs, licking her slow, tongue hard as her clit was becoming, her back arching as she dug her hands in his hair, pulled him up to her face. Kissed him.

"Together," she said breathlessly. "This time. The first time. Together."

She wasted no more time talking and pulled down his underwear. He moaned as she grasped him—hard and getting harder—and guided him to her softness.

She was everything he'd imagined a thousand times. *Jessie, oh Jessie.* A perfect fit as if they were made for each other.

And they were.

He bit his lip to stop himself from cumming too soon. "Don't move," he whispered. "Let me look at you." He rose above her, and what he wanted to say was… Oh Jessie, I'll never be able to leave you. Not now. Not ever. But what he did say was… "I love you." For it was not one thing, but everything.

And she reached up and drew him back in.

Sometime in the middle of the night, he woke to find her gone. Her pillow still bore the indent from her head, her smell—

their smell—was all over him. He threw on his jeans and followed the trace of it to the balcony.

The neon signs were all off. There was no passing traffic, even the distant highway was deserted. She didn't turn as he approached, only gripped the handrail tighter.

"Don't think I've ever seen so many falling stars."

She was right. There was no asteroid shower, at least none the observatory had broadcast about. It was actual stars that shot across the sky. So many. Raphael didn't put much belief in signs but recognized one when it came.

"Are they dying?" She seemed sad at the thought, as if some pile of dust a million miles away was a beloved pet, "or, just moving on?"

He put an arm around her to comfort and warm her, and her head fell softly on his shoulder.

"Come with me, Jessie. I can't make it without you."

"Yes, you can."

He turned her chin towards him. Her lips were slightly parted, and he wanted her again. Wanted her always. "Maybe, I don't want to."

She touched his face. Stubble sandpapered her soft hands. "My family needs me."

"You can't live your life for other people, Jessie."

"Except if it's you?"

Raphael dropped his hands. His arms fell to his sides. "But… but you want to be a singer. Make records. You've always said it was your dream."

She sighed. "I'll get to my dream one of these days. I know I will. We're only eighteen; there's plenty of time.

He could always tell her everything and anything, but some things he couldn't put into words. How did he explain why he had to leave? Would she understand if he told her he'd explode if he didn't? How did he tell her she was the most important person in the world to him but not the most important thing?

"I gotta go, Jessie. Cause if I don't go now, I never will."

And that was the truth. They'd get married, have a few kids; she'd work at the diner, maybe sing a few songs at Tom's on Friday and Saturday nights. He'd work at the ranch tending cattle while Travis gave him shit about being his boss, and he'd drink every night, avoiding home and the screaming kids until one night he'd down a bottle of Jacks and drive to the tracks, stop in the middle and wait for the freight to bear down, its bright light a super-nova in his brain before it splattered across the windscreen.

Same as his dad.

She kissed him. Of all the ways she'd ever kissed him, she'd never kissed him like that. She pulled away after a moment or ten, looked up and into his eyes and if she asked him then, said, "Don't go. Please don't go," he would have stayed. Would have done anything for her in that moment, her eyes a mystery he could spend his whole life unravelling, but she didn't. All she said was,

"I know."

PART THREE

First Light

Most folk thought Dakota had always been old and alone. Sure, she was old, but alone? How could anyone be alone in the desert? There were always people passing and if there weren't people, there were animals and if not animals, spirits, and if all else failed, the occasional alien.

Most folk also thought Dakota strange, and that was a fact. Most had their faces buried in phones or the TV or other people's business. Not Dakota. Never had a phone in her life. Folk needed to talk, they knew where to find her. To most, that was insane, to Dakota, it was the only way to stay sane.

None of which was to say she didn't have a need for companionship. Her days of the hot and heavy had passed some years before, but she still had urges, and morning masturbation and chamomile tea usually set her up for the day fine and dandy.

But not always.

She never spoke of the one man she had loved. It wasn't that she thought of him, not often, anyway. It was that she didn't want to sully perfection with substitution. She had kids, well, her younger stepbrother's kids, to look after, and that filled a gap in the longing for something bigger and stronger than her own heart beating for itself. Mostly, but not always.

So, when Kim Hyun-Ki, the Korean astrophysicist, happened upon her garden one autumn evening, she offered him a cup of tea same as she would anyone, but after, she made him dinner.

He too was alone, if you called studying the cosmos alone. He'd come to the observatory in the middle of the desert as most serious astrophysicists did at some point in their careers. A rite of passage much as a year in Chile. Many made discoveries: asteroids, stars, planets, even distant galaxies from time to time. Despite the isolation, most came away from their sojourn transformed positively, because the further away something was, the closer they came to understanding the limits of certainty and the enormity of possibility. That glimpse into forever touched upon the present in such a way they felt small and yet infinite. Unfortunately, the yearning for definitive answers only led to more questions, which was frustrating at best, obsessive at worst.

"Sounds like torture," Dakota said, dipping her toes in the pond as the toads burped and bounced. "Peeling an endless onion."

Hyun-Ki's English wasn't great, and he had long ago stopped making an effort to communicate except in the universal language of math and coordinates. Yet, there was something about the way the water rippled around Dakota's long, slightly curved toes, how like tiny black holes, her eyes absorbed the light instead of reflecting it, that awoke in him a desire to tell someone—a living human being and not a scientific journal—all he had seen, all he had imagined in his long life, and all the dreams he had dreamed but never shared. Was it aging and the encroachment of death that prompted this or a late embracement of life?

Lost in thought, Hyun-Ki did not reply, and while Dakota was generally contemplative, she felt an overwhelming need to fill the silence.

"The vastness of possible is constrained by the limits of tangible," she said. "When I was a child, I looked at the sky and saw stories: Náhookòs Bi'kà', the warrior, his partner, Náhookòs Bi'áád, the central fire of Náhookòs Bikò'… all imaginary, yet each rooted to Earth. As I grew older, I began to wonder if there were things that couldn't be imagined somewhere out there…"

She opened her arms to the sky. Held them for a moment or two as if to capture something lost, despite never having been found.

"Of course," Hyun-Ki replied. "That curiosity is what drives both scientists and artists. We must constantly challenge conviction. Ask, 'what if'?' Stretch our imaginations beyond our limited perception of possibilities. Seek the proof."

"But how can we prove anything when our own eyes might deceive us? The very stars above, for example… are they living or dead, their light only reaching us now."

Hyun-Ki thought he understood the answers Dakota sought, but it was challenging to find the right words to introduce complex concepts in a way the lay person could understand. The universal translator app on his phone would have been useful, but it created distance and was frequently inaccurate.

"Nothing in space ever truly dies, for matter is eternal whatever its form," he said, at last. "The universe bears witness to an eternal cycle of death and birth. How a star dies and what it becomes depends on its size: small stars burn out and larger stars explode."

Dakota chuckled. "The bigger they are, the harder they fall?"

Hyun-Ki nodded, nervousness gone. He was blessed with the eloquence of scientists speaking on their favorite subject. "And fall, they do. The debris from supernovas can move towards us or away. It can form neutron stars, or black holes which devour all life around them, or the matter can coalesce to form new stars and planets, perhaps even dimensions, or planes of existence. Maybe even, pathways in time itself."

Dakota looked into his eyes, pupils dark and wide in the night and saw his excitement. His belief was not in the limitations of life but the transformative potential of death. The possible beyond the visible. And something became clear to her as things often did, the older she got—if something could be imagined, it existed, if only in the universe of our minds.

She leaned her head back against her chair and looked up again. "But which are dead? Which are still living? Which are being born?"

"Do you want the short or long answer?"

"Whichever is easiest."

"Every star you can see with the naked eye is almost certainly still alive. With a telescope, it's different, the stars I observe with the telescopes at the observatory could be alive… or dead."

Dakota took some comfort in that. As the earth darkened, and the sky brightened, it seemed appropriate to ditch the tea and break out the good bourbon. She poured them both a tumbler and moved her chair closer.

"Even so, do I see the stars as they are or as they once were?"

"It takes time for their light to reach us, so we do not see them as they currently are."

"So, they *could* be dead?"

He smiled. "Could be, but unlikely. Stars live for billions of years. The time it takes their light to reach us is—with the Sun, it's eight seconds, other stars... years. Improbable that they've died in the intervening time."

"But not impossible?"

He nodded. "Nothing is impossible."

With his graveyard shift hours and daylight slumbers, the sun made infrequent trespasses against Hyun-Ki's skin. Dakota could have been deceived into thinking he was much younger than her, but as their eyes met over raised glasses, his pooled with decades.

"Time is a funny thing," she thought, not realizing she'd spoken aloud, which she often did, to the saguaro, the coyotes, the night sky, and now, him. "So, life out there..." She waved her hand across the sky. "when extraterrestrials look towards Earth, do they see our past?"

He chuckled. "That's a bit more complicated."

Evening had long settled into night, and although he planned to, both knew he couldn't possibly walk back to the observatory at this hour.

"I've lived my life attempting to understand existence but now..." He was not well-versed in the ways of love: only child, never married—only a few brief and furtive love affairs that led to nothing when he was younger—childless; so, he spoke only of what he wanted in that moment. Without fear, without thought of past or future. "I'd like to hold your hand," he said.

Dakota held out her hand and met his somewhere between them. Her sun-hardened skin was wrinkled and shar-pei pooled around her knuckles; his were soft and smooth. They sat that way for some minutes, as tingles that could not be explained by night's chill crept up their forearms and tickled their hearts.

Eventually, he stood and led her some distance away from the house and its ambient light.

"To answer your question: the earth does not emit its own light. What is bright here is not visible from space; earth reflects the light of its star, the Sun. And with that comes refraction and distortion. The math gets fairly complex. It's said math is the universal language, but a more advanced civilization could speak it well beyond our comprehension. The short answer is we don't know if they see our past, our future, or even if they see us at all."

Somewhere in Eternity

Time passed as time did, not in a line but a loop. Anticipation drifted from hope to despair where Michael settled for some time, for search as he might, he could not find her again. He lost his appetite and his ability to concentrate and when he wasn't searching, all he wanted to do was sleep. There, he sometimes found her in his dreams, and hope was reborn.

He told no one except his family and only them because he had to explain to father why he needed his quantum transporter. The first time they met, he had been twirling it around his wrist as he worked on his geo-plotter. His mind hadn't wandered, it had been PULLED, and his body followed.

It was sudden and terrifying until he saw her. She was his anchor in the violent storm of passage, and the moment they touched, the iridescence of travel vanished, and he became whole as if she defined him. How would he ever return home, material as he was? Did he even want to return? His indecision seemed to last an eon, though it was only a moment or two, his heart fluttering as their eyes met before she fainted into his arms. As he held her, long blonde hair silk against his skin, he *knew* her, as if they merged in that moment, his energy fusing with hers. Knew where she lived, her hopes and dreams, simple as they were, but were the simplest dreams any less noble?

He thought to stay. For a while. Learn more. For there were layers upon layers of her mind he didn't explore—though he could have—it was too intrusive, better for her to reveal herself to him over time. Over a lifetime.

He laid her gently on her bed, then retrieved her sister and her friends for he knew from her mind they were in danger. After, he stood silently, staring down at her as she slept—soft evening air cool, an owl hooting in a tree, some creature scurrying up a cactus—and marveled at her beauty. Although he'd seen many beautiful girls, her whole being seemed uniquely matched to his own. He lost all track of time other than the soft beats of her breath, until his father tracked him and pulled him away, back to his own time, place, planet, parallel.

How this had all happened, he could not explain and neither could father.

He searched for her, but without her coordinates each trip was random, hopeful. Futile. Any time he asked his father for help, he was subjected to eternal lectures on time and space, wormholes, quantum fluctuation and given countless math problems. He did them all, clinging to the belief that if he solved them, he'd find her once more.

He never did.

It seemed an impossible task, for the universe is endless and constantly expanding, but he was determined. He clung to the hope he'd find her before her time had passed. Fortunately, he had the father he did, with access to the transporter equipment Michael needed. Few could travel so easily. Unfortunately, his father threatened to take this equipment away.

"It's dangerous. You won't receive your reserves until you're sixteen. Anything could happen."

"I'm very careful, father. Nothing will happen."

"No one is careful at fourteen."

Their eyes met, but Michael did not look away. His father sighed.

"You've travelled to dozens of worlds. Now it's time to accept you will never find her. If she ever did exist, she might no longer. Maybe, it *was* all a dream..."

The dream theory again. "It was no dream!" he shouted and stormed out of the room.

He had walked dozens of worlds to find her and would walk dozens more. Hundreds. Thousands. His parents spoke of safety, of responsibility: taking up his father's work, marrying and continuing their lineage. Their world needed Michael, not another. Certainly not some backwards civilization in a warp of space-time.

"Possibility is infinite, but life is not," his father told him, "Even for us. Some have very limited time in any and all dimensions. The probability of finding a random uncharted time and place is…"

"I *will* find her, father."

Father looked to mother as if to say, I've failed, you try, but mother only shrugged and said, "Time folds and unfolds. If it's meant to be… it will be."

It was. Of that, Michael was certain. He would find her again, somewhere in eternity.

One Moment Over and Over and Over Again

The train was boarding. Both Jessie and Raphael stood on the platform but only one had luggage.

Stay. Please stay. Jessie sucked back the tears she couldn't stop from falling. She would die before she voiced her plea.

"I'm going to make something of myself, Jessie. For me. For you. For us. I won't be back till I do."

She touched his wet face. "You're gonna be a big star, baby. I know it sure as sunshine."

He took her in his arms and held her close as the train whistle blew, and the porter called, "All Aboard."

Raphael pulled back, held Jessie's face in both hands, his green eyes turning blue.

"I'll send for you soon as I make it. I promise. I love you, Jessie."

Her words came out weepy. "I love you, too."

Don't go.

But he went.

Ten Years Before the End

Sarah sat cross-legged on the bed holding a sobbing Jessie in her arms, the yellow cotton bedspread soppy from her tears. She tried to comfort her best she could, but Sarah had worries of her own. Worries that weighed so heavy, Jessie's tears drew them out like a poultice.

"I'm pregnant," she blurted out.

Jessie pulled back in stunned silence.

"What?" she burbled, snot running, tears spilling. "I thought…I thought you were on the pill?"

"I was."

"What the fuck? Did you miss any?"

"Nope. Not once."

It was Sarah's turn to cry. The two of them fell once again into each other's arms, seeking solace neither could give, only misery they could share. Some minutes later, tears exhausted, hunched sobs retracting into shuddering chests, Jessie retrieved a box of tissues from the bathroom, and they dried their eyes.

"What do you want to do?" Jessie asked.

Sarah blew her nose and sniffled twice before answering. She was a beautiful girl—Jessie reckoned the prettiest in town, though Sarah said the same about her—even with her puffy eyes, dripping nose, and the shadow of doom hanging over her.

"I can't have it, Jessie. I can't. I want to go to college. I got accepted into Halbrook only last week. With a full scholarship." Sarah's parents weren't as poor as Jessie's, but they weren't rich either. Halbrook was the top veterinarian college in the state and not cheap. Sarah loved animals more than anything. It had been her dream to be a vet long as Jessie had known her, which was forever.

Sarah grabbed Jessie's hand. Her fingers were ice-cold despite the heat of the room and her rising panic.

"You can't tell anyone. No one, not even Raphael. Especially, not Raphael."

Jessie patted Sarah's clawing hands in reassurance. "Don't worry, sisters before misters, remember?"

Sarah loosened her death grip and nodded. "I trust you."

Branches clattered against the window as a cardinal landed and burst into song. Pa was going to have to do something about that tree soon, before it burst into the apartment. Pa needed to do a lot of things around the motel and diner, not much of which got done, what with mom and Bobby gone and his grief lingering.

But Jessie couldn't think about that. Not then. She didn't ask if Sarah had told Travis; she already knew the answer. Travis would insist they get married on the spot and that would be the end of Sarah's ambitions. Travis was wrapped up in Sarah so tight, she was nearly a second skin. Sarah loved him, of course she did, just not in the same way.

"What are you going to do?"

There weren't many options. The tablets that used to come over the border were impossible to get anymore. Last local fella caught with them was sent up to Eyman on a ten-bill ticket.

"I thought, maybe… maybe you might talk to Dakota."

Jessie knew that was coming and dreaded it. "She doesn't do that. Not anymore. Not since she lost Mary Belle." Mary Belle, two years older than them but none the wiser. Her death had been quick, but it hadn't been easy. Once Dakota made up her mind about something, that was that, especially about something big as this.

"Please, Jessie."

"I'll help you with the baby. Or you could give it up for adoption."

Sarah's face fell. "Travis would never allow it." The blinds went down in her eyes. "Suppose I can try it myself. Heard there were herbs you can take…"

"Do you want to die?" Jessie leaned in, face scrunched and tense as Sarah went quiet. Too quiet.

When she did finally speak, it was in an eerily calm voice, as if confirming what her mind had already made up.

"I can't have it. I can't be stuck here forever, married to Travis, rearing his babies up at the ranch. I want something out of life, something that's me and mine, not his and ours. If I've got to be a mom at eighteen, might as well start engraving my headstone."

She wasn't wrong. There were two futures in the desert if you had neither skill nor wealth: poverty or marriage. Either way, you were no free woman.

"Don't, Sarah. Don't. We'll figure something out."

That something happened to be a travelling man who passed through from time to time. In his creased suit, loose tie and sweat-stained cuffs, he stood out amongst their usual customers. He'd left a business card with Pa at the diner last time—what, must be two, three years ago—Pa had tossed it in the trash and sent the fella on his way. A curious Jessie had fished it out: *Services for Ladies in Trouble* and a number. At the time, she hadn't thought much of it other than to wonder if trouble meant what she thought it meant, but she'd kept the card all the same.

"Don't worry, honey; I think I know who can help."

It was hard to arrange, harder still without anyone being the wiser but a week later, after school, but before Pa took his evening break from the diner, someone knocked on the door of Room 28. Jessie chose 28 because it was at the end of the long side of the L with an opening to the back and about as far away from their apartment as you could get. It hadn't been rented out in ages and was mostly used as a storeroom for cleaning supplies and stuff guests left behind. She'd spent the day cleaning, clearing boxes of detergent and stacks of musty towels from the bed, put on fresh sheets and had a large bowl of boiled water at the ready.

The man who arrived was of an age eighteen-year-olds classified as "old", which meant anyone over thirty. His eyebrows were thick salt-and-pepper, and hair sprouted from his ears and nose, though when he took off his cowboy hat, his head was bald.

He rolled in a suitcase and prepared a drink which was smoky and smelled bitter. He held the glass before Sarah, sweat beading on his forehead as late afternoon sun beat against closed curtains and the ceiling fan sputtered. The AC was off as it might be noticed or at least heard and call attention to them. Pa was forever turning off the units in vacated rooms.

"Are you sure you want to proceed?" the man said.

Sarah looked at the glass, at him and finally, at Jessie. Jessie kept her face neutral. She'd already made her opinion clear.

"Once you drink this, there's no going back."

Jessie bit her bottom lip and whispered in Sarah's ear, "I don't know. I've a bad feeling. You can still change your mind."

Sarah took the glass with trembling hands and downed the contents in one gulp. Nose twitching from the smell, she gagged and nearly puked three times but managed to keep it down.

The man set up quietly and quickly, but it still took some time. His hodge-podge of equipment was old movie, mad scientist, but everything seemed clean.

"Do you have the fee?" the man asked Jessie, because Sarah had become drowsy and slightly delirious, rattling on about riding wild mustangs off into the sunset and never looking back.

Jessie handed him the envelope. He counted out the twenty-five hundred dollars, which amounted to all of Sarah's life savings and half of Jessie's, then pocketed the bills before snapping on a pair of rubber gloves.

"I will begin."

Sarah's cold, clammy hand clenched Jessie's, her nails gouging flesh. Nails pink and pure and fingertips white in the beam of the man's head lamp. Jessie kept her eyes open and trained on Sarah's, stroking the damp hair from her strained face.

The sounds. Oh, God, the sounds: Sarah's screams muffled by teeth-clamped cloth, the whirl of the machine, the pumping suction, the god-awful noise as the fetus was sucked up a tube and splashed into the container with a wet plop.

Jessie couldn't look, the sound was bad enough, but Sarah did. Her eyes went wide as she panted in pain, then closed, and she refused to open them until the man had packed everything up.

"She may bleed." He pulled the suitcase handle and rolled it to the door." Here's a couple of pills for the pain."

The pills were bone white in Jessie's palm. "Are you a doctor?" She asked him at last when she probably should have asked him first.

He shrugged. "Used to be… before everything… I was put in prison for helping girls out." He patted the suitcase. "Now I do what I can with what I've got."

Which ended up not being enough.

Sarah's cramps started not long after the man drove off down the road, his black Impala a sidewinder searching for its next strike. She insisted the pain was bearable, but the drugs hadn't worn off yet.

"He said a little cramping was to be expected." She stuck two maternity pads in her underwear. "Funny, huh? Maternity pads." She hadn't cried up to that point, but her eyes had a far-away stare. "I'll never unsee it, Jessie. If I live to a hundred, I'll never unsee it or unhear the sound of my…."

She pulled up her jeans but couldn't do up the button. Her stomach had been flat before but was now distended. "I did the right thing. Don't worry."

Typical Sarah, comforting everyone else when she was the one in need of comfort. Jessie opened her arms, and Sarah fell into them, and the tears she'd been holding back flooded out.

Sarah spent the night so Jessie could keep an eye on her. Once Pa and Alice came home and finally went to bed, Jessie snuck a couple of Pa's beers. They turned off their phones, sat on the sofa, hand-in-hand and watched an old black and white movie on the TV. About the time Paul Newman was shoveling a dozen eggs into his mouth, Jessie nodded off.

It was the heat that woke her. Sarah's hand on fire in her own.

"Sarah?" Jessie shook her, but Sarah only mumbled incoherently.

"Sarah!" Jessie hissed. She was burning up worse than sunburn on a summer's day. "Sarah, oh my God, wake up."

Finally, Sarah opened her eyes enough for Jessie to see the pain in them. She grabbed her stomach and groaned. Blood had soaked through the maternity pads, her jeans, and the blankets on the couch.

"It hurts, Jessie. Hurts so bad."

Sarah barely made it to the bathroom, Jessie's arms the only thing holding her up. Hunched over on the toilet, she gasped and groaned, crying out with each cervix-spasming cramp. Her body caved in upon itself, as heavy blood clots hit the bowl.

"I have to take you to the hospital. This isn't the way it's supposed to be."

"No! They'll arrest me and throw me in jail. And you, too, Jessie. Don't you remember Tabitha Marks only last year. Rotting away in Mercer Mental Hospital under lock and key?"

"That's cause she played the lunatic card to stay out of prison."

"Yeah, and she'll never get out. Even if she does, her own parents want nothing to do with her." Sarah groaned again before another clot plopped into the toilet. "I'll be okay. I'll be okay, just help me to bed. Okay?"

She was very pale and had changed her maternity pads for an actual towel. Her sweat-curled, long brown hair clung to her face and neck. Jessie brushed it back and tied it up with a hairband.

"Least, let me tell Pa."

"No!"

"He'll tell no one and will know what to do. "

Sarah clung to her arm, fingernails indenting but not breaking the skin. "No, Jessie, you promised me. You swore."

Jessie put the back of her hand to Sarah's forehead. Grimaced. "You're burning up. You might die."

"Let me sleep. Please, Jessie. If I'm not better by morning, you can tell your Pa."

The second Sarah lay back and closed her eyes, her ragged breath coming out in locomotive puffs, her hand went limp in Jessie's.

Jessie ran.

When the ambulance arrived, the sheets and mattress were soaked with blood. Sarah's pulse was thready and weak. They worked on her fast and furious but by the time they reached the hospital, she was gone.

When Hate Set Up Home in Your Heart

They stood over Sarah's coffin.

"Couldn't even mind your own woman. What kind of man are you?" Cal hissed in his ear. His thick fingers dug under Travis' collarbone as he clenched his shoulder.

"She's so pale," Travis muttered. She'd always been tan and toned and beautiful.

"That's cause she's dead, Travis boy. Dead and gone. Now whatcha gonna do about it?"

Travis stroked the side of her face, but her once soft skin was rubbery and cold. He resisted the urge to shudder, swallowed vomit down. They'd screwed only four days ago, an eternity really, her underneath him, serious, not laughing as usual. He should have known.

Cal led a reluctant Travis away from the casket. Past Sarah's parents—dead-eyed and stiff—shaking hands. Her little sister, Lisa, the cousins, aunts and uncles from across the state, everyone from school. Even Raphael had returned for the funeral.

Jessie.

Cal spat. "She actually had the nerve to show her face."

"It wasn't her fault. She tried to stop Sarah. She called the ambulance.

"You believe that, huh? You've always been a pussy and now I know you always will be."

Cal flicked his cigarette and ground it out with the heel of his boot. Tendrils of smoke trailed from its intestines. A smoke. Travis needed a smoke. A drink. A fucking hammer to his skull. When Raphael came over with open arms and hooded eyes, Cal spat again and walked away.

"Travis, man. I'm so sorry. Jesus. I can't imagine what you're going through."

No, you fucking can't. You never struggled with girls; they all swoon when you walk by. Had the prettiest girl in town on your arm, and you up and left her behind. Sarah was all I had. All I ever had. She was sweet and smart, and she loved me.

Travis rolled the ring in his pocket. Round and round in his hand. The gold was warm, the diamond cold. "I was going to ask her to marry me."

"Oh, man. Man, I'm so sorry." Raphael pulled him in for a hug, but Travis' arms remained limp.

Travis wanted to punch him. Punch someone. Something. Break the world and grind the pieces to dust between clenched teeth. A roar big as the desert sky and just as blue boiled and rolled inside him. He shrugged Raphael off.

"Yeah, sure man," was all he said.

Raphael deflated. Poor Raphael. Everyone always worried about fucking Raphael. Not today, sunshine. Friends for life? Fuck that bullshit. Travis strode off.

Jessie, at least, had the sense to keep her distance, no decency but a shred of fucking sense. Raphael sat next to her on the low stone wall in front of the funeral parlor. Held her hand. Her warm, soft hand, which was not folded, cold and limp over her chest. A hand that would stroke his face, cook him dinner, jerk him off. A hand to hold as he squeezed, clasped, slapped, fucking pulled her hair, pulled her into his arms and kissed her.

Fuck Jessie with her blonde hair and baby blues. Fuck Raphael and his movie star looks and pop star charm. Travis had more money than they ever dreamed of, and he'd make sure he put it to good riddance to bad trash use.

Never Let Me Go

She told him everything. Knocked back one shot of tequila, then another, then started to cry.

Raphael held her close as he could without suffocating her as she buried her face into his chest. There was no point in saying what he thought—Jesus, Jessie, you should have convinced her not to do it, told someone, called an ambulance—why blame when nothing could be done. Or undone. Or atoned for. Other than to stake deeper regret in her heart.

"What did you tell the cops?"

Jessie snorted her snot and coughed. "What Pa told me to tell em: I knew nothing until she came to me looking for help, and I immediately got it for her."

Raphael rubbed his thumb and ring finger across his forehead. He did this whenever he was stressed out, as if he could rub the tension from his brain before a headache took hold.

"And they bought it?"

"Pa burned everything in the room. Destroyed the security camera footage. Said why should three lives be lost over a mistake."

"A mistake?"

"Oh, fuck. Fuck. Fuck." Jessie burst into tears again. "She made me swear not to tell anyone."

He stroked her hair and made comforting sounds. Fucking Sarah. Why put your best friend in that kind of situation and leave her with such a burden? "It's not your fault, baby. It's not your fault."

It took another ten minutes before Jessie's sobs subsided to sniffles, then silence. The motel was booked out due to the funeral. Raphael was in a second floor single with wood paneling and paintings of some brittlebush Alice must have done. They covered the walls as ubiquitous as the shrub in the desert. He'd never seen them before and the longer he stared, the more the petals looked like tongues and the brownish yellow heads like eyes.

Jessie pulled back suddenly, wiped her face with the back of her hand and squared her shoulders. "I'm gonna tell them everything."

"No, don't."

"I can't live with it. It's my fault. It's all my fault."

She brushed down her crumpled t-shirt and adjusted her tits. She did this whenever she made up her mind about something and was determined no matter who said what about it.

"No, Jessie."

She backed away from him. Barefoot on the hot concrete landing as she stepped out the door.

"Don't try to stop me, Raphael. I can't live with this."

He grabbed her hand as she turned; pulled her back into the room before she walked herself straight to the state pen. She tried to beat him off. Her strength stemmed from despair, not rage, and therefore, was no match for his determination to save her. She soon gave up; her punches became slaps, and her shouts turned to sobs.

"You think Sarah would want this? Do you, Jessie? Do you really?"

"No," she said finally, "she'd fucking kill me for even thinking about it."

"Exactly."

"Hold me," she said, finally pliant against him. "Hold me and never let me go."

He held her that night and the next but never was forever, and he had to leave before he couldn't. It was not the time to tell her he regretted moving to California every second of every day. That he was lonely and alone. He wouldn't give up. Not yet. One look in her glazed eyes told him she might.

"Come with me, Jessie. Leave all this behind. There's nothing here but sorrow for you now."

She could but wouldn't. Everything's a choice, and she didn't choose him. It was only ten years later he realized he'd chosen for both of them.

Time to Die, Motherfucker

There was an old barn at the far end of their property. Cows once over-wintered there. Later, it was a scrapyard for scattered farm equipment, tractors, and a rusting pickup on blocks, cab clear and clean except for the condensation ghosting the rolled windows.

That afternoon, it also housed the abortionist.

He sat tied to a chair in the middle of a dirt floor, all stained cuffs and collar and muddy eyes. The abortionist screamed but no one heard as his voice was muffled by duct tape. His eyes though, his eyes spoke volumes.

"Well?" Arms crossed over bare skin, jeans tight over ribbed belly, Cal sneered at the gun in Travis' hand. "You want him dead, so kill him."

The gun was heavy. Travis' hate and rage heavier. He'd shot his brother a thousand times in the dark recesses of his mind. Shattered his hard jaw, blown open those squinty eyes, shaved the perpetual stubble shadow and left a gaping hole in the back of his ape-sized skull. Travis seethed with frustration that all he could do was imagine.

An owl hooted in the rafters and slivers of sunlight seeped through dry, contracting roof timber.

"He took your woman… murdered your child." Cal's voice was a snake-hiss catechism in his ear. "You've been crying ever since for revenge. Well, you gonna be a man or a piece-of-shit mouse?"

Since they arrived, Cal had been casually swinging a rusty crowbar he'd pulled from a mangled pile of metal. The Abortionist's wide eyes followed every arc, tortured with the knowledge it would eventually land but not knowing where or when.

Cal ruffled Travis' hair, his stubborn cowlick defiantly springing back into place. "I ain't got all day, boy. You either gonna take care of your business, or I'm gonna have to let this... murderer... go."

There had been killing in Travis' brain ever since Sarah's funeral, but it hadn't quite reached his heart. It trickled somewhere in his veins along with a growing desperation to be anywhere other than in that barn. He'd shot things before, just nothing living and wasn't sure he wanted to start.

"What you think your woman would say, you standing here about to piss yourself?" Cal laughed and swung.

Connected.

The chair trembled as the Abortionist shook back and forth in agony as the crowbar crushed every bone in his right hand.

Cal's eyes narrowed. There was a fine mist of blood sprayed over his white T-shirt. "Won't be using that hand to kill any more babies."

"Stop it, Cal." It came out no more than a whisper.

Cal curled his thin lips into what he probably thought was a smile. Travis shivered. He'd seen that look before and not only once. There was a flush to his brother's sunken cheeks as he kicked an old metal pail with his black boot. It sailed at Travis, whizzing past his head as he warded it off with a bare arm.

Travis sucked in a gasp at the sharp pain as it connected with bone. How many bruises did he have from that bastard? Over his life? The gun trembled in his hand. Sweat pearled on his fingers, stung his eyeballs.

Ten years between them. For ten years, Cal was the only child. The golden child. When Travis came along, he was competition, and there was only one way to deal with competition. Travis had blanked most everything from his childhood, but he'd never forgotten the look in Cal's eyes that first time, the stone in his hand. Travis couldn't have been more than four. Pa told Cal to mind him while he and Ma entertained their guests. Cal's smile. The narrowing of his dark eyes, the shadow in them. Not annoyance. Hate. Previous pinches, slaps, never left a mark—Travis was just a cry-baby. But that day, Cal had stormed off, and Travis had followed. Followed him to the barn—this barn—and Cal had led him into a dark corner behind the pickup, picked up a large stone and said, "I'll bash your fucking head in you tell anyone. Now do as your told."

So, he did. Then Cal did what he wanted. Not once but many times. So many.

Until he met Sarah.

Travis quiet in the back corner of third-grade class. Soft-eyed Sarah crouching next to him. "Why are you so sad?" Soft hand on his hunched back. Her touch. Her one gentle touch. No need. No greed. No seed. He started to cry and couldn't stop. Big blobby tears drooled down his cheeks and onto his pale blue polo shirt with the embroidered eagle, and she took his hand. Took his hand and wouldn't let go. Said, "It's okay. It's okay." When he walked home, she followed, two steps behind. Said nothing the whole way only hummed a tune. Something they learned in school that week—she'll be coming round the mountain when she comes—and he paused, her voice an angel opening the gates of hell to rescue him. She sang and oh God, her voice, so big and strong and joyful, and he turned, her skipping along, swinging her book bag. Her smile, glorious as sunlight in a puddle, and he knew then, knew more than he knew pain or loneliness or despair, knew there was beauty in this world, and he held out his trembling hand as she skipped over all sunshine hair halo.

And she taught him how to say no.

And yes.

Sarah, oh Sarah, I could take anything long as you held my hand. Be anything. Do anything. Now you're gone, and I didn't protect you. I didn't save you after you saved me. This monster, this demon from hell, for that's what he was—look at him with his thick horn-rimmed glasses and overlapping teeth, the sweat stains, not yellow but brown at his armpits and cuffs, the smell of shit streaming down his legs as he witnessed the shift in Travis' eyes, heard the click of the safety. Eyes wide at his own imminent demise as Travis pulled the trigger.

Twice.

Next Time

It was the song that made him famous in twenty worlds. Unwritten, except in his heart, it burst from a burning yearning frustration at not being able to find her again *yet,* and although he refused to admit it, he was beginning to wonder if he ever would.

He'd just returned from his fifth timeline on the hundredth world. His parents had been threatening to lock him in his room until he came to his senses and at least ate something, let alone did his school lessons. What with exams coming up, how would he ever make it to university, let alone the Cadets and yes, of course, everyone has their own goals, ambitions, and journey, but did he understand he was throwing away a very promising future at the Quantum Labs because once, he maybe saw a girl in a phone booth in another dimension?

Yes! YES! She's real. I know it. And I will find her.

This is an obsession, not love, you don't know what or who or when or why she is or will become. She could be dying, dead, done.

No, you're wrong.

Wrong or right, you keep this up and don't study, I'm confiscating the transporter.

I dream of her, Michael would say, and his brothers would roll their eyes and his sisters sigh. And the dreams are so real. Real as me here now. Are dreams merely portals we've not yet tapped?

Mother would smile as if she knew the answer but would not say. Father remained silent at first and only frowned, until mother nudged him, and he said, "The universe is limitless. There is neither beginning nor end. Same as consciousness. This is why you must accept the futility of finding her again, if she exists in corporeal form at all. You must protect yourself and your dreams. Do not get dragged into another consciousness for you might never return."

What his parents called discussions but were really demands for the surrender of the transporter followed.

"You've been searching long enough."

"I'll search forever."

"You have a week."

A week? A week? He had no name. No time. No dimension he could identify. How could he find her in a week? He snorted. Opened his mouth to protest; took one look at his parents' faces and shut it again. He stormed off.

He would find her.

Someday.

Somewhere.

Sometime.

NEXT time.

Next time will be different. I'll find her next time. He said the same thing each time he failed, and it became his nickname at home. Each transporter trip took two minutes though it felt much longer, two days maybe. Two minutes, the length of a commercial break or the time it took mother to decide what they would have for dinner, his siblings to complain, and his father to blink from behind his teleprompter where he read ten different versions of the same news, and they'd all take one look at Michael's face and know he hadn't found her AGAIN and "Next time, don't come back," his brothers sniggered because they were older, and crueler, and his two younger sisters patted him on the back and said: "Next time, Michael, you'll find her next time."

And in that space between his deflation and their consolation, his sisters held his hand as mother said: "Your studies, Michael, why don't you get through school and put your brilliant mind towards the geo-plotting device you patented. Our world needs the ability to map universes, and track jumping histories. Then you might find where she is, or at least, was. Maybe even where she will be."

But that's infinity. No one can map infinity. It's impossible.

Think of all the impossible that became possible. Believe…

And on the last evening of that one week, when he still hadn't found her, he walked down the crowded boulevard after school under cherry blossom trees in full bloom, petals drifting like snow, people passing, lost in their own worlds on the way to home, work, to wherever they went in the city on the Hill, and his heart was so full of longing and despair, he burst into song before it broke. Not a song, but THE song of his heart, and the words came without thinking; the melody flowed with feeling.

The words were simple, made up as he walked along—streetlights and shop lights blinking on, the air calm but full of city noises—but the sound he made as he sang, sang with all the yearning in his heart: for her, for her eyes—full of fear but then of wonder because the second they touched, he knew she felt the same—the sound was faith that dreams were not imagination but other realities merging. The unconscious borderless, limitless. And he would find her again. He BELIEVED.

I believe
The worlds I wade
The wars raged; chaos engaged.
I believe
I believe you are out there.

Out there, you emerge from a swirl of dust
Beauty is not skin deep
It glows and gleams,
A measure of the treasure of your smile.

I will find you.
Someday, somewhere, sometime, next time
I believe…

And though it takes a thousand years
Though I shed a million tears
Though we live and die and live again.
I will find you

Someday, somewhere, sometime, next time
I believe
Oooh, I believe…

A great need rose in him with all the passion of his youth, not just for a girl—THE girl—but for a life yet to be lived, an adventure to be earned, heartache, heartbreak. And his song as he sang, walking through the park, his mind, his heart, his whole being striving for another plane—her plane, her world—was defiance to all the naysayers of his family and his own encroaching doubts, and whoever heard him sing on that warm, spring evening was filled with a renewed belief in beauty, in love, in possibility and wonder.

And it so happened as he paused by the lake, swans and their cygnets paddling past—eleven of them, such an impressive brood—the slant of the setting sun catching his blue eyes like sea glass on the shore, that first one, then many girls—mostly because even in his time he was a beautiful young man—were entranced by his voice, so pure and profane, and he was filmed by many, and the videos shared a million times in one hour, ten million in two, and he was quickly found by those who sought to capitalize on the newest trend and within a month, he was a superstar, which was neither his desire nor his intention. There were endless offers, but there was only one girl in the universe for him and next time, NEXT time he would find her.

Light in Your Darkest Hour

The night of the fire, Jessie was on the toilet pissing on a stick. The line came up straight away, solid blue. She stared at it, hand steady, heart lurching. Thought, there's two sides to every line and both tell the same story.

You're fucked.

Cold porcelain could not cool the flamethrower flush of dread. Fuck. Fuck. Fuck.

She smelled the smoke two seconds before she heard the screams and in those two seconds, reckoned all manner of mishaps: a guest squirting fire lighter on a lit BBQ, a tossed cigarette igniting brush, a blown car engine, all and everything in those two seconds except, the motel being on fire.

Jessie hurried out into a night red as sunrise or sunset. Stood frozen before flames dancing from the blasted-out windows of Room 28. What the fuck? What the fuck? Her disbelief was a form of denial, an inability to deal with two major fucked-upped forms of shit in two minutes.

"Pa, no!"

Alice clung to Pa for dear life, holding him back from the open door where smoke billowed, and flames danced.

"Pepper's in there and I'm getting her out." Pa pried Alice's hands from his arm, pulled off his shirt and covered his face.

"Don't, Pa!" Jessie screamed as she ran. She wasn't about to lose him too.

The heat was immense, a portal of hell. There were paint and cleaning supplies in that room. Someone had set this fire, and she thought she knew who. There was no way Pepper was still alive in that. No way. Fire engines sounded in the distance. The water would cost a fortune if there was even enough.

A bark. A desperate whining yelp. That's what did it. "Pa. No." Jessie closed in, reached for his strong, sinewy arm. Missed.

And he was gone.

Alice and Jessie looked at each other, then the doorway. Pa danced around the burning bed, scooped up Pepper and lava-hopped across the carpet. The fire engines stormed into the back lot just as Pa went down, overcome by the smoke and in the moment it took Jessie to judge whether the firemen would get there in time, Alice darted in after him.

"Alice!" Jessie lunged, but someone grabbed her and held her back. Someone with pale skin, sandy-colored hair and bright blue eyes who seemed to shimmer in the glow of the flames.

"Save them, please," she screamed as the roof collapsed.

PART FOUR

The Beginning of Time

Many years ago, in a time unremembered by humans but which the hills still talk about, a leopard came to the desert. Though they did not recognize it, the other creatures scurried from its scent: the snakes, gophers, and rats to their holes, the birds to their nests, even the insects stilled.

Muscles dense as gold, coat black as night, the cat did not know he was a cat. He was born of darkness and impervious to light, left no footprint on the sand and cast no shadow for he was shadow.

As he moved across the desert, the birds stopped singing, the snakes stopped hissing, and the gophers ceased their chattering. The air itself held its breath.

The leopard did not eat. Did not drink. Only padded over dust and stone for a hundred days until one night, he came upon a young man camping under the stars. The man was not afraid of the leopard as it curled next to his fire and even offered it some of his food which the leopard declined.

The young man was not prone to talking. Yet, that night, beside a warm fire and under a full moon, he felt the burdens of a life already lived and a future still to unfold. His regrets and fears were as big as the desert was empty, and as the fire crackled and embers glowed, he opened his heart to the leopard.

When he was done, the sun crested the horizon, and the man felt the weight of his world lift from his shoulders. Gone was the need to fulfil expectations, including his own. The world was open, anything possible. His heavy heart light for the first time in a long time.

Thus enlightened, the young man asked the leopard, "What is it you seek?"

"I seek nothing. I only am." And with that, the leopard ate the young man.

"Wait. What? What the fuck, Bob. Where's the lesson in this fable? The hell?"

Bob kept rocking back and forth in his rocking chair. "The leopard doesn't care. The leopard was hungry and ate."

"But the man offered him food."

Bob shrugged. "He wasn't hungry then."

"So that's the lesson? Some fatalistic bullshit?"

Bob stopped rocking. "No lesson, man, except maybe, there's no happy endings… and watch out for black leopards."

"Leopards? There's more than one?"

"There's always more than one."

Travis popped his can of cola. The hiss and fizz were the sweetest sounds he'd heard in ten years, along with the sound of his boots as they thumped on the bone-dry deck of the General Store. He didn't know Bob or his friend, two old-timers with nothing better to do than shoot the shit and spit chew in the spittoon, bullseye every time. He debated mentioning there were no leopards round these parts, never had been, never would be. Stories were stories, most of em bullshit, and he'd heard enough bullshit in the pen to know it when he heard it.

He'd been a quiet one inside—always one or two in each block—didn't say much, kept to himself, shanked the first bastard who tried to make him squeal like a pig. Didn't take much after that. Pa's money and his quietness were the icing on the respect cake. Before long, he had his own gang of loners, misfits, and murderers who didn't fit in anywhere else. Within a few years, he had an empire.

He hadn't planned it. What he had planned was to wrap a sheet around his neck that first night, then the second, the third. He had been prepared to take his own life but refused to let anyone else take it, and when that motherfucking wet-back tried to fuck him up the ass, he put out his eye.

They came for him after that, course they did, but the guards had been paid off handsomely. His father had bought the story of the Abortionist killing Cal and him killing the Abortionist. He had to buy it; Travis was all he had left.

He began his ten-year bid as a kid, came out a man. A worse man than he'd gone in but smarter. Crueler. Darker. A car was waiting for him when he got out. No mother or father, only a limo. Bob and his friend made a show of how much they weren't noticing it or Travis.

He crushed the cola can and tossed it in the trash. He was going back but moving forward. What had he missed in ten years?

He was about to find out.

The Past is the Only Hope for the Future

It would have been very easy for Alice to feel sorry for herself and she did… for a year…or two. It began with rage, a churning inferno in the pit of her stomach at what had been taken. Not lost, stolen. Hard to throw much of a tantrum, though, when your legs were useless lumps. Instead, she smashed the odd glass of lemonade, ice cubes skittering across a floor she could no longer stand upon, beat her pillow with her fists or screamed. A lot.

She refused to eat, to blink, to speak for the first few weeks as she lay in the hospital, casts up to her waist and on both her arms, bandages everywhere else. Miraculously, her skin was red but not burnt, but that was the only grace she got. She worried about being a nugget, terror howling through her like the wind through Redwing Cave on a winter's night. Wouldn't be hiking up there anymore. Ever.

Thank fuck it turned out only her legs were fucked cause at least she could kill herself if it came to it.

Couldn't go to Pa's funeral. Had to watch the live stream, everyone solemnly passing his closed coffin—was Pa really in there? Really? Hardly. It was all some sick joke, hah fucking hah—same as when the kids from school came to visit. Some of them anyway. She would remember each and every one and what they wrote on her four casts.

She said nothing to her friends. Nothing at all. Eventually word got round, and Alice was left alone with their fading cast tags and the nurses who changed her bed pan and bandages and washed what was left with a yellow sponge, each damp stroke cool comfort for it provoked the memory of a dream.

A dream of a man who ripped the burning beam from her broken body with a mighty roar, tossed it aside like an empty can and lifted her in his arms. His eyes as he looked down at her. His blue eyes gone smokey black.

The heat. She shivered just thinking about it. The air itself on fire: nose hairs crinkling, her long hair crisping, skin red and clothes smoking. How did he not flinch from it? He held her close yet gently as he waded through burning timber, past a toxic-fumed mattress, paint cans about to explode and out the door.

"Pa!" her burnt voice crackled as she clutched the collar of his sooty white shirt. "Save him, please."

He lay her flat. Touched her limp arms, and a tingling went through them like a shock from a faulty light switch, then moved towards her legs.

"Please," she cried and pushed him away.

He went. Where firefighters wouldn't, where Jessie couldn't. As flames roared, hoses whooshed, and Jessie screamed. He turned at the doorway to look at her and said: "Stay alive. I will return. I will find you. Just stay alive." Then he was gone.

The First Time He Broke a Promise

That taste. That bittersweet taste of almost. Sure, it was more horror than suspense. Still, less frightening than reality, and reality was the producer wagging his cock in front of his face, and Raphael having to decide just how much he wanted that maybe part. Would he get down on his knees, put a cock in his mouth and think horror wasn't a monster in a dark closet but a two-bit producer with bad breath and stinking, saggy balls who preyed on dreams? Or would he tell him to eat shit?

It wasn't that Raphael was above using his looks and goods to get where he wanted, he just wasn't *that* desperate. Yet. He survived—barely—by working as a late-night bartender at a dive bar off Pico which was how he met Ash. Twenty, tiny and tipsy. She was slumming it; he had no choice.

Ash knocked back a shot and wiped her mouth with the back of her hand. "You need to know the right people." Her reddish-brown hair, limp with grease or sweat—it hardly mattered—framed dull brown eyes. Despite the wear and tear, she was not unattractive.

"And are you the right people?"

She leaned forward on the bar, elbows on bottle-bruised wood and gave him a good view of her ample tits. "I could be."

Raphael coughed and averted his eyes. It had been three long years, but he hadn't cheated on Jessie once. At the start, they'd talked on the phone every day—two, even three times—and each time, he wanted to return home. He nearly did when he heard about the fire. Not that Jessie or even his best friend told him. No, he had to hear about it from Dakota. He dropped everything, got in his truck and called to say he was on his way, but Jessie got into a feral panic. Said she had enough to take care of without taking care of him too.

"I'll be alright. You just make sure you make something of yourself before you ever come back here again."

That hurt. A lot. But what did he have to offer her? Not much... nothing. And until he did, he didn't want to burden her further, even with phone calls. Their frequent video calls turned to sporadic voice notes, then texts, and finally, silence. For what? Months? A year? Longer?

He kept meaning to call, but every time he picked up the phone, he was too embarrassed to admit his failure. Too scared to find out she'd moved on, met someone new. As long as they didn't speak, he could continue to believe she waited for him.

Coward he was and knew it, but he would make it, he would, and he'd come for her then. Make everything up to her.

His conviction about the future lasted slightly longer than their communication. Excitement had ground to frustration wrapped in a threadbare motel blanket of loneliness. Recently, the loneliness had devolved to isolation: late nights on the balcony, star-staring while questioning his choices and his stoic belief that something big was in his future, big as in billboards, magazine covers, and silver screen stardom. Didn't matter if millions had that dream before him. Most of them either hightailed it back to their small towns with their big dreams between their legs or were sidewalk-slouched, twisted up in something, *anything,* that kept the dream alive.

That would never be Raphael.

Ash stroked the back of his hand with a ragged fingernail. She was a couple of steps from that street, a throw-away girl in a throw-away town.

"My Aunt Meg is the manager of Requiem."

"Requiem?" He pulled his hand back and dried glasses while not looking at her tits. He'd no money to spare for whatever habit hadn't quite taken hold of her, and he wasn't about to screw her. Too many better-looking and cleaner women had already offered.

"It's only the hottest restaurant in town. All the industry big shots eat there: producers, directors, stars. A gig there, handsome fella like you is sure to get noticed."

"A gig? I'm no musician."

Ash rolled her eyes. "Waiting tables, man. Smile. Flash those wicked green eyes, flutter those long lashes and slip your business card into every alligator purse."

He didn't have any business cards.

"You got a reel?"

"Nope."

"Headshots?"

Those, he had.

"It's a start." Ash rolled a cigarette and licked the paper with thin spittle and thinner lips. "I'll help you, man, but look, it's a two-way street, you get me?"

He could guess what she wanted. Money, probably. Sex. He didn't have the former and wasn't inclined towards the latter; he'd made a promise to Jessie. Not one she'd asked for or had accepted, but one made, nonetheless. His hand and memories saw him through most nights. Possible junkies with probable dodgy muff weren't on his list of sights to see.

"I'll pass." He dimmed the lights for final call. Shitty infomercials on the cheap TV and canned soup and saltines waited for him in his room.

She jumped to her feet and grabbed his arm. Her red nail polish was chipped, the hangnails she'd been chewing, mangled. "I need a place to crash for a few days.

He was green but not fresh. "Yeah, don't think so. Sorry."

She wouldn't let go. He didn't want to strong-arm her but pried loose her fingers one by one.

"Why not ask your aunt?"

She let go, and her face sank along with her hand. "Don't want her to know I'm struggling. I only need a sofa or a floor. Get off the street. Shower. Clean up. Then I'll be out of your hair. I'll take you over to Requiem tomorrow. My aunt, she'll…" Ash paused, looked at him from under long lashes. Her eyes were clear but were they conniving? "She'll love you. She only hires the best-looking starlets."

"I got a girlfriend," Raphael said in a last-ditch attempt to dissuade her where his own soft heart wouldn't.

She smiled. "Don't we all."

*

Raphael waited tables. He learned quickly how to smile without raising his eyes too much, only his lashes, to recognize the most powerful called the least attention to themselves, who to say no to, who to say yes.

So, when Manager Meg said, "Why don't you stay on for a few minutes, Raphael?" after last serving and bar closed and dishwasher steam hissed in those fine hours between night and day, he stayed on. It was a team meeting, team consisting of Meg and Big Dick Rick, Raphael jerked off under his apron, never taking his eyes from Meg's—those olive pit-hole, kohl-black eyes—cause she was pushing forty and pills and pecker weren't enough anymore as Rick bent her over the bar and rogered her from behind, she had to have an audience.

And when he took Rick's place, she gave him the side gigs catering at the soirees in the Hills where meat wasn't only served on silver trays, and he serviced old broads with powerful husbands. Maybe he didn't want to whore himself out to sixty-year-olds pulled so tight they'd lost a layer of skin, but nothing could get the years from their eyes and the longer he looked into them, the deeper he sank, but if he didn't, someone else would. They waited at the open door, lined up cause Mrs. Bartlett loved a train, and her husband was the hottest shot producer in town, and when she tugged Raphael's hair, he raised his head from between her legs where he learned women over sixty don't need to wax cause they're bald anyway. And she smiled and said, you, only you, and the rest—cocks in hands pumping fast to try and stay hard—dressed and left.

Back down he went, tongue darting, slurping and moaning, groaning not to gag and, "Baby, Christ almighty, I want you so bad," and he showed her. Fuck, he was hard. Hard just thinking about the break, the make, the fucking snake. No thoughts of love, just tasting that fucking dream, and it tasted of rotten fish juice, and no amount of designer perfume was gonna take that stink away. Told her: I never seen tits fine as yours and pussy so warm and snug, three kids, I don't believe it, and she trailed a long, fake nail down the side of his face. Drew blood. Said, "I like you, what's your name?" and he told her, but she'd already forgotten by the time he zipped up. So, he slipped one of his new cards between her fake tits cause Ash told him you handed those fuckers out to anyone who took them, said, "Call me any time." And she did. The next day. "There's a motel on Sunset."

So he showered, shaved, practiced shady seductions in the chipped and shadow-stained motel mirror, ushered her in when she rapped three times on the door, led her to the bed, slipped off the expensive whore heels she wore for the side-dishes, massaged her feet, licked her toes as she lay back and moaned, and when he was done, or she was done with him, she ran her fingers through his hair as he absently licked her nipples like some yearling yearning for the womb and when she asked, "So, Raphael, you got a girl back home?" he said nothing cause even though they no longer spoke, Jessie's name was sacred. Sacred as moon and stars, and he couldn't tarnish it.

"Only you, ma'am."

A couple of weeks and half a dozen motel rooms later, she invited him to dinner.

"At your house?"

"It's not a house, darlin. It's an estate."

"Will your husband be home?"

She scoffed and nodded.

Raphael was desperate, but he was not insane. "Does he know about…"

"Us?"

He nodded.

"He knows you're a friend of mine." She rubbed at the crescent moon scar on his hand. "I told him you might be good for a project he has coming up."

"Really? Truly?" He tried not to let his excitement show, but it was impossible.

"Dress decently and try to keep your hands to yourself while you're there."

No problem, sweetie. "It's gonna be hard."

"It already is." She looked down, took him in her hand and started stroking. It felt good. It always did. She knew what she was doing even if he had to close his eyes and find Jessie to cum.

Her husband was a regular at Requiem but none of his dates were.

"Evening, sir," Raphael held out his hand, but Richard didn't take it, only clapped him on the back and led him into a room, which ran the length of a basketball court, or two. He'd never seen a room that big with so little furniture. There was only a long, white sofa, a couple of lamps and some sculpture situated before a wall of glass overlooking the valley where head and taillights glistened and gleamed in a sea of neon.

Seemed neither of them wanted a home, only a view.

"Richard, call me Richard."

Dinner was fat steaks and skinny potatoes with some greenery tossed in for show. They were already half in the bag from fine cellared wine, Mrs. Bartlett tonguing the rim of her crystal while twiddling the diamond rope necklace dangling between her tits. Raphael avoided looking at her as much as possible, which became increasingly more difficult the later it got and the drunker he became and by the time Richard had poured the whiskey, she was toeing him under the table.

Small talk expanded to life stories; Richard proud of his rag-to-riches background.

"Bullshit." Mrs. Bartlett said. "Both your folks were in the business."

"Sure, but they made me earn my own way.

"Honey, please."

Richard laughed. "Yeah, it's pretty much bullshit, but you must keep up appearances. How about you, Raphael? What's your story?"

He told them about flat desert plains and endless sky, of rattlers and sage and rocks and caves and bats and dust, and his eyes went all faraway to a night when the stars painted the sky with every future and every past. He didn't tell them how he had fingered the ring in his pocket, debating whether to get down on one knee and beg Jessie to wait for him. How he didn't because it would have been too selfish to tie her down like that. Instead, he told them about the carnival and the phone booth, and the night they all woke from the same dream with sand in their shoes and hair.

"So, you don't know if this phone booth where all your dreams come true is real or not?"

Raphael shrugged. "Back home, there's all sorts of legends everyone says they don't believe, but they all do. I saw it once. At least I thought I did. Chased it in my truck but like the end of a rainbow, couldn't ever reach it."

There was silence, but in that silence, communication continued between Richard and Mabel as it does with all long-term couples.

"Honey, why don't you show Raphael the view while I finish my wine?" Mrs. Bartlett said as she met Raphael's eyes.

Said view from the wraparound balcony was heavenly and just as fucking cold. Raphael shoved his hands in his pockets to try and stay warm and held his breath.

He didn't have to hold it for long.

"I'll get right to the point, Raphael. I've been looking for a new face I can make a star, and Mabel is right, you're an eye-catching bastard."

Raphael's teeth stopped chattering and something big blossomed in his chest. Like the magic phone booth, he couldn't quite allow himself to believe it was real no matter how desperately he wanted to.

"I hope you'll keep making my girl happy."

Raphael's heart winced, but his mouth replied. "Yes, sir."

"Tell me more about this phone booth. I reckon there's some story there."

Whether he believed in it or not, there and then, on heaven's terrace overlooking the land of dreams, Raphael told Richard Bartlett a story about a phone booth in the middle of the desert that made dreams come true.

And his did.

When the Time is Right

"Whatcha going to name him, Jessie?" It wasn't the first time someone asked her or even the tenth.

Jessie shrugged.

"It'll come to you, don't you worry. When the time's right, you'll know."

Jessie had no intention of worrying about it until she had no choice.

When it came, the birth was hard, and she was alone through most of it. Didn't call anyone, not even Dakota. She writhed in bed and swallowed her screams till they vomited out of her in a torrent of agony. Alice called, then crawled from the next room, dragging her dead legs behind her. The sheer panic on her face. "Hold on, Jessie. Hold on." Her picking up the phone, dropping it. "Dakota. Dakota, Jessie's having the baby." Dakota on speaker as she raced over, telling Alice what to do, most of which she couldn't. And, oh God, the pain of it. How was such agony even possible? How? How? She couldn't catch her breath. "Breathe, Jessie, breathe." Couldn't. Only gasp as the contractions thundered down her narrow cervical lane. Dakota leaning over her, long white hair a blizzard. "You have to push. Push!" I can't breathe. Can't. Her mind hovered somewhere above looking down. Shut off. "Jessie! Jessie!" Hard slaps to her face. "Push, girl. Push." And it went on and on for hours, it seemed. Days. Get it out of me. I don't care if I die, if it dies, if we all fucking die, just get it fucking out.

And finally, she grabbed her hamstrings, bore down with every bit of flagging strength she had and out it came.

Silence.

A flurry of activity while Dakota fished for something in her satchel. A crochet needle? Limp hair straggling across sweaty face, eyes scrunched, she fussed between Jessie's legs, elbows jutting, head bent, faint prayers or curses coming from pursed lips, as Jessie faded in and out.

"Done. You have a beautiful boy."

Dakota lifted the child, still purple, nearly black from the umbilical cord which had been wrapped twice around his neck—shoulda killed him, didn't—and she wrapped him in a clean towel. He gurgled, then screamed.

"Put him on your breast, darlin."

Don't want to. Don't want it. He was pain. Dark as her memories. Dakota said nothing, only eased the screaming infant into the crook of Jessie's arm and aimed his mewling mouth at her nipple till he latched.

Jessie didn't look at him. Not once. But she held him. At least that.

Dakota held up a filmy piece of long, wet tissue. "You'll want to keep this." It dripped onto Jessie's bare arm. "It's a caul. Your water never broke, and your boy was born with it intact. Means he'll never drown."

Jessie laughed hard and long. Couldn't stop. "Never drown?" What the hell was he gonna drown in out here? Even the pool was dry. It was the funniest thing she ever heard. Her laughs went all screechy, then screamy. Dakota looked like she didn't know whether to hug or slap her again. Pull it together, Jessie, you're losing your shit. I wanna lose my shit. I'm not ready for this shit. I'm only nineteen. How the fuck am I supposed to run a business, take care of a crippled sister and raise a kid all on my own? How the fuck? How?

Her laughs turned to sobs. The baby gurgling on her swollen tit looked up at her, eyes all big and wide, his tiny fists kneading her flesh, and she never asked for all this, but she got it anyway, and she was stuck, well and truly stuck. Just when her life should have been starting, it had all ended in a ball of flames. Everyone gone, Mom, Bobby, Pa, Sarah, Raphael... Travis, and she was left with the carnage.

*

Jessie hasn't slept. Jessie hasn't slept in a million years. Sun blasting, heat cooking, baby teething. Mornings at the motel, nights at the diner. Instead of sleeping, she stared at the ceiling and listened to the trucks crunching tarmac, the hiss of the neon sign, the baby's screams. He was a beautiful baby even with eyes clenched and mouth mewling. A beautiful boy.

She didn't know whether to love or hate him.

Alice shifted in the next room. Amazing how quickly she'd gotten used to the wheelchair. Refused any assistance from the get-go, falling and nearly cracking her head on the toilet rather than letting Jessie help her. Always the same—stubborn as hell with a temper just as hot. Still, she couldn't hide her tears.

Screams. The baby again. On his back in the crib. Jessie didn't pick him up, only stared. Tiny fists thrashed at the wind-up mobile dangling over him, glowing in the dark. Twinkle, twinkle little star, how I wonder what you are...

*

Even though her Pa was gone, he'd had friends and an insurance policy. While the husbands repaired the burnt-out rooms, their wives helped her, doting on the baby: "What you name him, Jessie?" Nothing. No name. She didn't know, didn't care. He was everything taken and nothing gained, only another mouth to feed. The wives brought food for the first month or so after the birth, home-cooked meals she'd stir around with a fork. Once their husbands were done, they moved on, and Jessie was left to face a future where she was the one responsible for everyone and everything.

She tried. God knows, she tried, but shit just got worse. There was not enough money left over to maintain the pool, so fewer families stayed. In their place, there were more loners and those just passing through, most with guns or ganja, or who knew what.

Then the working girls moved in. One by one till there were five down the back of the L, back where Room 28 had burned down and Pa with it. Back where Jessie didn't go no more cause even though no trace of the fire remained, the echoes of crackling flames, Alice's screams, and the thump of Pa's body as it hit the floor were loud as the trains which passed in the late hours, freight rumbling and rattling.

Maria and Carl kept the diner going, hired a few more locals, one of whom ran off with a week's takings right when the produce and butcher bills and paychecks came due.

At that point, Jessie gave serious consideration to drowning herself in the bathtub. She filled it with hot water, rising steam a congregation of ghosts, knocked back a couple of Alice's pain pills—can you believe this shit, Jessie? Can't feel my legs but my damn ass hurts all the time—and she slunk down, eyes open, blowing bubbles in the water. Baby screaming, Alice calling, and underwater it was all not mute but muted, a warble instead of a roar. It might stop altogether if she only stayed down, staring at the damp ceiling speckled with mold she couldn't remove no matter how much bleach she used, seeing Rorschach images of a life she shoulda, coulda, wouldn't have. Heart throbbing as her breath got thready. Stay down, it'll all be over soon.

Did she want to die? What did that mean, anyway? According to Dakota, death was merely a transition to another plane. Was it better there? Did it matter? She just wanted it all to stop. For a day.

Forever.

A thud and a blood-curdling scream drew her from the bath. She grabbed a towel and ran to her room. Nearly slipped on the wet floor. Paused at the door, afraid what new woe would greet her.

The baby had rolled off the bed, his screams muffled by a mouthful of carpet.

There are lines in everyone's mind. Lines walked daily between sanity and insanity, good and evil, happiness and despair. Most skirt the edges either way, at one point in time or another, and there was Jessie, tight roping all three.

Hair dripping, eyes dry, she knelt next to the screaming infant who was hiccupping tears. Was he hurt? She picked him up and held him at arm's length, his arms and legs thrashing. Everything seemed okay. No head bumps, no protruding bones. She stuck him on her tit as that generally shut him up.

"Jessie? Jessie?" Alice called from down the hall. "Is everything okay?"

"Everything's fine. Be there in a minute." Which meant anywhere from two to a hundred.

She never looked at the baby as he fed, only away towards the TV which she stared through no matter what was on, or at the blank wall where memories she wanted to forget played out over and over again.

The baby gurgled happily. No point in either of them crying no more. Either shit or get off the pot. He coughed. Retched. He was choking on his own spit up. Jessie pulled him off, patted his back, gently at first, then harder, hard as her heart pounded. His face was red and his eyes wide. There was no breath from him. No breath.

Breathe, she willed as she spread him over her arm and whacked his back. Breathe, she screamed.

Who cried harder when he finally puked all over her and caught his breath? Impossible to tell through her tears.

"Oh, my God," Jessie cried to a God she no longer believed in. "Oh my God, thank you. Thank you."

For the first time, she drew him in and cuddled him. Looked deep into his pooling, wide, green eyes, his mouth flecked with milk and spittle and saw not pain, but love. Felt her heart expand and fill.

"I love you, Ryan." For a name came to her in that flash of tenderness. "I love you so much."

Time to Pretend

"It's not a bang. Get me? It's a whimper. There's no asteroid on a collision course with earth. No zombies, no disease wiping out ninety percent of civilization, no mass infertility or dinosaur clones or alien invasion. No bombs, earthquakes, or tidal waves. Got it? It's one man. One. Lost. Broken. You, man. You. At the end of it all. It's not the whole world but it's *your* whole world and it's gone, man, gone. And all you've got left is this hope you can find this magic phone booth in the middle of an endless desert. Cause that's your salvation. Right? The endless rotary-dial roulette of possible parallels. And somewhere. Somewhere in time and space is your soul mate. And you run, then walk, then crawl until you find it, and there it is. There she is."

Chin on chest, Raphael said nothing. He couldn't tell the director, Marty Weaver, that's not what the phone booth was at all cause that's what it was now. He couldn't tell him because the movie was no longer his, he'd sold the concept for fifty grand and a starring role.

It had taken years. From the point he told Richard the story to being on set, and starring— can you believe it, Jessie? — starring in a big Hollywood movie with, get this, Chloe Rogers. Raphael was as high on life as he could be without leaving the ground, though truth be told, he did seem to be floating. At first, it was a challenge to act morbid, depressed, and desperate when all his dreams were coming true. Beaming in the bright lights, could he rise to the challenge? Find inner despondency in the wake of pure joy?

Lights bright and hot. Collar sweat. It's called acting, Rafa, baby. That's the assignment. Imagine it. Be it. But could he? Had he ever known despair? Had he really?

Yes.

It came that afternoon. A letter. Not a text or a DM or voice note or even an email. A letter sent via his management company. That's how serious she was. She must have known, must have smelled it on him even hundreds of miles away. How many times had he dipped his wick in someone else's wax in what? Seven, nearly eight years? Worse yet, how many times had he gone home? Never, not once, that's the answer. Not since Sarah's funeral. The shame of it. Guilt building bigger and bigger roadblocks until he couldn't face her, couldn't call her, couldn't tell her: Jessie, I'm selling my dick but not my soul, that'll always belong to you.

Clackers clacking, booms in his face, he had to imagine the place he left behind when all he wanted to do was forget. See the face of his famous co-star and love her. A stranger. A beautiful stranger but a stranger. How was it possible? Act, Rafa boy, act. And do it quick or you're done, this business ain't waiting for anyone.

So, he looked at Chloe close up, their noses nearly touching, her eyes green and glittering and saw blue. Saw warm tan and thin limbs, not pale, near translucent skin, didn't see brown hair but blonde and as he pulled his co-star into his arms and held her tight near crushing, lips close but not touching, he spoke, not the line but the lesson.

"I can't make it without you, Jessie. The money, the fame... none of it matters. There's no dream come true without you by my side. Come with me. Please. I'm begging you. I don't know where we'll end up, might be anywhere or nowhere, but we'll give it our best shot. Together."

Raphael kissed Chloe's thick pillow lips, imagining another's. He started to cry as he kissed her. Real tears, not some shit they'd sprayed in his eyes. He clung to her as the dream slipped away, riding a pony dead to the ground, the carcass left for the vultures.

*

"That looked real."

Ash watched him over her copy of the script. Slouched in a metal folding chair, sunglasses perched on top of her head, auburn hair messy-bunned, she smoked her cigarette languidly despite all the glares from the crew.

Ash glanced at Chloe Rogers, star of the minute, who was beaming at him.

"Got a new fan."

Raphael sighed. "It's called acting, Ash. Acting. Kind of like how you acted poor and desperate."

She rolled her lips and nodded. "Yeah, well, at the time, I was."

Apparently, it was a rite of passage for Hollywood brats to go off the rails and frequent shitty motels and trod alleys pockmarked by tents and needles. Who knew? Raphael certainly didn't when he'd given her a blanket and a pillow but not his bed.

"How's it feel?" Ash said.

"How's what feel?"

"All your dreams coming true, thanks, in no small part, to you know who."

It was no lie. Between hooking him up at Requiem, turning out to be Richard's business partner's daughter on a bad bender and helping him write the script, he owed Ash a lot.

"How can I ever repay you?"

"Well…" He knew that tone and knew it well, it always spelt trouble, or at least trouble for him. "I seem to have developed a crush on Chloe Rogers …"

"Pretty sure she likes cock, Ash."

Ash smiled. "We'll see."

*

Raphael left his movie star trailer with all the comforts of home and then some. He was suffocating and it wasn't from the heat. Ground lights lit something of a path around the other trailers and over to the set, but Raphael headed away from it all, off into the desert, Milky Way bright enough to guide him.

When he was far enough away to think he was alone, he came across Chloe Rogers perched on a large boulder, blowing smoke rings into the night,

"You need to get away from the world to see it." She took a swig from a tequila bottle and offered him the bare neck.

"Thanks, but I don't drink while filming," Raphael said.

"Dontcha now. Interesting."

They'd spent the day shooting the most intimate of sex scenes—tasteful, though barely—all grainy close-up art. He blushed remembering the bulge in his pants as she ground against him in silk, moaning while the corners of her mouth curled into a smirk at the state of him.

What was he supposed to talk about now? The weather?

"Don't worry, I don't bite." Chloe shoved over on the rock. "Unless you want me to." She full throttle laughed, thick brown hair cascading down her back.

He was half-terrified.

"Don't look like the most beautiful girl in the world now, do I?"

Actually, she did. In t-shirt and jeans, bare-faced and half-drunk, she was incredibly beautiful. He didn't want her though, despite the hand-job he'd given himself after their scene today. *Don't you? No, really, I don't.*

Chloe took another pull of tequila. "It's all smoke and mirrors. My shine was tarnished long ago. Now, I just know how to fake it. Got the best makeup people in the business: they white out those dark circles, cucumber those bags. Can't have ugly or old or God fucking forbid, both, females hanging about. Not a hope. Half-dressed and in distress is the name of the game. Once, I broke my ankle on set running in five-inch heels. Can you believe that shit?"

"That must have hurt. I always wondered why women run around in heels in films. Surely, they'd be smart enough to take them off?"

"Of course, they fucking would. But then you'd have no wank sock fodder. You think men have a hard time in this business? Women have to slice and dice and pump the voids with silicone."

"Really?" Chloe had no visible scars like those he'd seen neatly tucked on Mabel.

"Really. I haven't come to that crossroads… yet, but it's there on the horizon of thirty. Don't get me wrong, I wouldn't change my life of fame, fortune, and fucks for anything. But sometimes I wonder if I'd make the same choices now. They snag us when we're young and dumb and filled with a crazed ambition, driven to do whatever it takes to reach the top. I sucked cock just to GET an audition. Fucking pervs hitting on sixteen-year-old beauty queens with stars in their eyes but not on their doors. And it's not only the women. How many wanted you to suck their cock?"

Raphael shrugged. "Sure. But Chloe, you're the biggest star on the planet."

She was quiet for a long minute. On camera, they'd rubbed themselves raw against each other, shoved their tongues down each other's throats but what she was sharing under the stars, half a bottle in her, the rest about to go down, was somehow much more intimate.

"We all sell our souls eventually. Choices. Compromise. And finally, capitulation. Just remember, losing it all is never as bad as having it all."

The empty bottle arced through the air and landed with a thud.

"The world is full of men who take, Raphael. Don't be one of them. I fuck men, sure. Even enjoy it sometimes. But I only love women."

He helped her to her trailer, but she ended up in his. They talked till the moon dropped. He hadn't had a lick to drink, but his lips were as loose as if he was the one who'd finished off the bottle. It all came out: not his hopes and dreams but his guilt and regret. At some point, Chloe began to snore, but Raphael kept talking cause the shock of Jessie's words had worn off, and his mounting fear had to find a way out before it consumed him.

He was up at dawn to find coffee and something to eat. When he returned to his trailer to go over lines and wait for makeup to arrive, she was gone.

He read Jessie's letter again. And again. But no matter how many times he read it, the words didn't change. Why now? Had she met someone new? Had he really expected her to wait all these years for his sorry ass? He tried her again. Phone not in service. Alice, no answer. Travis, no answer. When Carl answered at the motel and Maria at the diner, both assured him everything was fine and congratulations on the filming and no, Miss Jessie did not wish to speak to him. They knew he would respect that and wished him all the best.

Chloe took one look at his face as he hurried towards set and led him away by the arm. "You're the lead, Raphael. You can't fly off in the middle of shooting."

"You don't understand. I have to go. Now. Right now. Something's wrong"

"Leave and the entire production shuts down."

"It's not far. I'll be back tomorrow." He paused. Would he? "The day after."

She looked at him as one would a toddler or an idiot or both. "Nothing's wrong; she just doesn't want you anymore. If she did, you would have heard from her at least once in the past, what? Seven years?"

"Don't say that."

"It's the fucking truth. People change. Consider yourself lucky; it could be worse. Your childhood friend could have sold the soft-core porn shots you did when you had a drug habit fed by a scuzzball manager who promised your tough titties the world."

"Jessie's not like that. She loves me and you can't stop loving someone just like that." *Really? After seven years? You sure about that?*

"Sorry, sunshine, but it happens all the time. Trust no one. No one. Assume everyone wants to fuck or make a buck, and you'll never be disappointed."

For a minute, a stone-cold minute, there was a sadness in Chloe's eyes. A sadness marrow-entrenched, and Raphael's pain sharpened in bas relief. He felt like throwing up.

"I still cry," she said, "and not only on demand. Tears cleanse the poison from your soul, but eventually you got to dry your fucking eyes and move on."

At which point, Raphael realized he'd been sobbing all along.

"You know there's nothing you can say or do that's going to change her mind. Right?"

"I gotta try."

Chloe sighed. "You abandon set, you'll never get another gig. This is the Big Time, baby. Fuck around and find out."

"I'm a nobody anyway."

"There's no shame in being a nobody, the danger is being a never was. You don't want to get blacklisted in this town. It will follow you to an inevitable early grave. You ready to give up everything? Are you really? After so many years of trying? And over a girl who point blank told you she didn't love you?"

So, she had been listening last night.

"You want to be an actor, forget that damn letter and pretend everything is hunky fucking dory. Finish the film. Deal with reality later."

"I don't know if I can."

"You have to. There's too much riding on this. Marty needs you. The crew needs you. And Raphael?"

She moved closer, long hair brushing against his bare arm, and he caught her freshly showered scent.

"Yes?"

"I need you..."

What time passed Raphael couldn't say. Only that he somehow made it through the day's shooting and woke the next morning in Chloe's trailer, limbs entwined, dick twitching at the memory.

Shit. Shit. What moral high ground did he stand upon? I only ever saw Jessie. Jessie. I called her Jessie the whole time. She didn't seem to mind.

Chloe's smile opened before her eyes. "Don't worry, it was just a fuck. A great fuck," she said as she finger-traced the hair on his chest, "but just a fuck."

He looked at her then, this beautiful woman, toned legs akimbo, hand stroking his morning-hard cock. Yeah, that's all it was. A fuck.

Her mouth moved upon him, and as he lay back, Raphael didn't close his eyes. Couldn't. Cause Jessie. Jessie was there. Here. There. Everywhere. The only place free of her was Chloe's face so he looked there. Stared as she worked on his cock, and she stared back, and even as he gasped and groaned, laid her back and licked her wet, Raphael didn't take his eyes from hers, and it was hot and urgent, both knowing it had nothing to do with each other. Only a fuck. A fuck.

He didn't want to hurt her. Didn't want to inflict his own pain upon her but... but my God, he wanted to ram his cock so far up her, he'd see the shadow of it in her eyes.

"Fuck me, Raphael."

He pressed down against her. Moved in that way Mabel taught him. Chloe blinked. Lips parted, sighed. He kept it up till she couldn't look at him anymore, only gasp. And when she was done and breathing hard, she rolled over and pushed that perfect peach ass that had launched a million magazine covers against him, and he'd never done that before. Never. Would never.

Chloe laughed. "Aren't you sweet? Now, fuck me, big boy, fuck me."

Raphael blinked, slathered Vaseline, closed his eyes and eased himself in.

"Does it hurt?"

"Only if you stop."

A discrete knock on the trailer door woke them. Raphael's heart pounded. Where the fuck am I? What time is it?

Chloe shoved his clothes at him, gestured towards the bathroom with a finger of silence on her lips. He sat on the toilet, not daring to dress as Chloe's PA chitter-chatted about schedule, makeup, hair, blah blah blah and in the murmur of their voices was a song and in that lullaby, a face, a name, a pain in his gut and suddenly it all crashed down, and Raphael heaved the remnants of his last supper for that's how he'd always remember it, the last supper before his world fucking ended, and whatever the fuck he ate burned his esophagus. Chicken, it was chicken. On his knees, he full-throat throttled chunks up and into the toilet. Didn't care who heard him anymore because he was dying, his insides splattered over the million-dollar trailer of the twenty-million-dollar actress he had just fucked up the ass.

*

Jessie.

Jessie, pick up the phone. Please.

But there was no answer because her number was no longer in service.

His stomach lurched again. He hadn't eaten in days, and the cast were starting to talk. The crew too. Marty took him aside. What are you on? What? What drugs you taking, Raphael? You're fucking strung out. Sorry, Marty, problems at home. Christ, don't fuck up my fucking film. No one gives a shit about your girlfriend problems. Grow the fuck up. Fuck you, Marty, he wanted to say, wanted to pull the cameras and lights and trolleys fucking down and wreck the place.

"I was going to propose, Chloe. Soon as filming was done. Had the ring and everything. It was my mother's mother's ring." He rubbed his ring finger. The pale crescent moon-shaped scar had never faded. They each had the same scar in the same place from the same time. Jessie…

"Raphael, snap the fuck out of it," her hand on his arm and all he could do was wish it was Jessie's. "Raphael, come on, we're almost there. Eight more weeks. Focus. Use your pain. Put it into your performance. It's what good actors do. They don't fake it, they channel it. My hospital bed scenes are next. Keep imagining I'm her. You'll win an Oscar."

Her smile was neither condescending nor pitying.

"Thanks, Chloe. I mean it. I owe you."

"Shut up and get over to makeup. You owe me nothing. Just one time before we wrap, fuck me. Not your ex. Fuck me."

Time to Move On

Raphael,

I hope you're doing well out there in movie land. Hear you got yourself a role in a film. It won't be long before you're a star. I know it.

When you left, I realized I didn't know how to live without you, and I had to find out. Truth is, there was only ever us, never me. Was that love or just habit? Either way, it wasn't good for me and probably not for you either.

I know you'll read this and maybe part of you will feel bad. Don't. It's been over seven years. I don't love you anymore and probably never did. You and me were a childhood romance, and we're not children anymore.

Don't take it hard, the world is opening for you. Go conquer it. If you ever cared for me, let me be.

Jessie

What the Fortune Teller Told Them Would Be

The boys squirmed on low stools, knees chest-high, wanting to be anywhere else. The girls tilted forward, mesmerized.

"It's a trick of the light," Travis hissed in Sarah's ear loud enough for everyone, including the fortune teller, to hear.

Sarah elbowed him in the stomach, and he nearly toppled backwards, laughing with Raphael behind the girls' backs.

Mistress Marlena didn't even raise an eyebrow, intent as she was on studying the frenetic silver flakes in her crystal ball.

"Looks like a snow globe," Travis said, none too quietly.

Raphael chuckled, and the girls glared. Mistress Marlena, however, did not break her concentration. The flakes grew thicker, and sparks began to emit from the crystal ball's surface like something in a mad scientist's lab. Mistress Marlena's eyes grew bigger, brighter; her pupils became whirls of worlds. Even the boys shut their mouths and sat up straight.

The lights flickered. The tent flaps puckered. The table shook. It felt like a rocket about to take off. The government launched them in the desert from time to time. It had been years since one had streaked across the sky, but they felt the same breath-held anticipation. The lights went out, and the crystal ball grew and grew till it filled the circumference of the table. Jessie clung to Raphael, Sarah to Travis.

"Place your hands upon the crystal ball, and I will read your future," Mistress Marlena intoned.

Raphael was the first to touch it. Static sizzled and his fingertips glowed as they connected with the crackling surface.

"C'mon, let's get out of here." Jessie tugged his hand. She thought getting their fortunes told would be a joke, something they could laugh about over a few beers and some smoke once they got out of this mess, but Raphael was mesmerized.

"Can you hear me? Raphael?" Jessie turned to Sarah and Travis, but they too had their hands on it. Jessie pulled harder. Her hand slipped. Connected.

Her skin tingled and eyelids fluttered. She no longer saw the crystal ball, Mistress Marlena or her friends. Instead, there was an opening to a dark tunnel surrounded by expanding prisms of light. Her friends paused at the mouth, hands on the edge, peering into the darkness.

Fuck. Fuck. She shouted as loud as she could, but none of them heard. Jessie slapped herself in the face. Hard. And she was back in the room.

"Raphael, wake up. We have to find Alice." She slapped each of the boys and clapped her hands in Sarah's face. "Snap out of it, guys." They blinked, shook their heads, and looked around, stunned. "Get your hands off that thing,"

There was a POP as each let go. The crystal ball shrank to its original size and was once more empty, clear glass.

Mistress Marlena's face was lit by a lone candle, her smile wide. She closed them quickly, but Jessie caught the malevolence in her eyes. It was a look she'd never forget.

"One of you will rise and fall.
One will become all they hated.
One will suffer endless loss.
And one will die."

The candle went out but instead of a thin trail of smoke from the extinguished wick, a thread appeared. It wound its way from Travis to Sarah, Raphael to her. The others swore she imagined it all, but not one of them could explain why, from that day forth, Jessie had a new scar in the shape of a crescent moon on her ring finger, as did the others, forever more.

A Black Hole at Night

There were only two times Hyun-Ki noticed he was alone: when he ate and when he masturbated. Neither bothered him, not really. It was an observation like all scientific observations: I am eating my food and taking notes or reading instead of engaging in conversation, using my hand instead of enjoying the pleasure of Dakota's lovely, warm mouth.

Hyun-Ki took a sip of coffee and finished the last bite of his yoghurt and papaya. He never noticed he was alone at all before he met Dakota. The concept was unfathomable when studying the cosmos, the intricate beauty of mathematics, and the poetry of physics. Yet there he was on a hot summer night, climate control cooled but the heat of the day dragged in the door like a stray. Alone.

Most days, he slept with the dawn and woke early in the afternoon. First, he reviewed data. By the time he finished and caught up on the news, it would be dark. Most waking moments, he was transfixed by the sky. Even in dreams, the sky screen played in his mind's eye and numbers crunched in his brain. However, once he began spending time with Dakota, other thoughts intruded, creating gaps in his concentration and within those gaps, hints of dissatisfaction.

In the warm room, well away from the room the actual telescopes were kept, which was hyperbolically cold as space itself, he tapped on the computer, analyzing data from a satellite, or interpreting images from the telescopes and making calculations, only to find himself some minutes, hours later, staring aimlessly at the screens. Instead of images and data, he saw his own reflection. He was old, wasn't he? It seemed unfair somehow, for he hadn't yet achieved his ambitions. Worse yet, the tedious nature of scientific endeavor, contrasted with the palpable emotions he felt with Dakota, was eroding his scientific curiosity and replacing it with a carnal one.

Computer images no longer brought the same flutter to his heart like when he pilgrimaged to Ulsanbawi Rock on Sokcho to star gaze. Or sat atop the mountain in Anbandegi, village lights dim as he lay on the car bonnet and bathed in the glow of Eunhasu, the Silver River.

Where had that wonder gone?

How he longed to revisit the firefly park at Yeongyang where he first learned to love the stars. It was the last place his parents took him before the accident. They slept under the stars, clouds of fireflies blinking and winking all around. He woke in the night, slipped from his sleeping bag and followed, trying to catch one in his glass jar, make a wish, then release it.

He walked through low fields as if in a dream, imagining the fireflies were twinkling stars visiting from the heavens. This, he thought, this is what it's like to be in space, drifting through darkness, guided by firefly light. At that moment, he knew what he wanted to be—a star traveler, but the death of his parents and his near-sightedness meant all he could ever do was observe the stars, not visit them… and dream.

There are no deserts in Korea though in the spring, yellow dust can blow in from the deserts of China and Mongolia, and he always wanted to experience the vast emptiness of such a place which is what first brought him to the observatory. Hyun-Ki missed his home, but it was not the root of his restlessness on that hot summer night. He fished around in his clothes closet, pushed his neatly pressed and hung chinos and button-down polo shirts to one side and there, behind the empty suitcases and still bearing the airline tags but now laced with a thin layer of dust, was his trunk.

It was old. Nearly as old as he was, but unlike other trunks which travelled the world, it had only one sticker on it, from KARI, the Korean Aerospace Research Institute. Most fellow astrophysicists assumed the trunk contained a state-of-the-art telescope. It did not. When he revealed its contents, gently peeling back the soft velvet blanket it was wrapped in, their eager anticipation quickly changed to astonishment and incredulity at the basic kit within.

To them, it was little more than a toy shop telescope with plastic casing and cheap glass lenses, but to Hyun-Ki, it was magic. Pure magic.

He pulled out the trunk. It smelled of chosen-goyo, a scent which made him long for the familiar when he spent his whole life exploring the unfamiliar. He removed the telescope tenderly. With its nicks and cracks and tripod with two wobbly legs, one held together with duct tape, its worth was little more than sentiment. It was light, but he carried it outside as if it was the weight of the gravity tethering him to Earth.

The sky was clear. Eunhasu, a torrent. He moved some distance from the observatory, through sage bushes and past saguaro sentinels, listening carefully. He had a healthy fear of rattlesnakes and venomous spiders, neither of which were a concern in Korea.

With each step, his mind, usually a constant cascade of probability, regressed or progressed, depending on your point-of-view, once more to those halcyon days of youthful possibility. He found a level spot, set stones along the legs of the tripod to brace it and unscrewed the lens cap. Stretched his arms over head and hugged the heavens, drawing them down to him.

The lens was integrated and not powerful. It could be focused to a limited degree, so it was with some surprise on that cool, early summer night, that he could not locate the crescent moon which dangled overhead like God's banana. There was nothing but darkness.

Hyun-Ki straightened. Rubbed his eyes. Aimed the telescope in this direction and that. Could find nothing in its sights currently visible with his naked eyes. The lens cap was off, the lens intact—he'd maintained it faithfully for over fifty years—there was not even a scratch. He wiped the lens with his eye glass cloth. No change.

Puzzled, he tried one last time. He was tired, used to computer projections he could magnify and enhance, perhaps his eyes, so used to the artificial, could no longer perceive the real?

Through the eyepiece, the sky darkness blossomed. Hyun-Ki held steady, did not blink though his eyes twitched. His mind raced. It wasn't possible to see an event horizon with this telescope. Even less possible for something to be emerging from it rather than consumed. If that's even what he was witnessing. There were no black holes visible with the naked eye. Or a toy telescope. It must be something else. Something remarkable.

Sweat gathered at his hairline and began to drip into the eye piece. He did not lose concentration, for the second he did, the image would vanish. There was no device to record his observation, no calculations could be made; he could only witness.

Concentration had never been a problem for him until recently, but no other observation had ever been as important. Every joint ached, every pore itched, every fiber of his clothing stuck to his skin. Just as he reached the point he could no longer tolerate the sweat-prickles in his groin, it happened. A pulse of white light jetted from the blackness.

Hyun-Ki reeled back. My eyes! Please, not my eyes! He couldn't see. Anything. Only a cloudy mix of pixels across his retinas. Not blind. Please, not blind. Eyes scrunched, he prayed and prayed.

By the time he opened his eyes again some indeterminable long moments later, his vision was returning. How could that have happened? A light from millions of miles away so bright, it affected his vision through a cheap lens? Not possible.

What was possible?

How many times had he asked that question in his lifetime? Hoped nothing was impossible only the knowledge lacking.

Still, this was impossible.

Initially, there was nothing visible in the sky. No sign, no echo, only steady stars in Milky Way soup. Until he saw it, a thin streak of white. A comet? It didn't lengthen as it approached, though it did gain velocity as it neared earth. It smashed hard into the desert, far enough away that he could not judge its distance, but close enough to feel the vibration.

Hyun-Ki brushed himself off and hurriedly packed his telescope. His first impulse was to tell the world, his second, to keep it to himself. The news was unlikely to remain secret for long. A minute? Two? Considering how policed the skies were in this country and across the world, by the time he returned to the observatory, he expected to be greeted by a cavalcade of excited broadcasts and private messages.

There was nothing. Only silence. Another impossibility. Had he imagined the entire thing? The red haze clinging to his peripheral vision said otherwise. He would set out in the morning with the Jeep. How he would find the impact site in all that vast wasteland was anyone's guess. Buoyed by wonder and filled with conviction, he experienced a sense of destiny. Perhaps the impossible *was* possible.

But it was not to be, for search as he might, he never found any trace of an impact. As the days wore on, doubt tainted conviction until all that remained was the straggling debris of his wonder.

The Big Time

Lights bright. Anticipation, a vacuum sucking any sensible thought from his brain. Limo slow, door ajar, out he climbed.

Pop. Pop went the camera flashes as the neon marquee hummed.

GRAND PREMIERE: THE PHONE BOOTH at the END of the WORLD

"Raphael."

"Raphael."

"Oh my God, Raphael!"

He held out his hand for his co-star to emerge.

"Chloe!"

"Chloe!"

"Here, Chloe."

One long leg extended from a sequin slit. Paused. Then the other. The dress sloped along her curves, every inch of her perfect. Sapphires and diamonds dripped from her ears and neck. *I ate that. Can you believe it? Had her begging for more.*

Camera flash. He blinked. She wasn't Jessie.

They say you fall in love with your co-star but all he had fallen into was her bed.

Was Jessie watching now? Could she see him on the TV, the news, all over the socials? Did she ever think of him? Ever? At all?

"So, Raphael, you wrote The Phone Booth and starred in it."

"Yes, but I couldn't have done it without my co-writer, Ash Tipton."

Who was nowhere to be seen. None of this industry bullshit for Ash Tipton. No fucking way. She'd been adamant until Chloe had asked what she'd be wearing. Never had a woman changed her mind so quickly.

"And what a film it is. The critics are raving. Is it true everything was filmed on location and not in a studio?"

"Yeah. Hard to get the feeling of wide-open spaces with a green screen. No matter how big the special effects budget is."

"So, Chloe Rogers is your co-star? Rumor is off-screen as well."

Raphael laughed. Who would believe the hottest actress in the world had pursued *him*? He didn't believe it himself. She was looking at him, over her shoulder, her laughter tinkling crystal, her hand movements ballerina delicate. She'd trained all her life to be a star and was hellbent on whipping his ass into the limelight. No complaints, but he wasn't exactly compliant. He didn't know the game and wasn't quite sure he wanted to figure it out. His haircut had been five hundred dollars, the tux, five grand, the cufflinks on loan worth fifteen. He was a rough and ready hick this town was trying to lasso, flying high and shooting for the stars. That night, he was one of em. And fucking another.

"Chloe is an amazing actress, and I'm incredibly privileged to have had the opportunity to work with her."

And there she was, draping herself on his arm. A natural beauty looking up at him with those big doe eyes. His cock twitched, but his heart did not skip a beat.

He looked away. Took in the fan swarms, the bulb flashes, the screams and roars.

"Raphael is the best actor I've ever worked with," Chloe said, mostly to get a rise out of her ex-fiancée who also started out a nobody before becoming a star but was now a junkie hoofing meth. "Pure, raw talent."

They were moved on to the next media outlet. New reporters, same questions. Turned this way. That way. "Look at each other." "Put your arm around her." "Raphael." "Raphael." Only Jessie had ever called his name so many times.

In the theatre, as the lights went down, and his name went up, Raphael pinched himself. Subtly, so no one would see. He reached into his tux—ostensibly for his phone to capture his name large in the opening credits—bunched his crisp white shirt between two sweaty fingers, grabbed skin. Pinched. Blinked.

It was real. Or as real as it was ever gonna get.

I've made it, Jessie. I've really made it. If only you were here, next to me now, everything would be perfect.

But she wasn't and never would be, ever again.

Chloe leaned towards him, all sparkle spangle and expensive perfume which smelled like rain through the trees and whispered in his ear, "Smile, this is the first best moment of your life."

So, he smiled. All through the film. Difficult, considering it was about him and Jessie and their friends, but he was happy, even though the happiness was tainted by what he had lost to attain it. When the crowd gave The Phone Booth a five-minute standing ovation, he felt a stranger in his own body, as if the applause was for someone he had possessed for a few hours. Chloe, Ash, Marty and the rest of the cast were used to this. They'd bypassed the excitement and taken the ennui exit.

The after-party was at Requiem, of course. Manager Meg sidled up to him, ran a hand down his broad back and settled it briefly upon his waist.

"Got a minute?" she said discretely through the corner of her bright red lips.

Aerobics slim and just as wired, he'd never been attracted to her, only did what was necessary. Who had used who? In the end, did it really matter?

"Sorry, Meg." He removed her hand but did not hold it. "Maybe some other time. We'll have lunch."

She gave him a *you wouldn't be here if not for me* death glare, smiling the whole time.

"Sure, Raphael. Sure. By the way, you're wanted in the private room."

The private room wasn't very private, crowded as it was. He knew everyone there from cast and production and crew. He allowed himself one flute of champagne and ignored the pill bowls and powder lines.

Arms were thrown around him, congratulations all around. The din was incredible, yet he could hear his own rapid breathing and the tremulous beating of his nervous heart. He didn't belong here, surely? This wasn't happening. It was all a dream. And like all dreams good, bad, or indifferent, there was a monster in the closet. There, in the corner.

"Raphael." Marty Weaver waved him over. The crowd parted for him for he was a star now. A star. "Come meet our executive producer, Raymond Barclay."

From the shadows, a figure emerged, face all geometry, eyes a darkness, extended pale hand cuffed by intricate tattoos.

Run. Run, Raphael, run.

The voice was faint in the shrill din. A rumor. Easily ignored. Raphael took the proffered hand, flesh hard, cold, and strong, and he shook it.

About Time

"About time my boy came home."

Travis' mother poured him a tall glass of cold lemonade and served him dinner herself, having sent all the help home for the day. Pa sat stone-faced at the head of the table staring at his plate which was heaped with steak, mash and fresh green beans, all Travis' favorites.

He'd grown so used to prison food, Travis figured he'd lost the taste for anything that hadn't come out of a box or a vat of oil, but he figured wrong. First bite of medium-rare—bloody juices dripping down his chin and pooling on the plate—and he closed his eyes and sighed. He didn't speak for the couple of minutes it took him to inhale the meal. The speed at which he ate more from habit than hunger; in prison, you ate fast so no one else ate it for you. Once done, he pushed his clean plate away and proclaimed: "That was the best damn meal I've ever had in my life."

"Watch your language."

It was the first time his father had spoken since they sat down, though he still refused to look at his son.

Mother beamed. She held out a silver serving spoon heaped with steaming mash.

"Seconds?"

Travis settled on mom's famous dessert, German chocolate cake, which he'd fantasized about for ten long years. It was even better than he remembered which was some feat. In the pen, memories and the hope to return to the source of those memories—for comfort or retribution—were the only things that had kept him going.

His father didn't touch much of his food and barely looked at Travis, only at the empty seat across from him where Cal once sat. Nor did he stick around for gin and tonics on the veranda.

"Don't mind your Pa, he'll come round. He was… okay… for a while but seeing you again… well, it's brought everything back. He loves you, and I know he's glad you're home."

Her hand on his forearm was meant to bring comfort as she squeezed but felt more like a claw. Nobody had touched him in a long time, and he both missed and loathed the sensation.

Sarah. Sarah was the last person whose touch he'd enjoyed. She'd never touch him again though, would she?

"Did you see your friend, Raphael was in a movie with Chloe Rogers? Can you imagine? Chloe Rogers."

Travis had done a lot of imagining about Chloe Rogers while in prison.

"He's not my friend anymore."

His mother paused mid-sip of her G&T, lips pursed over the crystal rim of her glass.

"Oh? You've been best friends all your lives." She put the glass down on a lace doily. "Did he turn his back on you, is that it? Don't pay no never mind. He's not been in another film since. Who knows what happened to him."

Travis shrugged. There was no way to know what Raphael knew or didn't know. He hadn't heard from him once in the past ten years. But water, bridge and all that bullshit.

"Left his girlfriend, what's her name?"

"Jessie."

"Yes, Jessie. Left her high and dry with a child. Went off to make movies and hasn't returned since. Poor girl, losing her Pa, and her sister in a wheelchair after the fire. Terrible thing. Don't know how she manages. You should pay her a call. See how she's getting on."

Travis' hand tightened around his hi-ball before he downed his drink and pushed back from the low, glass table.

"Don't think I will, Ma."

She looked up at him. At what point had her blonde bouffant become streaked with so much gray? When had her long, swan neck begun to crinkle like a crumpled sheet? There was still clarity in her eyes, but her body had begun its inexorable decline no matter the expensive beauty treatments and spa weeks. Surgery would be next. He was surprised she'd let it go this far.

"I thought she was another of your closest friends?"

"That's ancient history, Ma." He kissed her soft cheek. "Ancient history."

Ancient History

They were on the floor where he'd sunk to his knees. She held him in her arms as he sobbed. His head was heavy against her chest, hair stinking of nicotine and grief. His tears seared through her thin t-shirt as she rocked him.

"She's gone. Oh my, God, Jessie, she's gone. She's gone."

Jessie stroked his thick, black hair as one would a child who stubbed a toe, didn't know what else to do. Say. Other than cry herself. Cry from guilt and shame. She sobbed Sarah's name in chorus.

"I loved her more than life itself. I was going to marry her."

Jessie couldn't tell him what had really happened though every shuddering cry threatened to shake it from her. Travis' tears and slobber on her bare arms reminded her of Sarah's blood when she'd cradled her. *It's all my fault. All my fault. I should have stopped her. I should have.* She wanted to say. Would say, if he continued sobbing much longer.

He wiped his snot on her shirt, grazing her breasts.

"Sorry, Jessie. Oh God, sorry." He tried to rub it away but only succeeded in kneading them.

He paused. Looked up at her, eyes crystal with tears and desperation, grief a cold cutlass. His rubs became strokes; his lips moved to her neck. "I miss her. I'll never see her again." Hands on her shoulders, he pushed her down. Sat across her waist. Loomed over her.

She tried to push him away. "Travis, Stop. Please. Don't."

"Did you know? Did you?" His voice guttural.

"No." *You did. You did.* "No, I swear."

Jessie turned her head as he pressed his lips hard, brutal, banal against hers. Clenched her teeth and clamped her lips. He only pressed harder. Spittled against them.

"You were her best friend. How could you not know? Stop her? Tell me! I would have helped her. Why wasn't I there? Why? Why?"

He let her go. Began punching himself in the head with both fists.

"Travis, stop. Please stop. It's not your fault." She dared not touch him again and eased herself away on the floor only to meet the bed.

"Whose fault is it, then?"

He was breathing hard through clogged nose and clenched teeth. Jessie was alone at the motel. Raphael had left not long after the funeral. Pa was collecting Alice at school. The cleaners had gone and although Patrick was at the front desk, he might not hear her if she screamed. Which she wouldn't.

"It's no one's fault, Travis. Only a terrible accident."

He stiffened. "It was no accident. It was a crime. A dirty, filthy, fucking crime and I'll find out who did it if it's the last thing I do."

For a minute, it seemed he would hit something. Her. But then his anger was overcome by another wave of sorrow. His shoulders rolled and his head lolled, and he began to cry into his sleeve once more. Jessie put a gentle hand on his shoulder but did not hug him.

He stilled. Wiped his eyes with his sleeve. Stopped crying. Looked at her from under the canopy of his bedraggled bangs, eyes hard and sharp and dry. "You knew. There's no way you couldn't. You were her best friend, and she told you everything."

He was between Jessie and the door. *Scream, Jessie. Scream. Someone will hear. Someone will come.* But it *was* her fault. Wasn't it? He wasn't wrong.

"Didn't you?" He screamed at her.

"No, Travis. I swear I didn't."

But he wasn't listening. He crouched on all fours as she cowered in her guilt before him.

"You took my woman and my child from me. Now you're going to give me what's mine."

And he fell upon her.

PART FIVE

The Day They Gave Away

"She would have been really proud of you."

Alice brushed the thin layer of gravel and dust from their mother's headstone and sprinkled water over the desert flowers she had loved so much. Jessie stroked the engraved picture. How beautiful she'd been, how gentle.

"Do you think? I'm only graduating, not even with honors like Sarah or any awards like Raphael."

Alice shielded her eyes against the summer sun. Even with Factor 50, her skin was tightening, melanin roasting. "Not everyone's a bookworm, Jessie. You're graduating and that's the only thing that matters. You don't want to go to college anyway. You've only ever wanted to be a singer."

True. Jessie didn't see much point in spending another four years and money they didn't have doing more of the same bullshit at college. She shrugged. She could sing all she wanted but who would hear her in this wasteland? The coyotes?

Alice placed another bunch of flowers on their brother Bobby's grave. Hands shoved in the front pockets of her denim cut-offs, she closed her eyes and arched backwards, drinking in the sun.

"I wonder what Bobby would have been if he'd survived?"

Jessie curled her arms around her knees. Bobby hadn't died right way like Mom, and they'd hoped, hoped despite the doctors' grim predictions, but he'd never regained consciousness. Having that hope cruelly snatched away was so much worse than having none in the first place. Bobby never had big ambitions, not like his younger sisters, and he loved living in the desert. Always said it was where the magic happened.

"He'd be helping Pa, wouldn't he? He wanted to take over the motel and diner when Pa retired."

Alice laughed. "Was gonna turn it into a retro tourist destination. Had me draw up a logo and artwork."

"Remember the video he made?"

"How could I forget? All his high school friends in the pool and us serving them iced tea and lemonade on trays."

Jessie tossed a pebble at Bobby's headstone. "I hated him for that. You hear me, Bobby James?"

Alice laughed. "You loved every minute of attention from the Seniors."

"Did not."

"Liar."

Maybe. She'd been with Raphael long as she remembered, but it had been nice that summer she turned fifteen to have Bobby's friends notice her long, tan legs, blonde hair, and boobs that might not have been big but were perfect.

"He was gonna record me singing. Weren't you, Bobby? 'Gonna make a star of you, Jessie Ann, you just wait and see.'"

"They always believed in us both, didn't they? Hard to believe in myself anymore, now they're gone," Alice said.

Jessie stood. "We're gonna do them proud, you watch, baby sister." She wrapped an arm over Alice's shoulders and gave her a squeeze.

Alice looked up at her with glistening eyes. "We will, won't we, Jessie? We will."

A bright flash lit up the sky and the two girls stumbled back, temporarily blinded. They clung to each other. It took a few seconds, but their sight eventually returned to normal.

"What the hell *was* that?" Jessie said. She expected no answer and got none. They shrugged it off and headed home so Jessie could get ready for graduation.

*

"You still haven't done it with her? What the fuck, man. Are you gay? I mean, I don't mind; I'd still be your friend long as you don't have a thing for me. You don't have a thing for me, do ya? Oh hell, you do…"

"Shut the fuck up, Travis."

Raphael shot him a look but said nothing further. Travis would never understand they'd been waiting. Why? Who knew. They'd done everything—mouths, hands, fingers—everything but the deed. Tonight though. Tonight was the night. Graduation night. They had rooms at the motel, Travis and Sarah in one, Jessie and Raphael in the other, and while Jessie's father didn't approve, he reckoned he hadn't much say in it, now that they were eighteen years of age. Better safe under his roof than out on roads full of drunks. Anything was better than that.

The rest of the motel was booked out by other couples from school. Out front, there was a limo Travis' parents had hired from all the way over in Reservoir Heights. It would take them to the high school auditorium, then to Tom's and lastly, back to the motel.

"What's that?" Raphael pointed at the pill packet Travis had in one hand and the syringes in the other. "What the hell are you doing, Travis?"

"I'm just... just... nothing."

He tried to shove the packet back into Sarah's overnight case, but Raphael snatched it from him.

"You're just what?" There was one line of white pills and one of pink in the packet. "Travis?"

Travis couldn't meet Raphael's eyes as he hemmed and hawed.

"Spit it out."

One syringe was filled with a red liquid, the other, white. "What the fuck? What are you trying to do?"

Travis glared at him, desperate as a trapped animal full of fight. "I can't lose her. She goes off to college on her own, I'll never see her again. I love her, Raphael. I can't live without her. I don't want to live without her."

"So you're switching her birth control pills? Fucking hell, Travis."

Travis shoved the syringes into his pocket. "It probably wouldn't have worked anyway."

Unless Sarah was drunk, which she probably already was. Drunk, she might not notice her white pill was a little pink before she swallowed it.

"Travis, man, this is wrong. So wrong. You wanna trap the woman you love? Like this?" Raphael flapped the pill packet back and forth. "If you love someone, you don't betray them."

The fire in Travis' eyes flared briefly but hotly. He was used to getting his way, everyone knew that, but the four friends had reached a respectful equilibrium in their power dynamics over the years, acknowledging that sometimes it was important to let others win. Especially, if they were right. Travis held a deep breath and let it out with a pained sigh.

"I'm gonna miss her so much. I'm so afraid of losing her."

Raphael patted him on the back and handed him another shot.

"That girl loves you more than anything. No way that'll ever happen," he said with a conviction he didn't feel. People changed. Maybe Sarah would go off and meet someone else. Someone who shared her interests. Someone keener to save animals rather than kill them like they did up at the ranch. Maybe she and Travis would grow apart, like Raphael feared he and Jessie would. "There's more to life than another person."

"Just cause you're abandoning Jessie, doesn't mean we're all the same. Some of us keep our promises."

Raphael rolled the empty shot glass round his fingers. For a second he wanted to lob it at Travis' head, but that would have accomplished nothing other than ruining the entire night.

"Soon as I get settled I'm sending for Jessie. What? Would you have me bring her to a place I don't know, with no job, no nothing? Only my dreams?"

"Ain't she got dreams too?"

Yeah, she did. Jessie wanted to be a singer, and she was good. Real good.

"Not all of us have filthy rich daddies footing the bills."

"Or any daddy at all."

Raphael stopped fiddling and clenched the glass in his fist before settling it gently on the table and pouring them both another shot. He clinked his glass against Travis' "Don't be a cunt, Travis."

Travis raised his glass. "It's hard sometimes."

"Don't I know."

Two more shots dissipated the anger in both of them. The girls muffled laughter from the next room was both salve and stimulant.

"Listen, Raphael, I know it was wrong. Thanks for talking sense to me."

Raphael nodded. "Instead of trying to keep her, why not follow her? Go to college yourself. Would be good for you to get away from home."

Away from your family, he meant but didn't say.

Travis ran a heavy hand through thick black hair and sat back on the bed with a soft plop. Raphael didn't know this, hell, even Sarah didn't know all of it, but he needed to control what he could in his life because he controlled so little: everything done for him, decided for him… no say or deviations from orders. Maybe moving away from home would be the best thing for him. Leave his toxic family behind, get a small apartment with Sarah. They wouldn't need much: a hot plate, a fridge, a bed, a bathroom. He'd work hard. At what? His future had been mapped out since birth: be a rancher, take orders from Pa, then Cal, look after Mother. Breed. Rinse. Repeat.

"Haven't you ever wanted to be something other than what your family told you to be?"

Travis shrugged. "Always wanted to start my own business."

"You'd be great at it. Charm. Charisma. Smarts and a touch of insanity. Everything a budding entrepreneur needs. College isn't all about learning, you know. It's about making connections. I know you said you'd never go but think of it this way…" Raphael paused. Travis was tricky at times, took offense easily and held grudges. Mostly, he got over it quickly, at least with Raphael and the girls, but bluntness was always risky. "Instead of holding Sarah back, why not move both of you forward?"

Travis downed his dregs and licked his thin, dry lips. Next door, the girls were laughing so loudly the walls were nearly shaking.

"But you're okay with leaving Jessie behind? I thought you loved her?"

The AC cut off and the silence void was filled by their breath. They should be laughing and getting drunk like their girls in the next room. It was the time for celebration, not confrontation, but Raphael could not shrug Travis off with another shot. The bottle was empty anyway.

"I do love her." Raphael brushed down the wrinkles in his pants and straightened his tie. "I love her more than anything in the world, but I'm not Jessie and Jessie's not me. We've both got our own path in life and someday soon, they'll cross again, and we'll be together for good. I got my dreams, and she's got hers. I thought..." Raphael had started strong, convincing himself more than Travis, but it hit him like an eighteen-wheeler running a red—he was leaving, and Jessie wasn't coming with him. "I thought our dreams were the same, and they are... they are... but she's got to put hers on hold for a while, and I gotta respect that. Just like you gotta respect what Sarah wants."

"That's pathetic."

"That's love, Travis. When your needs aren't more important than those of the one you love."

"Bullshit, Raphael. Then why don't you stay? There's plenty of work at the ranch. You and Jessie could have a good life."

There was a knock on the wall, and Sarah's muffled joyful voice cut into the tension.

"You boys ready?"

Raphael tossed Travis his jacket and Travis shrugged it on. In front of the mirror Raphael slicked back his long black hair. Christ, he was a good-looking motherfucker. He was gonna make it in the pictures. Make it big.

"I got nothing. Not even a family, but I got a dream, and I'm gonna make it come true, so I have something to offer the woman I love. Don't take Sarah's dreams away. She's always wanted to be a vet, and you've always wanted to escape." There was impatient banging on their door by the girls. "Think about it, man. Okay?"

Travis went to the door and palmed the doorknob but hesitated before opening it. Everyone thought he always got whatever he wanted. But truth was, Sarah was the only good thing to have ever come into his life, and he didn't want to lose her. He looked back at Raphael's earnest face. Would he tell her about the pills?

"Don't worry," Raphael said. "You're my best friend, and I'd never betray you."

Travis opened the door, and the girls spilled in, Jessie heading straight for Raphael, teetering on her platform shoes, while Sarah settled herself under Travis' arm. Her sleeveless dress was long and silvery-blue. She pulled the bustier up and pushed her boobs down, then smiled up at him. Her shiny lipstick smelled of cherries and her breath of vodka.

Her eyes sparkled more than her earrings, more than her necklace, more than the crystals sewn into the bodice her beautiful boobs kept threatening to pop out of, and from her radiant mouth, came those words he'd heard so many times before—whispered, shouted while she laughed, cried—I love you, Travis, and she held his hand to her heart, her heartbeat tremulous as a baby bird's and said, "Do you know how fast you make it beat tonight," and he wanted to hold her in his hand and protect her until she was strong enough to fly away.

Only this time, he would follow.

*

The sun was still shining as Alice watched the limo pull away. A limo down from the city must have cost a fortune, but Travis' family had a fortune to kick around. Jessie looked beautiful. Her and Raphael were blessed in the looks department, for sure. Would Alice ever stop men dead in their tracks? Would anyone ever love her?

She walked over to the pickup. Stopped with her hand on the door.

There was still plenty of sun left in the day, and the heat showed no signs of abating. Steam rose from the road and a haze hung over the entire strip. Their town wasn't made of much: the motel, diner, Tom's Bar, Lincoln's, the ranch, a scattering of houses—they were even bussed to the regional high school—but as Alice stood where parking lot met desert, purple sage sprinkled like rain drops on a parched land, watching the limo head towards a bigger place, even though the sun nearly blinded, even though everyone always left and anyone who arrived didn't stay long, there was a beauty to the place: sky a kaleidoscope of blue, white, silver and gray, sun prisming, thunderheads clapping, rainbows stretching eternal, five weather systems in one visage. She loved it all: locals, regulars, the truckers passing through.

Even the strangers.

Alice drove fast and far. Something possessed her. A need to get away but not to. Windows open, air thumping, eyes peeled for road critters, she finally found what she must have been looking for.

She slammed on the brakes.

There was no good reason for a man to be nowhere-middled. Not one. She rear-viewed him, haloed in the fading light. He looked young, not much older than herself. Familiar. Someone from school?

Foot on the gas, keep going. Don't reverse. Don't. Ain't no good ever gonna come from picking up a hitchhiker, but he didn't have his thumb out, could barely raise his head. He turned and looked in her direction.

And she knew him.

Mom always told them they had three chances in life: the chance to change, the chance to do the right thing, and the chance to take a risk. She reversed. Tires kicked up gravel and blew sand. She rolled down the window and leaned out, bare arm burning on sun-soaked metal.

"You alright?" She looked him up and down. Jeans, a plain, white T-shirt. Boots. Covered in dust.

He looked at her, eyes ice blue. Hair a dirty blonde, sandy color. Thin, but his arms were toned, his chest defined. Alice had seen someone so beautiful only once before.

"Do I know you? I know you, right?" She scrambled out of the cab and hurried over to him.

He stared. It would have been creepy if her heart didn't race, and her breath catch. *Get in the truck, you fool. Get back in the truck and drive fast and as far from him as possible.*

But then, he said her name. "Alice." His voice no more than a hoarse whisper, his accent strange as if he knew the words but not how to pronounce them. "I found you on the last day..."

Delirious. Mad from the heat. But how did he know her name?

He sagged against her. Nearly went down. Alice threw his arm over her shoulder, her arm around his waist and half-dragged him to the pickup.

She opened the passenger door. "You're gonna have to work with me."

He grabbed hold of the panel. His breath was warm and surprisingly sweet against her face as she helped him into the cab, swung his legs in and closed the door.

Not a single vehicle had passed since she pulled over, and there was no sign of any in either direction. Alone with a stranger in the middle of nowhere.

He's no stranger.

His eyes were closed when she climbed in, his head against the window. Her arm hairs crackled, and her heart bucked and bounced as she stretched across to buckle him in. There was a shadow of fine hair on his chin, and his eyebrows were blonde and silver. His breath tickled her long hair across her cheek. Was he asleep? She reached out a tentative finger to brush a lock of hair from his eyes.

And they opened.

It was seconds before she retracted. Slowly, for every fiber of her being wanted to sink into his arms, face against his chest.

She blushed and fumbled with the keys. Dropped them. He caught them mid-air and handed them back to her. No one had ever looked at her the way he did, watching her every move, eyes soft in their assessment as he examined her face, her bare arms, her knee peek-a-booing from the crumpled hem of her cotton dress, before settling upon the droplets of sweat pooling at the base of her throat.

She hurriedly buttoned the top of her dress.

"Wait."

His hand settled upon her necklace. Pa had gotten the diamond set for her sixteenth birthday and put it on a gold chain.

Neither he nor the jeweler had believed she found such a perfectly cut and clear diamond in the middle of the desert but couldn't provide another explanation and even the police had been unable to trace it.

"Perfect," he said, hand falling heavy to his lap.

Alice tugged down the hem of her summer dress and gripped the steering wheel. She did not start the engine.

"Where did you come from?" she said.

"The desert."

His voice was parched, his lips dry. She opened a bottle of water and passed it to him. He tried to raise his hand but was too weak to take it, so Alice held it to his lips.

"Where are you going? Where can I take you?" she said.

He looked up at her from under long eyelashes. "Wherever you are."

*

By the time they reached Tom's Bar—caps in hand, robes crumpled and rolled—and settled into a reserved corner booth, they could barely move from the crowd pressed into every corner, including against their table. They'd already drunk so much in the limo that Jessie had the head-spins, so when Raphael went up to the bar, all she and Sarah wanted was water.

The two girls sat cheek-to-cheek, both trying to keep themselves and each other upright. Music played. It sounded like a band, but it was hard to tell. The crowd made music of its own: the chorus of voices, the trumpet of drunken laughter, the drum of hands upon a table. Jessie began to hum along to its rhythm, rocking against Sarah who grumbled and put out an arm to steady her.

An unseen force, a moon aura or wind of omen must have blown in from the desert that night. It came through the open window above their heads and cut through the din of noise and alcohol, bright and clear, and spun Jessie's heart round and round. She was overcome with an urge to sing. It had been so long since she had, since the accident when she lost not only her mother and brother but also her song.

"Stop, you'll kill yourself." Sarah clutched Jessie's arm as she crawled on top the unsteady table. "Jessie. Fuck."

Jessie shrugged her off. Who knew what came over her or into her, but she rose, and as the table rocked, Jessie found her footing and her song.

At first, no one paid her much mind, but as her heart opened, and her mournful song poured out, the band paused, and the room quietened until the entire brim-filled place was still, everyone with their phones held up and recording.

Jessie saw none of it. She only had eyes for Raphael frozen in the middle of the floor, hands full of drinks and eyes of wonder as he listened.

You say tomorrow never comes
But it's near, my dear, it's near.
We say we'll never say goodbye
But here we are, tonight we're here

Tonight, we will set the world alight.
Tonight, the world is ours
For tomorrow comes too soon.
And tomorrow, tomorrow, is yours.

The crowd hummed and swayed as Jessie continued:

I don't want to tell you
Goodbye
But must
Where will you go?
What shall I do?
How can I ever find my way back to you?

And as the chorus began again, the entire bar joined in, crowd parting as Raphael strode towards her, while Jessie sang with every bit of longing and sorrow in her heart.

I love you.

Oh, how I love you.

Jessie teetered and fell. Drinks smashed to the floor as Raphael caught her. Her song and their kiss were filmed by at least one hundred people and within one hour, had gone viral across three media platforms, and before Jessie and Raphael left for the night, five managers had rung Tom's looking to speak to Jessie, all promising to make her a star.

*

Alice led him to the pool and helped him sit on the edge. She rolled up his trouser legs. The material was thin but the softest fabric she'd ever felt. She eased his boots off and his feet into the water, herself into the pool. He looked down at her as she rubbed the desert from his pale feet.

"Can I touch you?" he said.

Alice nodded, not trusting herself to speak. His hand trembled against her cheek as he cupped the side of her face. Alice sighed but did not close her eyes, only swam in his, would drown if she had to, if only to feel his touch forever.

In the desert, a phone begins to ring...

PART SIX

Late Night Confessions

"You were on fire!"

Michael scowls and brushes down his still steaming clothes. "I found her. I finally found her." He gives up trying to minimize the damage. His clothes are ashen or ashes, his skin pink or red. "She needs me. Desperately. And you dragged me away."

He strips to his underwear and throws the rest into a pile his mother douses with water. She calls him. He does not find her; she draws him to her. He can still feel her, a tenuous connection, but the need still there, maybe even greater than before.

"You took the transporter without permission," his father says.

Michael shrugs. They hadn't hidden it very well or securely. "I need to go back." He eyes the transporter gripped tight in his father's hand. "I can find her again if I try immediately. I know I can."

"Have a shower at least," his mother pleads. Her eyes go wide as she catches sight of his tattoos. "What happened?"

He thinks to lie, to tell them of a car accident or a mountain falling on top of him, something, anything, but he's never lied to them before and much as they would prefer it, he isn't going to start.

"I had to save her."

This incites a gasp from his mother and a grunt from his father.

"You were only just given them," his mother says.

"Well, if I run out, I guess I'll have to live and die same as everyone else. Like normal people who don't have rich and powerful parents."

His parents share a glance before turning back to him with narrowed eyes and straightened shoulders.

His mother takes his arm and draws him close. She tries to moderate her tone, but it gets shriller with each word. "Who is this girl? What do you even know about her? She's not of our time or place." Her words tumble over each other as his determination solidifies.

She lets go of his arm and looks at her husband who hasn't said much of anything to that point, busy as he is staring at Michael's arms.

"So much gone."

"She would have died."

"Your allowance can never be replenished. You know this."

"I never asked for these reserves, and now I know where they come from…I don't want them."

His father snorts. Michael has only seen him angry once and that was when his older brother, James had been drunk and joyriding in Dad's car. He had crashed into another car driven by a pregnant woman and every ounce of his health reserves was handed over to revive her and her baby. Dad had looked like he wanted to finish James off, his hands clenched so hard into fists, his nails drew blood. James had calmed down after that—he had no choice—there are state-of-the-art hospitals, but some things doctors and surgeons can't fix, only your reserves, and his were gone.

It isn't anger but fear causing his father's nostrils to flare. Still, Michael wishes he'd understand. When his parents are like this, there's little point trying to explain, but he'll try. He leads his father outside to the garden, and they stand under the moons as the trees sway and leaves rustle in a slight breeze, one steadfast in his determination, the other in his disapproval.

His father breaks the silence. "We've tolerated this obsession long enough."

Michael bristles. It's going to be harder than he thought.

"Father, do you remember our talk about soul mates? Your conviction that there is an equal opposite for every living creature somewhere in the universe? How the odds of finding that mate are infinitesimally small? That we can only hope to find the closest approximation?"

His father sighs, breath a heavy steam in the cooling night air. "So, you're going to tell me this... girl..."

"Alice. Her name is Alice."

"This Alice is your soul mate? Does she know anything about you? Does she even know where and when you're from?"

It's Michael's turn to sigh. His father's next words will be: you're only sixteen, what could you possibly know about the human condition in your coddled life on top of Cherry Blossom Hill? What could you know about love? Of struggle? Of sacrifice?

His father had been born in the desert valley. A life sentence for most, but he hadn't let circumstance stand in the way of his intellect and ambition. He lied, cheated, and stole to climb the Hill. Reached the very top echelon of Quantum Labs. Married a woman he hadn't loved but had grown to love. Had five, count them, *five* children, none of whom were eliminated, and their health force redistributed, only to be squandered by irresponsible idiots who think they met their soul mate in another dimension.

Michael hears all of this in the slow, steady breath of his silent father. Some of it inferred, some imagined. His father is man of few words, but those he does speak bear the weight of that silence.

"Many lives were volunteered to give you those health reserves you squandered on a stranger in another dimension, who may be in the past or future, unborn or dead even as we speak."

No, I would know if she was dead. I would know.

Michael looks out over the trees in the direction of the long plains, lakes and desert beyond. Fires burn here and there. The faint refrains of his hit song can be heard through the open windows of a passing car. Michael's world is limitless. His father has ensured that, but the world they live in is not.

"Do you know, father... sometimes, in the early hours when it's neither day nor night, when the world is quiet except for the sound of my own breathing, I think I hear them—the ghosts within me. Do you know what a burden that is?"

"I lost everyone once and couldn't bear losing everyone again. And for you to give it away..."

The night birds call to one another; a lullaby of peace imagined but not gained. Michael knows his father once had another family. Out in the desert where the fires burn. He climbed the Hill to secure a place for those he left behind, only to discover none had survived.

"I would give all of it away and will."

"Obsession does not bridge worlds; it destroys them."

"I will do anything for her."

His father turns to him. His eyes seem smaller and the dark circles under them bigger. "Alice?"

"Yes, Alice. She lives in a desert."

His father blinks.

"Maybe, you're one of the lucky ones. Maybe, out of all the infinite times and dimensions, you have found your soul mate. Maybe…"

"She is."

"And if you locate her? What will you do? Stay there? Bring her here? Have you thought this through?"

No, he hasn't. He's been so focused on just finding her. Michael shrugs. It doesn't matter. He'll figure it out. They'll figure it out.

"Sometimes the quickest route looks the longest. Study. Go to university then enroll in the Cadets. Work on your geo-plotting device. If you can map her coordinates, you can transport to her at will."

"How can I map her coordinates if I can't find her in the first place?" He rubs his temples. Takes a deep breath. "I can still sense her. Out there. It feels as though I can nearly reach out and touch her."

"It must be frustrating. So close and yet, so far." His father pats his arm to comfort, but it's only condescension to Michael. "We all make choices in our lives. Even when we think we have none, there is always a choice. Only remember, with all choices, there are consequences. When we follow our heart instead of our head, those consequences can be tragic."

"Please, father…"

"I do this reluctantly, but I am confiscating the transporter, and this time you won't find it. Once you've graduated from the Cadets and completed an internship at Quantum Labs, you can have access again."

Michael's head throbs, and he begins to sweat. "That will take years…nearly a decade…don't…please."

But his father's heart has hardened. It's clear in the set of his chin and the distance in his eyes as he sees not his son but a past that does not bear repeating.

"I am not you, father; I won't fail."

His father closes his eyes, and Michael is immediately regretful.

"I'm sorry. I didn't mean that."

"Yes, you did, and I meant what I said as well. The quickest and sanest route to achieving your goal will be learning and expanding existing technology. You are capable. You've proven that. I won't let you throw your life away over some impossible fantasy."

"That's my choice!"

"And this is mine."

At that, his father turns and walks back towards the house. Stumbles. Nearly falls. Michael rushes to his side. How frail he has become. How old.

"Please, take some of my reserve, father." He holds out his hands.

"No, son. I don't need it, but you will. There are those in this world who wish me ill. Who would and will harm my family if given the opportunity. Confide in few here. Trust no one, anywhere. Not even this Alice."

"I trust her. I can and will save her."

"But does she want you to?" There is a sadness in his father's eyes that speaks of old hurts and new fears. "Michael," he says softly, more to himself than his son, "there are no saviors."

The First Time isn't the Hardest

Jessie reads Raphael's last email. Again.

For a town full of stars, you can't see any in the sky. Have they all fallen to earth? I miss you. It's all going to happen, Jessie. We'll be together again soon.

R

She gave up missing him long ago. Now, he's just a memory. A snapshot in an old photo album, or an apparition in the corner of her eye, gone when she turns to investigate. She can't touch him, not anymore. For a while, she could feel him. She'd close her eyes, kiss the back of her hand and imagine his lips. Now, it's only her hand. She can't allow herself to pretend. To hope. Once, there were dreams; now, there is duty.

Rust stains crawl from the plug hole like all her hope went down. She takes enough from her wages to cover her room and board at the Deuces Wild Motel off the strip, everything else goes back home. People depend on her, and she can't let them down. The diner has to reopen, the motel needs to be spruced up, and then there's her medical bills…

Occasionally, a whale sits at her table—big cigar, fat fingers, tiny dick—and if they win, they might toss her a couple of pumpkins. Once, even a five-k chocolate. That paid for the diner's new windows. She saves ten bucks every week towards her 'get the fuck out of the desert' fund. That's the new dream—move to the coast, open a desalination shop. Learn how to swim.

She talks to Ryan and Alice every night on the video phone. Wishes she could touch them. Can't. There is no one to touch. No one to touch her. Fraternizing with guests or gamblers is strictly forbidden and it's a rule Jessie is more than happy to abide. She hasn't been with anyone all the years he's been gone. Hasn't wanted any man to touch her.

Then one night, a long lean man in a good suit whose only flash is a Rolex and shoes made from soft leather sits at her table. Wins big, loses bigger. Draws a crowd. Takes a liking to Jessie. His eyes meet hers, and they aren't predatory, only appraising. When he smiles after losing another twenty-k hand, there is no malice or chagrin, only a sense of calm as if he's doing the backstroke in the hotel's infinity pool.

He rises from the table and talks to the pit boss to settle his account. Neither despondent nor emotional like she's seen some. Shoulders straight, head up. Women stop as he passes. Stare. Same as Jessie stares as he walks away.

The pit boss has her clap out. Speaks to her quietly in the pit.

"Mr. Cremins has requested a private table."

"Excuse me?"

"The choice is yours."

The boss hands her a room key—2570, the penthouse suite. Jessie looks over at the floor manager who makes a point of being busy at another table. This is a high-class establishment, no fraternizing with the guests, yadda, yadda, yadda, but apparently there are different rules for sons of water barons.

Jessie fingers the five-k chocolate he tipped her. As inconsequential to him as a pillow mint but would pay for an air conditioner and a new door for the diner. He will almost certainly give her more, much more. For what? A quick fuck?

She takes the private elevator to the penthouse suite. She will decide what to do by the time she arrives. It's fifty-fifty when the elevator dings open and by the time she arrives at his door, his odds have gone up.

Jessie has no illusions. There are no saviors, only other lost souls, some with a lot more money than her, but as she knocks once, twice, an image forms in her brain—a knight in shining armor—and this illusion solidifies her tentative knock. This goes well, she might even be able to finally go home. This dark-eyed stranger with a fat wallet and a kind smile, will give her a break. The world will finally give her a break.

It's better that she doesn't know him. Will force herself to forget him. Jessie knows the price she will pay but doesn't understand the consequences. Not yet.

He opens the door. Young. Handsome. Not beautiful like Raphael. There is something in his eyes that belies beauty—history, and none of it good.

She takes the champagne flute he offers and takes in the view. Neck crawling and skin tingling, she feels as reckless as the twenty-fifth floor balcony. Lower floors have no balconies or windows that open because jumpers are bad advertising. The penthouse, well, the penthouse it seems, provides everything for its guests, even that option.

He slides open the balcony door. There is a heater, a thick woolen blanket, an ignored dinner and guttering candlelight. He turns off the room lights, and the Vegas strip dances for them.

He strokes her cold skin with warm thumb. "Beautiful, isn't it?"

"Yes." Jessie looks up at the hooked sliver of a moon. "Beautiful."

He kisses the spot on the back of her hand his thumb has warmed. Lifts her hair gentle as a cool breeze on a hot day. Kisses the inside of her neck. Her shoulder. Turns her—hand in the small of her back—draws her in. It's been so long. Jessies closes her eyes. Pretends this one night is all a fairy tale. She knows otherwise, of course. Does it matter? Does anything?

Instinct tells her what he wants. What she needs to live in the after.

"Take me," she says.

And he does.

*

She does not sleep. Has a shower in a bathroom bigger than her entire motel room. Catches herself from all angles in the mirrored walls. Likes none of them. Briefly considers smashing each pane like a crashing, cokehead rock star. Instead, she squeezes some of his toothpaste onto her finger and rubs it on her teeth to remove the taste of him best she can.

He is on the balcony, still and staring off in the distance as the curtains slap in the early morning breeze. He hands her a thick envelope.

"I know the world doesn't deal much in cash these days, but I find it a lot handier than digital."

Jessie is too old to be demure, too young to refuse, and too stubborn to care. No blushes when she takes the envelope. There is a line, and she's crossed it, and there is no going back, only forward.

On her way out, crossing the hotel plaza, she pauses at the two-story high fountains as they erupt in a shower of laser lights. Looks up. He seems a bird as he leaps. A bird folding its wings and nose-diving from the penthouse. It takes forever for him to fall, and she begins to think him suspended like Wile E. Coyote in the Roadrunner cartoons. Transfixed, she waits for the inevitable splat. It is loud, a sound she's never heard before and hopes to never hear again. Unlike the coyote, the high roller does not get up again. Does not even twitch as blood runs from his mouth, his ears, his pores, his open skull.

The Rolex on his wrist catches the ghost of the laser light show. Blue, green, yellow, orange. Red. One eye dangles from its socket; the other is buried under what remains of his handsome face. Roadkill. He looks like roadkill hit by a semi. An hour before, those warm, strong arms were wrapped around her tight as a promise, loose as one he never meant to keep. His breath soft against her neck as he whispered of all he had seen, all he had done, and her heart had gone pitter-patter, first as he reached around and stroked her clit with lazy but expert fingers, then from having sex with a man. Not a boy who loved her, nor one who raped her, but a man.

It doesn't take long for the crowd to gather—closer and closer—heads preening for a better look. Careless whispers. Shouts. Jessie is frozen. Her brain sputters to a halt in the impending chaos as sirens sound and black-suited security men with earpieces and microphones swarm to block the morbidly curious and cameras.

A shadow forms amongst these black suits. Is it the gambler's soul? The gambler. His name. What is, was, his name? The shadow coalesces, becomes substance: a man, tall and slender with moons for his eyes. He looks at her and no one else. Jessie's breath catches, and her blood shrivels. She can't breathe. Can't breathe. Can't breathe until another figure approaches the shadow man. Says something quietly in his ear. Looks at Jessie.

Travis.

What on earth is he doing here, and who is that he's with?

"Miss? Miss Williams?"

The spell is broken as security leads her away. Take her to a windowless room with two cold metal chairs and a small table between. They take her envelope and her job. Tell her to leave town today. Right now. Forever. Or she never will.

She doesn't have to be told twice.

Late Night Deals with the Devil

Travis is in Vegas to find Jessie. Work up the courage to approach her. All wrongs have been righted except this one. He spent five years in prison praying for her to suffer like Sarah had. Worse. But something changed in the second half of his incarceration. He became harder and meaner in every manner except in his feelings towards her, and when he found out about the kid… well…

Redemption seems too much to hope for, but if she forgives him, maybe he still stands a chance to be what Sarah thought he was, not what he is.

He never suspects someone is also watching him.

Each night, he sits at the same baccarat table. The baccarat area is roped off, the floor slightly sunken. He has no clue how to play baccarat only that the minimum bet is a grand. He throws down five. Bets on the player every time. Loses. A lot. Enough to notice. Enough for the pit boss to notice him. Notice him noticing Jessie.

A waitress leans over, whispers in his ear, "Can I get you anything?" Her tits are full and round moons over the tray of smokes, mints, water and candy that hangs from her neck. Travis meets her eyes and says no thank you. Puts a hundred buck tip on her tray.

His luck changes.

First, Raymond sits next to him at the low table. Travis doesn't know his name is Raymond, that comes later. What he does know is, when Raymond sits, everyone else gets up. Not all at once. Most shift uncomfortably for one deal. Two. By the time the shoe is finished, the other twelve seats are empty, and onlookers have given their table a wide berth.

Travis knows darkness, and he's intimately familiar with shadow. Neither bother him. Much. Raymond is dressed in an expensive black suit, the tailoring fine, too fine even for Vegas high rollers. Italy, maybe. Japan even. Travis ignores the ink miasma on Raymond's wrists when his cuffs retract as he places his bets. Pretends he doesn't hear the tinnitus of muffled screams. Doesn't shiver at the coldness running up his left side even though there's two chairs between them.

Travis quickly claws back his losses and is up at least twenty grand. Raymond's bets are modest and the only thing he's rolling are chips between his fingers as he watches Travis watching Jessie.

Second, Richard sits at the table.

"This seat taken?"

It's a stupid question. Obviously, no seats are taken, the pit boss just doesn't want to piss the shadow man off by closing the table. Might have been different back in the mob days though Travis has his doubts; the mob knew better than most the zero-sum game.

Richard sits between Travis and Raymond. Travis does not know his name is Richard yet, that comes later too. In the meantime, Richard doesn't shut the fuck up. He's not nervous, though he should be the way the shadow man glares at him as he rambles on about the time he was in Monaco and lost a million on one blackjack hand and another half on two girls and five guys in his hotel room after, and do either of them know where to have a good time? He's not nervous at all, only hungry. Travis has seen the look before, in a cellmate who wrapped a bedsheet noose around his neck while jerking off. Travis got sick of watching his eyes bulge and throat gurgle as he came and one day finished the job.

Travis is distracted by the crowd around Jessie's table. It's a low stakes table high rollers wouldn't normally sit at but there's one there now. The look in his eyes is also familiar. Travis saw it many times in the can; the gambler has given up and is just trying to decide on logistics. His eyes settle on Jessie.

Travis pushes his chair back but a hand on his shoulder keeps him from rising. The cold from that hand seeps through his clothing and leeches to his bones. Travis has never felt such cold before and is certain it will kill him and quickly.

Raymond leans over and speaks softly in his ear. "I can get you what you want."

He meets Raymond's eyes but anything he finds there is nothing he wants, only fears. In the choice between following Jessie as she claps out and heads towards the elevators or speaking to this devil in a good suit, Travis has no choice. Not if he wants to live. And for now, he does.

Travis knows nothing good in life comes for free and even shit has a heavy price tag, but he follows Raymond and Richard to the intimate high rollers club, where they talk over Irish whiskey and sushi. Turns out Richard is some hot shot Hollywood producer. The same hot shot who produced Raphael's hit movie.

Small world.

Travis is smart enough to know when he's being set up, but canny enough to get out of it. If he wants. He decides to hear them out.

After three whiskeys, Richard drops the stupid act and gets down to business. They are looking to fund an enterprise. All Travis has to do is let them set up shop at his ranch in the desert. The ranch he has told neither about.

"What's in it for me?" Travis says to Raymond, but he already knows the answer.

I can get you what you want.

They retire to Richard's suite to share coke, champagne and a couple of hookers. A bit on the young side for Travis' taste but legal. Supposedly. The girls know their stuff anyway and are paid well for their bruises. If Travis hears screams while he's in the shower, he does his best not to let on. When he returns to find two puddles of clothes and a lack of girls to wear them, he mentions neither, only sniffs at the faint smell of smoke.

Travis is at the window weighing his options when something falls from above. It goes by fast, so fast he isn't sure what it is until he hears the thud. There's no balcony in Richard's suite but there is a floor-to-ceiling window. He can see what's left of the body on the ground below and next to it, a shock of blonde hair.

Jessie.

Travis walks to the elevator as quickly as he can without running. Richard is in his boxers, soft belly protruding, snoring on one couch. Raymond sits on the other, fully dressed and eyes closed. The elevator dings open, and Travis presses the button for the ground floor. He is not surprised when Raymond's hand stops the door from closing.

Neither speak on the journey down from the twenty-fourth floor and their silence is filled respectively by regret and intent. Travis has a knife strapped to one thigh and a snub-nosed revolver in his breast pocket. He knows neither will do him much, if any, good. He hopes he doesn't have to make the attempt.

Raymond gets to the body first, but he's not looking at it. Travis sees Jessie. Sees Raymond seeing Jessie. *Go,* Travis tells himself. *Get the fuck out of here while he's distracted. Disappear.* Travis has plenty of money and options. He owes this freak nothing, and Jessie even less.

He thinks of the puddle of clothes in Richard's room. Closes his eyes so he can pretend he doesn't see himself being a stupid fuck as he leans into Raymond and says quietly in his ear.

"I'll do it."

Coffee Break

Travis is waiting for her outside the Deuces Wild motel, leaning against a stretch limo, smoking. Sun in her eyes, Jessie doesn't realize it's him until he calls her. Instinct says run but where to with no job, no money, no phone?

She refuses to get in the limo but agrees to a coffee in a small diner off the strip. She's been there before but not too often. They'll know her well enough to describe her if it comes to it but not where she works or lives.

They sit across from each other in a booth. Travis with his elbows on the table trying not to twiddle his thumbs. Failing. Jessie has her hands on her lap. Clenched. It is the first time she's been this close to him since...

No, don't remember. Put it out of your mind. See what he wants, for sure as shit, he wants something.

"Jessie, I..."

The waitress arrives and takes their order. Jessie should eat. Her room is paid till the end of the week, but she won't be staying, and the only sustenance she has is a box of graham crackers, a bottle of vodka and a carton of smokes. She orders a coffee. Black.

Travis orders the same.

He sips his slowly, appears about to speak after each swallow. Looks at her each time, then looks away. Outside, night shifts are ending and morning shifts are beginning. She'll have to go back home now. There's no place else. But how would they survive? The diner still isn't operational. The hospital bills aren't fully paid. There was an insurance policy, but it didn't cover half of shit. Realistically, everyone will be better off if she is dead.

"I met Ryan," Travis says finally.

Jessie doesn't look up from her refill. Keeps stirring her spoon round and round and round.

"I had a DNA test done."

Jessie stops stirring. Stops breathing. Says nothing. Waits.

Travis leans forward. His thin lips are pressed tight as his eyes. "He's mine, Jessie. Ryan is my son."

Up to that point, Jessie had reconciled that possibility with her ability to live with it. Faced with his claim, she says the only thing she *can* actually live with.

"I don't believe you."

"It's true, I've got the papers."

"Show me."

He sits back and reaches in his pocket. Draws out a document from a lawyer and places it on the table between them. Jessie stares at it like a rabid coyote. Doesn't raise her eyes. Doesn't say a word even though inside, she's screaming.

"Marry me," Travis says, and his voice is some damp squelch from a muddy well. He reaches across the table, hands open. "I'll take care of you both. We'll be a family."

She looks at him. Doesn't flinch as the memories of Ryan's conception flood back. Stares him straight in the eye. Recognizes the hope blanketing utter despair, the need for her forgiveness to save him.

Barbara Byar

Never

July 11th

Comings and Goings, The Diary of Ryan Williams, aged 10

Mom had to go make some money. I'm to stay here, help Aunt Alice, Carl, Maria and the others at the motel for the summer. She should be back before school starts again but in case she's not, I promised to go to school. That's the most important bit. *Stay in school, Ryan, it's the only way you'll be able to go to college and get into the space program.* I'm only ten, I'm not worried about college yet, but I'm gonna work hard because I want to be an astronaut someday. Make my mom proud of me.

Dakota introduced me to Hyun-Ki. He hasn't let me see through the big telescopes yet. Have to start small. Learn the basics. Instead, he let me look through his own personal telescope. It's not very big, but I can see things through it I can't see with the naked eye. Seeing the stars and planets close up makes me want to visit them more than ever. Trouble is, I can't explore from earth, only observe, and I want to travel the stars, not watch them travel across the sky. Someday, it will be possible, and I want to be ready. Hyun-Ki doesn't really have much sway, but he's got a couple of friends at the space agency and said he'll put in a good word.

Mom said she'll call every day. I wanted to go with her, but she said Vegas ain't no place for a child. I'm not a child anymore, not really. Ten is no baby.

She left after my birthday. We had a big BBQ with all the family, and everyone from the diner and motel. Many don't work here anymore, not after the maniac incident, but Mom is gonna make money to get the place fixed up, and we'll be back in business. Aunt Alice said she'll take good care of the motel. Carl and Maria are helping out until the diner is fixed. Aunt Dakota will do the books. We'll be alright. Everything will be fine. Don't you worry about us, Mom.

I met this guy. Mom said not to trust any adult except Aunt Dakota, Aunt Alice, Carl and Maria, but he seemed harmless. He was at the shop and bought me an ice cream, said my hair was messy. It felt creepy when he touched it, and I swear he pulled some off my head. He apologized. Said his ring got stuck. But I didn't see any rings on his fingers.

*

When Ryan finishes his homework, he goes looking for Aunt Alice to see if there's anything he can do to help out. Some things cost money they don't have, but his labor isn't one of them. He wants to get the diner up and running again as soon as possible, same as everyone else. People need their jobs, and he needs his mom.

Aunt Alice is behind the front desk. Her wheelchair won't fit in the small space behind the counter, so she sits on grandpa's old chair with its saggy middle and wooden arms nicked by the knife he always carried. Aunt Alice is fond of telling him grandpa stories and sayings. Such as, you hope for the best to come through the door but prepare for the worst. How each nick in the chair represents a time Grandpa had to emphasize his lack of tolerance for bullshit as he called it.

There is also a gun hidden in a locked drawer under the desk. Never bring a knife to a gun fight—another one of Grandpa's sayings. That gun has been needed more than ever once news spread the old man and sister were gone, leaving a cripple in charge, but Aunt Alice also has zero tolerance for bullshit, which she had to demonstrate ten times before that word also got around.

"My legs may be useless but my trigger finger ain't."

She hasn't killed anyone, least not yet, but that one fella passing through from Oklahoma sure was never gonna walk right again neither.

The bell over the door clangs and one of the ladies who lives at the back end of the motel comes in to pay her rent. She is tall with long legs and once she spies Ryan, she pulls her shorts down and her tube top up. In the daylight, she looks a lot younger than in the shadows of night, about Aunt Alice's age. Maybe they went to school together.

Ryan is a curious child, not prone to keeping his questions to himself, but before he can open his mouth, Aunt Alice says, "Scoot now, Ryan. Go see if Carl needs any help over at the diner."

Carl is busy painting over the graffiti on the boards covering the bust windows. The boards are supposed to be temporary, same as the CLOSED sign hanging on the door. Carl is a big man and looks hard but is soft as marshmallow, least with Ryan. Ryan never knew his grandpa and didn't know his Pa, but Carl is the closest thing to both.

Carl pulls down his mask and wipes his face with a kerchief he has round his neck.

"No school?"

"It's summer."

Carl takes off his baseball cap and runs a hand through his thick salt-and-pepper hair. Ryan has shot up in the last year, but Carl will always be a giant to him. Gone were the days he'd get a hug; now, it is a hair ruffle or a hand on his shoulder. Mom still gives him hugs. Maybe not the kisses she used to speckle all over his face, but plenty of hugs.

He misses his mom.

Carl must have read it on his face cause he gives his shoulder a squeeze and says, "Your mom is working real hard so we can get this place back open for business. Lots of hungry truckers with no place to eat." He smiles, thick moustache covering most of his top teeth as he does. "That's what family does, we take care of each other."

Carl gestures towards a pile of tools and cleaning supplies. "New glass will be here next week. Now how bout you pick up that brush there and start going over that picture of… what is it?" Carl squints.

"Looks like a cat or something," Ryan says. A big, long cat to be sure, but a cat, nonetheless.

Carl pops his baseball cap back on. "A leopard. That's what it is, a leopard."

A couple of hours later, Ryan's arm sagging along with the sun, Carl stops sweeping the parking lot long enough to thank him for his help and send him on his way.

"Straight home now, Ryan. You hear?"

Ryan has always followed the rules set by the adults in his life but once he hit double-digits, a sense of willfulness crept into the part of his brain controlling his limbs. And so, once he safely crosses the road, and Carl returns to sweeping, Ryan keeps going.

His intention is to visit Aunt Dakota, but that is until he hears the drones. Like monsters in a closet, he's rarely actually seen one, only heard them. He's has been told ten thousand times and will almost certainly be told ten million more, to never go near any drones and if any fly overhead, to run as quickly as he can for cover. But he is halfway to Aunt Dakota's and there's no cover to be found, only a half-hearted sage brush clinging for life to the dregs of last month's rain.

He tries to play it cool, but Ryan's heart races at the wheeze, whirl, hum of the approaching drones. Fortunately, they pass right over him and keep going towards the train tracks where a handful of freight cars have been uncoupled for a good few days. He can see them, barely, just not make anything out except for the sound of gunfire.

At ten, Ryan has some sense, but the sense of self-preservation is not one of them. Intrigue, mystery, now we're talking. In the desert, the boring old desert where he has no friends and nothing to do, gunfire and three drones is the highlight of his summer.

Although Ryan is reckless like most kids his age, he isn't insane. He waits till the shooting stops, and the drones scream away back towards the distant mountains and the cop shop at Healy Pass before he heads towards the freight cars.

There is a body, alright—a man slumped, head shoulder-lolled. Rivulets of blood seep through holes in his chest. Two kids are trying desperately to cover the wounds but don't have enough hands. Ryan rushes over to help them.

The girl is sobbing.

The boy is shouting, "No, padre. No, padre, no."

They look at Ryan, first in fear, then desperation.

"Help him, please." The girl says. She looks about Ryan's age, the boy, a year or two older. Tears cut canyons through their dirt-caked faces, and their eyes are dust-storm wild.

Ryan doesn't know much about dying, but he knows about dead. Plenty of road-kill critters crawl to the side of the road to die. Their father is gone. He wants to tell them they'll be okay, that he has no father either. Sometimes, it's a big hole which needs filling but most of the time it's okay, he has his mom, Aunt Alice, Carl and Maria, and Aunt Dakota.

They are alone.

"What're your names?" Ryan says.

"Estella," the girl says through her tears as she sinks back in the sand, deflated, "and this is my brother, Daniel," she adds when her brother doesn't answer. "Can you help my father, please?"

She clutches her brother's hand, and they scramble to their feet. Is it some sixth sense that warns them of the approaching vehicles or the heightened senses of those whose lives depend on listening for predators?

A cruiser and a black sedan approach, kicking up a maelstrom of dirt in their wake. When Ryan turns back to the body, Estella and Daniel are gone.

Ryan has experience of guns, but he's never had one drawn on him. A little warm pee trickles down his right leg, and he trembles and shakes as two officers approach, roaring questions at him.

"Rrrryan…Williams. My name is Rrryan…Williams."

"Now, now. No reason to frighten the poor boy."

Two other men get out of the black car. The one who spoke is familiar. It's the guy who'd gotten his ring stuck in Ryan's hair. Travis is his name. The other is just scary. He doesn't have fangs or horns or even weird clothes but where everyone else casts a long shadow in the late afternoon, the tall thin man *is* shadow. When he smiles at Ryan, his thin lips pinched tight, Ryan's heart freezes and breath catches and neither start again until he's broken his gaze.

"I can vouch for this young man. He's not who you're looking for. There's two others. They can't have gone far."

The officers quickly lower their guns and nod to Travis. Hopefully, Estella and Daniel have hidden themselves well or are far away. It's hard to find someone in the desert if they don't want to be found and their tan and brown clothes blend in. Maybe... maybe, they'll be lucky.

They are not.

It takes the officers five minutes to find them, during which shadow man watches Ryan while Travis talks on his phone.

"Richard, hey yeah. Wanted to give you a head's up. Looks like we'll have veal and lamb on the menu this week. Which do you prefer? No problem. I'll make your reservation and forward the details. Usual place. Yes."

Travis claps his phone closed and crouches next to Ryan. He takes his cowboy hat off and holds it in one hand while holding the other out to Ryan. "Come on, I'll give you a ride home."

Ryan looks at the clean, pale hand with its neatly manicured, white-tipped nails but does not take it. Travis' smile seems genuine, but it's hard to believe anything good will come from getting in the car with him and someone who looks like Slenderman with a human face mask.

"Where are they taking them?" Ryan says as the cops shove the screaming girl and struggling boy into the back of the cruiser. "They've done nothing wrong."

Travis wipes his hand through his hair and puts his cowboy hat back on. "Don't you be worrying about them. They'll be well taken care of. There's always families looking to take orphans in." He looks over at the body and raises his eyebrows. "Now, you don't want to be out here alone with a... deceased person, do you?" He offers his hand again.

"Back away from the child, Travis."

Aunt Dakota. Everything tense in Ryan loosens all at once, and he really does think he'll pee his pants, this time in relief, not fear.

Travis winces before he straightens and turns towards Aunt Dakoka. None of them heard her car approach, as it arrived just as the cruiser left. The shadow man hasn't spoken once, and doesn't seem much concerned about anything, not even the revolver in Aunt Dakota's hand.

"Dakota. Lovely to see you. It's been ages. You're looking as youthful as ever. This young man happened upon a crime scene, and I told the police officers I'd make sure he got home safely. Didn't know he was a relation?"

Dakota's eyes slide over to Ryan who wants nothing more than to be by her side.

"Thanks for the offer." She holds out her hand, and Ryan runs over and grabs it in relief. There isn't a lot he knows for sure but one thing he does, is Aunt Dakota can beat anyone, even a shadow man. "But I'll take him from here." She leans over and tells Ryan to get in her car.

He doesn't have to be told twice. He scrambles in and rolls down the window so he can hear what's being said.

"Sorry to hear about your mother and father, Travis. Tragic."

Travis lowers his head and kicks at a stone with the toe of his black boot. "Thank you kindly, Dakota. It's been hard alright."

"Seems there's a lot of fires when you're around."

"Don't know what you mean by that, Dakota."

"Oh, I think you do."

The smile on Travis' face makes Ryan think of a rattler deciding whether it's too hot and tired to strike.

"Hear you're making a whole lot of changes up at the ranch." Dakota takes a good look at the shadow man. "Got a new foreman and all."

"Well, you know what they say—out with the old, in with the new. My parents were always reluctant to diversify, but sometimes it's the only way for a business to survive. You're welcome any time. I'll give you a tour. We'll have lemonade. Catch up properly."

Dakota nods and walks slowly back to the car. Ryan holds his breath until her hand is on the door. Neither Travis nor the shadow man make any move against her, but all the hairs on Ryan's sweat-drenched body stick up straight in the air.

Travis calls after her. "Don't worry about the cops. I told them Ryan had nothing to do with it. They won't be troubling you."

Dakota opens the car door. "You don't need to tell me that. I know this child had nothing to do with gunning down an innocent man looking for a better life for his children."

Travis looks over at the dead man. The blood has stopped flowing and has begun to congeal. Vultures circle. Funny how they can smell blood from miles away.

"Looks like he found it."

Dakota doesn't say much as she drives, and it isn't till they pass the coroner's van screaming down the road that she says anything at all. When she does finally speak, she pulls the car to the side of the road and takes Ryan's face in her trembling hands.

"You seen that man?"

"Travis?"

"Don't play stupid with me, Ryan Wiliams; you know which man I'm referring to."

Ryan gulps and nods best he can with Dakota holding him so tight. Her lips are parched and pursed as she looks at him. "You stay clear of him no matter what you do."

"The shadow man?"

"That's no man, Ryan. That's no man at all. That's a leopard, and he's hunting."

When Dreams Became Nightmares

"Where is she?"

Alice looks Raphael up and down. Folds her arms. She might be in a chair, but her sneer looms over him.

"What do you care? You went off and left her when she needed you most. You made your way, now Jessie's making hers. Leave her be."

Still as stubborn as she ever was.

"Alice, please. I have to find her." He holds out the bible, open to Jessie's inscription. "I think she's in trouble." Alice stares at the book for a few seconds before she scoffs and pulls it from his hands.

"You're some asshole, Raphael. You know that, right?"

Yes. Yes, he does.

"She doesn't want you to know and made me swear not to tell you or anyone else but..." Alice smacks her palms on the arms of her wheelchair and half-rises from the seat. "I can't go looking for her, and she needs finding. You think you got problems, Raphael? Do you? Try having no legs." She sinks back and growls. Opens and shuts her mouth again two more times before she finally lets the words out. "She was in Vegas up until a few weeks ago. Something happened. Something bad, was all she said, and I haven't heard from her since."

"Where in Vegas, exactly?"

"I'd tell you if I knew. Carl's already gone out to look for her. Far as he could make out, she's no longer there but where she is now, no one can figure." Alice's voice rises with each word, panic in the unsaid. "She's not answering her phone, and it's going straight to voicemail. Been like that for weeks."

At that moment, sun blazing through streaked glass of the reception window, glare eating what two brain cells he has left after all the booze the night before, Raphael's head hurts more than his heart. It's late afternoon, and he's only just woken from his stupor. He'll head out in the morning to look for her. In the morning, everything will look better. All he has to do is get through the night.

Despite the heat and the whiny whirl of air from the wobbly fan, he doesn't take off his t-shirt or jeans when he returns to his room. He doubts he'll ever get naked again except to shower. He sweats. Not only from the heat but the memory. Everywhere he looks, eyes closed or open, all he sees are the girls: Chloe and Ash, all diamonds and rubies and sequins.

Raphael remembers everything he wishes he could forget…

Black tie, darling. Secret party. Hush. Hush. Don't tell a soul. He laughed. Who would he tell except them? Into a long, black limousine, one either side of him. Music soft. Champagne popped. Funny tasting. The girls' laughter, soft rain on tinted windows, "That's because it's expensive," Chloe whispered in his ear, took his hand and slid it up the long, narrow slit of her dress. She wore nothing, not even pantyhose, and he slid two fingers in. He could never, would never get enough of her pussy, warm velvet glove, tailor-made for him. The sequins of her dress caught the dim cabin light and glitter-bombed the roof with their reflection. Stars. We are stars. We are everything.

Raphael looked over at Ash, who smiled. Ash, who moved to the other side of Chloe, slid a shoulder strap down so Chloe's plunging neckline plunged to her waist. Kissed Chloe's cleavage, nipples hard and wanting, back arched, breath taut. Kissed her lips, ruby red and trembling. And they moaned and groaned against each other…

On the threadbare bed on the edge of the desert wasteland in the room where he lost his virginity to the love of his life, he's getting hard just remembering. What the fuck is wrong with him? Getting hard remembering how he hunched her fifty-thousand-dollar dress around her hips. Slid his tongue in as Ash teased her nipples with tiny bites. How could he have fucked her so many times and wanted her so many more…

Chloe, he begged. She groaned, Ash's tongue shoved down her throat, one hand kneading Ash's tits, the other stroking his cock. He was hard as a rock when she released him, cock twitching. She buried her face in Ash's pussy, expertly highlighted brown chignon, loose and tumbling. A diamond earring skittered across thick carpet as Ash pulled Chloe's head close and rubbed her crotch against her warm tongue. Met Raphael's eye. Me, her eyes said. Me first and me always. And he should have known then, in that moment. When instead of closing her eyes, she stared at him as he entered Chloe from behind, pumping hard and cumming harder still, all three at the same time, Ash watching him till the end. Till she couldn't breathe or see, only scream.

Everything blurred after that. The three of them a tangle on the seat. The smell of leather, cum, and Chloe's perfume. The tinkle of her laugh and the hum of Ash's. The drizzle of champagne down their raw throats. The slow stop of the long limo, somewhere dark. Somewhere quiet. He managed somehow to tuck himself and his shirt in as the girls fumbled and laughed. Chloe, it was Chloe who put the blindfold on him. Told him it was a surprise. How many more surprises did he need? They held him, Ash on one arm, Chloe on the other, both giggling as they led him stumbling and tripping over uneven ground. There were trees. Lots of trees. He felt them, tall and encroaching. Heard the leaves rustling. Why didn't he listen? He did not know the language of trees, but he knew the whisper of warning.

The pungent smell of earth. People.

The girls handed him over to someone else. Someone in robes who unmasked him, gave him a cup, more a bowl, warm in his hands. Drink. So, he drank, and it was bitter, and it flushed through him as he was led to a platform. Not a platform, but a dais and upon it a table and upon the table, a woman all porcelain skin and long limbs. Beautiful. The crowd murmured. Chloe, his lover, his friend, Chloe there, purring in his ear. Diamond crusted fingers fumbling with his zipper, she eased out his cock and put her mouth upon him. How could he be hard when he could barely see, when his head throbbed like a traffic jam. Someone else at his back, licking his balls, his asshole. Man, woman, no way to know. Hands everywhere. Silence except for sucking, stroking, the wind through the trees. He was hard. So hard. They led him to the table. To the girl. Young. Too young. Tiny buds where her breasts should be, soft fuzz where her bush should grow.

"For you, Raphael. All for you. A virgin sacrifice." The voice was warbled yet familiar. Richard. Richard there. Raphael tried to raise his head, but it was heavy as his dick was full. Either might explode or both. Richard in his ear. "Isn't she beautiful? How I wish I were you."

Raphael stumbled back, nearly breaking his cock as it jerked out of Chloe's mouth. Chloe sighed and looked up at him from her knees, her irises consumed by her pupils, wide and soft as velvet. Soft as her pussy. Every nerve on fire. His cock. He reached for himself. Someone held down his hands.

Richard drew him to the table. "She's waiting for you. All her life, she's waited for you. For this moment. To offer herself to you."

Who would know? Richard. Chloe. The crowd around them. The dark shadow of a naked man looming at the girl's head, skin covered in hundreds of swirling tattoos, his dick in one hand, gently stroking, a gold chain in the other, glinting in the torchlight.

"All you have to do is take her." It's Chloe. Beautiful Chloe, who he wants, might even love. A little. The biggest star on the planet. Is this the price she paid for her fame?

"Chloe, no."

He struggled to keep his head still, blinked and blinked and blinked, but his vision would not clear.

"It's okay, Raphael. Only once. Just the once, and the world will be yours, and you and I will be king and queen of it all."

The girl on the dais did not blink. Did not move. She could be a doll, not real at all but then the shadow man leaned over, whispered in her ear, and she raised a slight hand towards Raphael, gestured. "I am yours," she said.

Raphael stumbled back, soft and flaccid. He did not want to rape but rescue her. Save her from these monsters with their beautiful faces and bodies. He took the offered hand and pulled her up, but she was limp, unwieldly. He pulled her into his arms as the crowd circled. Searched for a way out. Stumbled. Something knocked him on the side of the head and down he went, the girl tumbling out of his arms only to be scooped up by the shadow man. The last thing he saw, the last thing he will see till the day he dies, was the naked man covered in tattoos and bathed in darkness clasping the gold chain around her neck and swallowing her whole.

Raphael shudders awake as he does most mornings. Where is he? Where? Home. Safe. At least from them if not his own mind. He splashes water on his face. Dresses.

He woke in a different motel that night. Everything gone. His phone. ID, Cards. Keys. Everything. Biggest star on the planet for a hot five minutes, and then, he was nothing. Had he imagined it all? Had it all been a bad dream?

No. He played it back. The next day, everything even more grim in the southern California sunshine.

Richard buzzed him in when Raphael arrived at his door. Mabel was nowhere to be seen, but the shadow man sat in a chair on the balcony overlooking the valley. He did not acknowledge Raphael's presence and for that, Raphael was grateful.

Richard did not offer him a seat or a drink, merely stared at the frying pan in which he was scrambling eggs, "You should have done it," he said. "You wanted her. There's no denying it."

"No, Richard, you're wrong. You're very wrong. I don't know what Chloe and Ash gave me but no. Never."

Richard pursed his lips and tap-tap-tapped the spatula on the side of the pan before setting it gently on a rosebud-shaped dublé.

"Be glad my Mabel has a soft spot for you and forget what you saw, forget my name and forget this town. Otherwise, you will be forgotten forever. If you get what I mean, and I think you do."

"But the movie. The magazines. The TV spots. The interviews. My agent…"

"Your agent was very disappointed in your latest performance. I daresay you'll see the press release in the morning dailies. Something about substance abuse. Rehab. Too famous too fast. Gone to his head. The usual." Richard met his eyes for the first time since Raphael arrived. There was a hardness there he'd never seen before, and Raphael finally realized Richard wasn't only a successful producer but a ruthless one. "Get in the car you came in and get out of town before said car wraps itself around a tree. You won't be the first small towner who let fame go to his head, and you won't be the last."

With that, Richard scooped the scrambled eggs onto a fine china plate and served them to the man in the chair.

Ash and Chloe were coming in as Raphael went out. Hand-in-hand, bright, sunny, laughing and either very much in love or doing a great job acting it. Ash refused to acknowledge him, only gave Chloe a long, deep kiss before letting go of her hand and brushing past him.

Being used was one thing. Being betrayed quite another. "Guess it's neither looks nor talent that got your name in lights, Chloe."

She smiled and gently touched Raphael's cheek.

"We could have done great things together, you know. Pity."

Some black bile shifted in Raphael's stomach. How could something so beautiful be so ugly? He removed Chloe's hand and pushed it down.

"Don't ever touch me again."

"Oh, don't worry, darling, I won't." She moved past him, then stopped, hand on the door.

He didn't want to turn. Couldn't bear to think he could be fooled so thoroughly. Never think with your dick, Raphael. Lesson learned. The hard way.

"I do like you, Raphael. A lot. We had… fun. Just remember, there's plenty of beautiful and talented people in this business but only a few make it to the top and even fewer stay there. You ever ask yourself why?"

"There are limits, Chloe. Come on. I don't believe this of you. Come with me. Get out of here before it's too late."

Chloe shook her head, tendrils of hair cupping her high cheekbones as the afternoon sun grazed her eyes. It might have been sadness in those glittering greens, regret even. "It's already too late, Raphael. It's already too fucking late."

Was it? Was everything too fucking late? No, he would find Jessie. Dreams were bullshit, Jessie was all that mattered. All that had ever mattered. How could he have ever forgotten?

The End of the Road

Ryan overhears everything the fella in Room 33 tells Aunt Alice. Mom's in trouble, which is all he needs to know.

He returns to their apartment, for even though mom's been gone over a month, it will always be their apartment, and he sits on his unmade bed biting his fingernails. What happened? Something bad, he knows that much. Aunt Alice won't tell him anything, that's for sure. Ryan's mind races with the possibilities. All bad and worse. He's got to do something, anything.

Once everyone's asleep, even Carl, snoring in his chair, he sets out. They'll look for him, for sure, but not till at least noon when Aunt Alice goes to rustle him out of bed. That'll give him about a twelve-hour headstart. He left a note but that won't make no matter; Carl will be on his tail in no time.

It's crazy to think he'll make it to Vegas on his mountain bike with nothing more than a backpack full of water bottles, some beef jerky, a tire repair kit, and fifty bucks he borrowed from the petty cash drawer. But he's reminded of another of Grandpa's sayings: 'You gotta do, what you gotta do,' and finding mom has to be done.

Once he's past the observatory and into open desert, he loses signal and turns off his phone. He's tired before he knows it. Nearly starts to cry when his legs begin to ache, then go numb, but fear pedals his wheels. Mom. Have to find mom.

He doesn't get far the first night and cowers in a ditch with some gophers. His pillow, a large flat stone and his blanket, a jacket he'd hastily tucked in his bulging backpack. He freezes anyway. Sleep won't come, mostly due to fear of things unseen but very much heard, but once it does, it's disrupted by the constant chattering of the gophers who don't take kindly to his intrusion.

Adrenaline wears off by the second afternoon, and he's tired and hungry and very much alone. Ryan's never been alone. Not really. Home is always a few minutes away. The place he returns to, not runs from. He half hopes Carl will track him down.

Occasional cars and trucks do whizz past, thunder on an endless flat road. The noise is scary but not as scary as the drivers who slow. Open their doors. Ask him if he wants a ride. As the sun crests noon and starts heading down, he's tempted, sorely tempted to take up one of the offers. Any truck or car or pickup would get him to Vegas within hours, but his mother didn't raise no fool. Most shrug and continue on their way when Ryan says thanks, but no thanks, but one fella doesn't take no for an answer.

It's a fancy car with a fancy California plate. Black. Tesla. Not many of those around anymore. It's quiet as it idles just ahead on the shoulder. Ryan stops. There's something about this car that gives him the creeps. Maybe it's the blacked-out windows, maybe it's cause his skin is fire ant crawling. He straddles his bike and surveys the terrain and his options. There are no other vehicles on the road or in sight. Off-road would be hard to navigate, mountain bike or not. No point in turning around either, the Tesla would only follow.

There's no choice, he's going to have to pass it. Leisurely. As if he's no care in the world about the potential sex beast, serial killer, child molester who waits patiently for his approach.

The car window eases down slow and quiet to reveal a man in a suit. Why any fella is wearing a suit and tie in the comfort of his own vehicle all the way out here is anyone's guess, but Ryan has no interest in knowing.

"Where you headed?" The voice is friendly enough, but the man's smile is too big, his eyes too small.

"To my dad's place."

The man sniffs the air and looks up and down the road. The sun is kissing the horizon, and it will be dark soon. Ryan could vanish into thin air without anyone being the wiser.

There's a taut pause between them. Things can go either way. Hopefully, the right way. Hopefully, the fella says, "Suit yourself, little buddy," like others have, and roll up his window, step on the gas, haul ass out of there and leave him the hell alone. Ryan hopes wrong. Something clicks in the man's eyes, and night draws down upon day. When he unbuckles his seatbelt, reaches over and opens the passenger door, his fake grin morphs into something Ryan has never seen before, a pained hunger about to be satisfied by a Ryan sandwich.

Ryan high-tails it straight into the dirt. The creep can easily track him with all the dust he's kicking up, but the Tesla isn't up for off-road and will quickly get marooned. Nonetheless, Ryan keeps pedaling fast as he can, ass hurting and teeth gnashing from all the stones and shrubs he can't avoid because of his speed and the growing darkness. He keeps going and going and going as if his life depends on it, for sure as hell, it does.

He finally stops when his legs have gone all wobbly, leans over the handlebars and gasps for breath. He doesn't stop long. The desert wakes when the sun goes down, and there are noises in the growing gloom. Most he can identify: critters, the wind, a few birds fluttering from bushes as he passes. Some, he can't. Dusk bruises everything purple except for a crack of light clinging to the horizon and headlights on the now distant road.

He keeps going. Takes his time pushing his bike through soft dirt and over hard stone. Stop, and he'll be dinner for the cackling coyotes or worse, a skinwalker. How many times has Aunt Dakota told him never to wander the desert at night? He is tired and cold; his phone is useless, and he finished the last slurp of water earlier in the afternoon. Maybe Mister Tesla wasn't some child-napper kiddie-fiddler and was just being kind. Kind enough to give Ryan a lift and a meal.

Yeah, no.

Ryan sighs. No use feeling sorry for himself. Like mom always says: there's no presents at a pity party. Dying of thirst, he is eyeballing a cactus and fingering his knife, when he realizes the tentacles of light clutching the horizon aren't from the sunset but a settlement of some sort in nearby hills. There will be food there. Water. Safety.

He pushes on. Nearly walks himself and his bike into a big crater. If the moon hadn't peek a booed from behind a cloud, he would have sailed straight to the bottom. Broken something. Maybe everything.

There are plenty of craters in the desert—space debris is always falling from the sky—but this one is different. The pulverized dirt and stone is faintly incandescent for a start, and the mist rising from the bottom isn't ground fog, but something from a bad dream. Heart racing, Ryan backs away quickly and gives it a wide berth. He's curious but not crazy. Whatever fell from the sky is probably not something he wants to encounter.

Finally, he connects with a one-lane back road which winds through small, deserted hills and about when his strength and hope are gonna give out, he arrives.

Turns out it isn't much of a settlement, just some abandoned, dust-bowled buildings, a gas station, motel, and diner. Same kind of set up as back home, only further off a main road and less populated. Soft refrains of country music drift from the open windows of the diner. There are a few cars in the parking lot, including a police car.

And the Tesla.

Ryan ducks behind a dilapidated metal shed. It takes a while to work up the nerve to peek around the corner to see if there's any sign of the Tesla creep.

Nobody. Not a soul in sight, only a waitress in the diner wiping counters.

Still, he hesitates. How hungry is he? His gurgling stomach says very, but his thirst is the deciding factor. He needs water soon, or he might get dehydrated and that's no joke. Ryan shrugs and steps back onto the road. Even if weird Tesla man is there, what is he going to do with a cop around?

A pickup approaches. Ryan hears it before he sees it. The motor is old, not smooth like the Tesla or hornet-humming like a cop cruiser. It rumbles up the short hill and into the bowl of the settlement, exhaust coughing and suspension humping over the mostly dirt and gravel road. The driver parks in the lot and sits in the cab for a few minutes, looking around. There're no streetlights, only the light from the diner and a curtain-muted glow from a couple of the motel windows, so it's hard to tell much about the driver except it's a fella.

The driver finally gets out. He's wearing jeans, t-shirt and boots. Not cowboy boots but black leather boots bikers wear. He's seen them at the diner sometimes when they pass through town. They look tough, and their bikes sound tough, but they're mostly big old softies. This guy doesn't look like a biker though; he looks like a movie star.

Ryan's belly rumbles. He decides to follow the guy into the diner.

As he makes his way across the road, a window opens at the corner of the motel, slowly, inch-by-inch as if the person opening it is afraid to be heard. A head appears. Squeezes through the gap. The head is small. Not an adult, but a kid like him. A girl. Framed by dark curtains he can barely make out her face but something about her is familiar. Could it be? Closer and closer he moves, quiet as a mouse and making himself just as small.

Estella.

Her eyes widen at the creak of a door behind her. "Vete rápido," she whisper-hisses at him through the cracked window. "Quickly. Quickly. Go."

What is happening? Judging by the sweat of her hair, the white slip she wears and the terror in her eyes, nothing good.

Ryan gestures urgently with his hand. "Come with me. I'll get you out of here."

Her eyes are as chipped as the paint on the window ledge, and her smile as threadbare as the curtains. She retracts into the room. "I cannot. Now, go. Before it's too late."

Before the words even finish leaving her mouth, rough hands cover her mouth and pull her back into darkness.

A Moment in Time

Sex sweat is always sweet in the desert heat. Bodies glide a gloss in low light, droplets bead and flick from damp hair as heads are thrown back, and sighs bellow. Dakota and Hyun-Ki have been fucking long enough now they've learned each other's preferences. How Dakota likes him to "grind the coffee" pressing down upon her mound and softly rotating while her hands grab his firm ass. How Hyun-Ki likes his nipples twisted and his balls sucked, not together but one at a time. The sensitive sweet spot of Dakota's inner thigh, the web between Hyun-Ki's toes. They are like horny teenagers, and Dakota doesn't remember ever being so satisfied.

Unlike any lover before, Hyun-Ki makes sure she cums first, unless, of course, she wants to be bent over and fucked, hard. Which she does occasionally. This night is not one of those times. This night, she feels the weight of the world shift and lift as if a lid has been raised from a boiling pot and something living is about to be thrown in, or something dead removed. Tonight, she clings to him as she has no other man before, as he whispers Korean endearments in her ear.

After, Dakota lays in bed listening to Hyun-Ki's soft snores. There is comfort in his arm so casually thrown across her chest, the soft drool from his mouth on her bare shoulder.

"I love you," she says, for the first time in thirty years and for the first time, she feels old enough and wise enough to mean it.

He tilts his head back and their eyes meet. Worlds and lives are exchanged in one, long glance. More than anything that could or would be spoken. Nonetheless, he says, "Saranghae." Which she assumes means the feeling is mutual.

Tempted as she is to kiss him deeply and completely and begin sweating once more, Dakota gives him a quick peck and goes to the window. Her nakedness glows in the starlight and if there are pale craters of cellulite on her thighs and gentle rolls on her hips, neither she nor Hyun-Ki pay any mind.

"There is a moon coming. A powerful moon," Dakota says.

Hyun-Ki nods and stretches toned arms overhead. "A super moon is predicted next week. We have not seen this alignment of planets and moon in five hundred years, and it will be another five hundred before we see it again."

The night is still and full. There is no sound of howling beasts or passing vehicles, only the distant clitter-clatter of a playing card thwacking against the wheel of a mountain bike.

"Ryan has gone to look for his mom," Dakota says.

"Should we go after him?"

She pauses. Considers. "No."

"He'll never make it."

"He's not meant to."

Don't Want to be Lost in Time

The further from the city, the kinkier they are. Sure, there's the lonely cowboy, but there's also the angry asshole whose wife won't blow him and why the hell not? He works all day while she sits around getting fat and letting the kids go feral. Nothing to do with the fact his balls smell, and his cum tastes like rotten eggs left in the sun. Some like it rough, and those Jessie avoids. There's a look in their eyes and a hardness to their chest she's learned to spot a mile away or at least through the peep hole.

She moves around, mostly to outrun pimps looking to add her to their stable, the law looking for a cut, and the cunts looking to beat up a whore. No matter what motel, she stays in the same room number each time. Figures it's her lucky charm as she's not dead yet. Room thirty-three reminds her of Raphael who she tries not to think of when some gorilla with bad breath and a worse attitude is on top of her telling her to cum, you stupid bitch.

Her clients find her online, and she screens them as much as possible, but there is no way to see the evil lurking in men's hearts except if they show up with a knife, a garbage bag, and duct tape. The money is good, especially for kink, but like every working girl, Jessie has her limits. She never takes a day off, figuring the more men she fucks the quicker she can stop fucking any at all.

One morning, sunup and her first client not due for a couple of hours, Jessie grabs a coffee in reception and sits in the metal chair outside her room. An old woman sits in a similar chair outside the room next door. Jessie isn't one for talking, and this woman doesn't seem the type to make friends, but Jessie asks her for a smoke and the next thing she knows, she's dragged her chair over to Beth's and is listening to her spill her guts.

"You don't know me from Adam and that's just as well, but this life is finally catching up with me, and I reckon I've not too many more of these," Beth waves to the sun rise, her coffee, and her smoke, "left before I'm checking out for good. I want to tell my story cause if even one person knows it, it all won't have been for nought. Cause the dying's worst fear is neither heaven, nor hell, nor riding eternal dream beams, but being forgotten."

Beth doesn't say anything for a minute or two. Is she looking for permission? Jessie has heard enough sob stories in the past month to make her want to shove BBQ skewers in her ears, but Beth does seem frail enough—skin pale and hands trembling, lips thin, and hair wispy—she might up and blow away at any minute.

"Tell me," Jessie says to be kind.

A nod and a clearing of the throat is all the preamble Beth gives before she begins…

"I'm not special. Nothing to mark me as any better or worse than anyone else. I've no fame or fortune. No great accomplishments. But I was here. I existed. I touched people and made and broke things.

"I had dreams. We all do. Only thing keeps anyone going. If you got no dreams then you got no future, only a past full of regret. When I was a little girl, I wanted to be a ballerina. Imagine that. Little old me in the middle of the desert, a million miles from any ballet studio. I watched them on a TV show one Christmas. The Nutcracker, it was. Thought it was the most magical thing I'd ever seen. All I wanted was to be Clara. Still do."

At that, Beth stands on the dusty wooden planks of the path, which extends from room to room, brushes her baggy cotton dress down and does a pirouette. It isn't graceful or even pretty, but Jessie claps at the beauty in that bent body straightening for one brief moment.

"Didn't fall and break a hip. Miracles never cease." Beth laughs. "I tried my best with what I had. Taught myself by watching videos. Danced in the desert under the light of the moon with rodents and coyotes as my audience. I'll tell you, I never felt so alive. Believing.

"But life sneaks up on you and snatches those dreams away. You meet a fella, and he's tall and broad with chocolate eyes, and a smile just as sweet. He tattoos your name above his heart, and you tattoo his over your ass. Soon enough, his dreams become yours, and by the time you wake up in hospital with two broken arms, a rod in your spine, and promises it'll never, ever happen again, it's too late. The only dreams that will ever come true are nightmares.

"I have kids. Two. One's in Eyman, the other… I dunno. Don't see either, not for years. Can't remember the last time we spoke. Drugs for one. Alcohol, the other. Broken people spend their lives either trying to mend the damage or finish the job. You never have kids thinking the end of their road will be a bottle or a needle. Never even enters your head, even if you're on both, yourself.

"No, the baby growing in your belly, that's your hope. Hope things will be better, brighter for them than it ever was for you. All your hardships, your sadness rolls away with each contraction, and they pop out thick with blood and mucous and when the nurses wipe them clean and hand them to you all swaddled and smelling of new, it's like God washed away all your sins, and you can start over. In them. With them. For them. All your dreams become making all their dreams come true.

"They might not want to know you, but your kids will always need you." Beth cracks open a beer and takes a long swig. "You're young. Beautiful. Same as I was before the bricks of regret built a palace on my shoulders. Once I killed that bastard husband of mine, I thought about killing myself too. Sometimes, staying alive is the biggest sacrifice you can make."

Jessie knows the words to that tune. Mom, Bobby, Pa, Sarah… Raphael. She pauses then; his loss hadn't hurt the most, but it did hurt the longest. Beth looks her up, down, and sideways.

"I see you had your heart broke too. We all have one time or another. Leave you, did he?"

Jessie nods but says nothing. Saying anything would make it present instead of past. She can forget the past but isn't sure she can live with it in the present.

"Sometimes we think there's no getting over 'the one' and maybe we never do. Maybe that's why it wasn't hard for me to take up this profession. Wasn't easy, but it wasn't hard either. I did what I had to, do what I must. I tried all the usual: waitressing, casino girl, stripping, then one night a fella who wasn't bad looking and had kind eyes asked me for a private dance. Gave me a big tip, enough to pay the rent. I thought it was an easy way out of the mess I found myself in. Figured selling my beauty was the only way me and my kids could get by. I figured wrong, and you're wrong too. This is no life for anyone, Jessie darling. You still have every chance in the world; don't throw it all away until all that's left is begging some stranger to remember you."

"I have a kid," Jessie says. "He's young still, only ten." A kid she hasn't talked to for how long now? Days? Weeks? Longer? It hurts to miss him, and she misses him fierce, but she can't talk to him. Not now, not any longer. Not while she's doing what she's doing. He can never know, even if it's all for him.

"A good age. The best even. They're not babies, but they're not yet men."

"I'd do anything for him."

"Even this?"

"Even this." Jessie pauses. She tries not to feel ashamed—she needs a lot of money fast and other than robbing banks, this is the quickest route—she mostly fails. A whore is a whore no matter the score. Will she ever be able to face her son again? "But I won't be doing it for much longer."

Beth takes a sudden interest in some cracked skin between her thumb and forefinger. She sucks on it as if to extract some festering poison, then spits.

"I said the same for years."

"Then why?"

"Why do I still do it?" Beth shrugs. "It's not the money. Though that's part of it. My age, what else am I gonna do? There's every kind of kink, and granny sex pays the rent. But it's not the real reason. The real reason is hot cocks and cold hearts remind me that once I thought I knew what love is."

Dinner Time

Night is falling and so is the fuel gauge. His truck is the most reliable thing in Raphael's life right about now, but it can't run on fumes, least not for long. The phone signal went about an hour back and although he's on the highway, he feels lost. He hadn't thought this out well—does he ever think anything out well—and now, here he is, in the back of beyond without a hint of civilization or even another vehicle in sight.

The low fuel warning light blinks on. There's maybe twenty more miles in the tank. He scans the horizon and then the rearview in case he missed anything. Spots a weak glow of light in the hills off to the north. Too small to be a town and too far off the highway to be a rest stop. No options mean it's the only chance he's got. He takes the next exit.

He leans forward, chest against the steering wheel, willing his truck to climb to the top of the winding hill. If he makes it, he can coast down from there. Luck is on his side, and he reaches the small settlement before the tank runs out.

The place is quiet and something feels off. He can't quite put his finger on it, but hopefully he'll be gone before he does. There are no streetlights and only one powerline that reaches out from the hills like a stray hair. No sign of any townies, and the few remaining houses are boarded up. Other than that, there's a motel with a dark lobby and a closed door, a well-lit but empty diner, and a barn with a couple of old-fashioned gas pumps out front.

Over at the pumps, the signs say Self-Service and Pay at the Diner. He fills up both the tank and the jerrycan he keeps in the bed of his truck. Looks around. Spots the kid crouching next to a shed that looks like the next breeze will blow it away.

On the run. That much is clear.

None of his business.

He heads into the diner to pay for the gas and get a bite to eat. Only person in the place is a waitress behind the counter wiping down a countertop that's already clean. She looks up, looks him over. She is tall and skinny, her eyes small and beady. Her uniform is one of those old-fashioned soda-counter outfits with a pink apron.

"You here for the veal or the lamb?"

"Can I get a burger and fries please, ma'am?"

She points at the menu on a chalkboard hanging over an old-timey register. There are only two things written: VEAL. LAMB.

Weird.

"No, thanks. I'll just get a coffee and pay for my gas."

She meets his eyes as the coffee pot percolates behind her. "All out."

Raphael nods and hands her cash for the gas. Turns to leave. *Keep going. Out the door and out of town asap.* He might not have always known when demons were wearing people masks, but he knows now.

He pauses at the door. Turns back. "How about a room for the night?"

"No vacancies."

There are three cars in the parking lot, one of them a state trooper's, and there must be at least ten rooms in the motel.

"Well, guess I'll be heading on. You have a good night."

Raphael may have made dumb moves in the past, but those had been from naivety, not stupidity. He is no longer naive. Veal or Lamb… young meat. *No. Get the fuck out of dodge. Now.*

As he returns to the parking lot, he hears the muffled sound of crying. A kid. *Where's that kid?* None of his business. *You can save this one.* He gets in the pickup but doesn't start the engine, though really, he should. *Get out of here now and don't look back. You've got to find Jessie.* Last thing he needs is to draw any more attention to himself, especially in the middle of nowhere with the highway a good ten minutes away.

Just as he decides someone else's business is none of his, especially if a trooper is involved, there's a knock on the cab window behind him. Raphael nearly jumps out of his skin but manages to summon the courage to turn and see who is in the bed of his truck and if they have a gun pointed at the back of his head.

It's the boy.

"Mister. Mister," he hisses. His hair is full of dust and his eyes of desperation. "You've got to help me, please. I'm begging you."

A limo with California plates pulls up and five men get out. Two with black briefcases, three in black suits, and none with good intentions. God damn it. Raphael slides open the window.

The kid hesitates. "You're not one of them, are you? I can tell."

Raphael isn't one of them, but he ain't no fool either. He has two bullets, that's it, and he has to save one for himself. The boy trembles at the hatch, hands bunched into fists as he watches the men head into the motel.

"No, I'm not," he says and motions the boy in. He's not about to take on the suits, their goons, and state troopers, but at least he can save the boy.

Soon as the boy climbs into the cab, Raphael moves to start the engine, but the boy is there before him, yanking the key out of the ignition and shoving it deep in his pocket.

"Give me the key, kid."

"Sorry, mister, I can't. My friend is in there. Please. You have to help her."

He doesn't seem like a bad kid. In fact, there is something familiar about him. Something in the eyes. It's not the color or the pearling tears but a determination and stubbornness that reminds him of Jessie. Jessie. He has to find her, not fuck around and find out.

It would be easy enough to get the keys off the kid who's hunched against the door like a beat dog hoping for a scrap but expecting a smack.

Raphael sighs. "I'm no hero, kid."

Nope. Not even a little bit. Only a loser with nothing left to lose and a jerrycan full of gas in the bed of his truck. Big pleading eyes look up at him.

God damn it to hell.

"Kid, stay in the car and be ready with that key when I get back." Raphael slides from the cab, boots landing on dirt with the thud of a dead body hitting the ground. Fuck. Fuck. Fuck is wrong with him?

There is no sign of any life, even the waitress seems to have vanished. There's quiet and there's too quiet, and he can't shake the feeling he's being watched as he scoots down next to the limo and slashes a tire. He cocks an ear. No one's shouting or shooting so he moves to the next vehicle and does the same and then the same again.

He finishes with the trooper's cruiser, then retrieves the jerrycan in the bed of his truck. Debates which car he'll set alight when he hears sounds he'll never forget. Kids, man. Kids. Screaming. Men laughing.

Burn it. Burn it all down.

Instead of one of the vehicles, Raphael splashes the gas on the corner of the motel where the windows are dark. Pulls out his lighter, sets it alight and scurries back to the pickup to watch.

It doesn't take long. The old, dry wood catches quickly and spreads fast. All hell breaks loose: screams, shouts, breaking glass.

Two kids climb through a smashed window, grazing their legs on ragged edges. A boy and girl hold hands and run as if their life depends on it. Both naked. The boy is covered in blood and holding a knife. The kid in his truck runs out to help them.

"Where's the key, kid? Where's the motherfucking key?" Raphael roars as flames crackle and climb.

But the boy isn't listening, he's helping the others onto the bed of his truck. Raphael climbs behind the wheel right before a handful of angry men, including one state trooper emerge from the burning building.

Fuck. Fuck. Fuck. "The key, kid. Give me the fucking key."

They almost make it. Almost. Raphael is peeling out of the parking lot in a cloud of dust when shots ring out. None hit his tires, thank fuck. The kids aren't so lucky. The girl starts screaming as the naked boy goes down with a thud. Raphael can't stop. Can't help. All he can do is drive.

He heads for the highway but doesn't get on it. Too obvious. There'll be an APB out before he even hits the on ramp. He'll need to take his chances and head deeper into the country where the roads are mostly dirt and houses are few and far between.

The kid bangs on the window.

"We need a hospital. He's dying."

Raphael chances a quick look over his shoulder. The kid isn't dying, he's dead, but there's no time to say so. No time to stop. In the rearview, the girl sobs while the living boy tries to console her.

After two hours, with no sign of pursuit, he stops to get his bearings. The moon is cloud-bound overhead, and a light fog has settled upon the desert as if all its ghosts are assembling. Two of the kids are shivering over the body of the third.

When he sees the light, his first thought is to avoid it. You run into two types in the middle of bumfuck nowhere: survivalists or cults, one will shoot, the other will try to convert you first. There's no explaining away a naked kid or a dead one to either.

Still, when no good options remain, desperation is your gambling hand. The adrenaline has worn off, he's exhausted, and the kids are freezing. Maybe a farmer or a native or even an artist lives here off the beaten track. Maybe, for once, Raphael will get lucky.

He pulls up the driveway. A curtain drops and a light goes on. The front door opens to reveal an old man holding a shotgun and pointing it at Raphael.

Not so lucky.

Raphael hisses at the kids to stay quiet and low, then gets out with his hands up and his chin down. "Sorry to disturb you, sir. I know it's late, but my phone's out of battery, and I'm hopelessly lost."

All true. Raphael neglects to mention the three kids, one dead, in the back of his truck. The important thing is to get them to shelter before he's got three corpses to deal with.

"Got no time for strangers. Be on your way," the man says. He has a heavy accent. German or something. A German all the way out here. Go figure.

"Please, I've kids who need help. I mean you no harm, I just..."

Raphael sinks to his knees. After everything that's happened the past couple of weeks, he hopes the German *will* blow his head off. Let someone else worry about the kids and the body he's somehow accumulated in the past few hours.

No, he can't die. He has to find Jessie before it's too late. He can beg though.

"Mister?"

It isn't Raphael the boy is addressing but the man with the gun. By the determined set of his eyes, it's the cold that's rattling his limbs, not fear. He is tall for a kid who can't be more than twelve, and thin. Too thin. As if trouble has been calling to his door as much as it has Raphael's. He has to admire him, going up against a shotgun with no way of knowing whether it will be used or not. Brave kid. Or stupid. Or desperate like the rest of them.

"Mister, please. My friend is hurt. Hurt bad, and we really need help."

If the kid's pleading doesn't do the job, Raphael is out of options. Luckily, it does. The German lowers his gun, hesitantly at first, then with the conviction of someone making a bad bet with good money, he holds the door open and lets Raphael and the living boy inside.

Raphael figures the truth, crazy as it is, will be the best way forward with a German named Frank who retired to the desert some years ago with his Philippian wife who passed away only last year.

Frank believes everything Raphael tells him, which is mostly the truth. Once Raphael finishes, Frank gets a heavy blanket and helps him gather up the girl. She refuses to leave her brother, and it takes some convincing to get her into the house and a warm bath where, if she can't wash away the pain, at least she won't freeze to death with it.

The body is another story.

"It's not a body," the kid says. He's been mostly silent, choosing to listen to the adults before deciding whether they could be trusted or not. "His name is Daniel, and his sister is Estella."

"And what's your name, kid?" Raphael says.

The kid purses his lips. No way to know if whatever comes out is the truth or not.

"Ryan," he says.

"Well, Ryan, hard as it may be to believe or accept, Daniel is dead, and the kindness of strangers only stretches so far."

"It's alright," Frank says. "I've wrapped Daniel up in a blanket, and we'll give him a proper burial in the morning."

With his bald head, pale skin and massive hands, Frank might be mistaken for someone who'd cut you up and store you in the freezer, and while the jury isn't a hundred percent out on that yet, it seems unlikely. There *are* good people in the world, Raphael, baby. Most of them just don't live in Hollywood.

"Thank you." Ryan says and joins Estella who's lying on a large, brown sofa wearing a robe four sizes too big, sucking her thumb and staring into the flames of a roaring fireplace.

Raphael doesn't want to think about what she sees there, but he has a pretty good idea.

Frank's curiosity as he looks at Ryan is matched only by Raphael's own. "You relations?" he says to Raphael.

"No," both he and Ryan say at the same time.

Frank nods. "None of my business anyway. I've seen strange things in my time out here, and I dare say I'll see stranger yet. There's no rhyme nor reason, right or wrong anymore, only lawlessness exploited by the bad guys. And it's only going to get worse, the less there is for the more.

Frank pours him a glass of whiskey. Neat.

"The world is full of bad guys," Raphael says as he raises his glass in thanks.

"Which is why I live as far away as possible from anyone."

They clink glasses and Raphael downs his in one go. He swore never to do drugs or drink again, but not much else can take the edge off an adrenaline come-down.

"You'll want to move your truck into the barn," Frank says. "There isn't much around these parts, and if people are looking for you, they'll pass by eventually. Best to move on before too long." Frank lowers his voice so the kids can't hear. "The boy will need buried well away from here. I want to help, but I can't have dead kids on my property."

Raphael nods and thanks him. There is no refuge in life, only brief respites, warm as the wood crackling in the fireplace before a cold morning hearth intrudes. He moves the truck, puts his phone on a charger, and bunks down on a sofa across from the kids. It's covered with heavy blankets and smells of smoke and dog. He fights sleep as long as possible, one ear listening for the kids, the other for approaching vehicles. The last thing Raphael sees before his heavy eyelids close is Frank sitting by the door in his rocking chair, holding his shotgun.

There's about ten beautiful seconds when Raphael opens his eyes again that he's still in his dream. A dream where Jessie is in the kitchen cooking up bacon and eggs and toast and Christ, he is starving.

"Hungry?" The gravelly gruff voice is unfortunately not Jessie's.

"Famished."

Raphael rises and folds the blanket. The kids are already at the table, Ryan ignoring his own heaping plate while trying to convince Estella to eat from hers. No sign of dream Jessie, only cold, hard reality. He debates for all of five seconds before choosing to confide in Frank. "I'm looking for a woman. Tall, blonde, beautiful."

Frank laughs. "Aren't we all?"

"Name's Jessie. Jessie Williams."

Ryan bolts to his feet. "That's my mom!"

A Long Time Coming

Alice's eyes burn with tears of frustration as she pounds her useless legs till bruises she can't feel shine purple. She can't reach Jessie. Can't go after Ryan. And Dakota? Fuck, Dakota.

"He's got to do what he's got to do."

"Damn you, Dakota, he's ten. What the fuck does he got to do in the summer other than ride his bike and kick a ball around?"

She starts working on Carl, trying to convince him to drive her around the desert to search. Jessie will never forgive her if something happens to Ryan. Hell, Alice would never forgive herself.

Carl goes out on his own cause someone has to mind the motel and that someone is Alice. He's gone two days before he returns empty-handed. Alice thanks him and serves him dinner before wheeling herself to the parking lot and howling frustration at the moon, and as she howls, a text comes in from a number she doesn't recognize. Probably spam shit. Desperation makes her read it anyway.

It's Ryan. "I'm okay. Don't worry. I'm going to find mom."

Alice rings the number. It rings out. She rings again. About forty fucking times. Finally, someone answers.

The voice is familiar as her own. "Raphael?"

Silence.

"Raphael, goddamn it. Answer me."

Raphael's voice is reluctant. "Hi, Alice."

If he was in front of her, she would have run him over with her chair and sat on his head for good measure. "You bring that child back here, Raphael." She debates saying the next bit cause it's not her news to share, but Alice knows it's the only thing that will persuade him. "That boy is Jessie's kid."

"I know."

He knows. What else does he know? "Is Jessie with you?"

"No. I'm still looking for her. There's been a problem but don't worry, her boy is safe."

"Don't you hang up on me, Raphael." Alice is practically screaming at this point. "Bring that child home."

"Can't talk right now, Alice. We're in a hurry. Gotta go."

"Don't you hang up on me—"

He hangs up.

Alice throws her phone into the brush, and it hits a saguaro before skipping across the dirt. "Argh," she screams, and Carl, Maria and one of the cleaners come running. "Help me, someone, please help me fix these goddamn, useless, motherfucking legs."

*

He comes out of the desert that night.

No one comes out of the desert. Ever. Though plenty wander into it, never to return. She recognizes him immediately even though he's too far away to make out properly in the dim streetlight. He probably doesn't recognize her. Not with her face all puffy from crying, and her hair pulled back in a tight ponytail. Not to mention the wheelchair. Under normal circumstances, she might hide herself away until she's presentable but right now, she is just so happy and relieved to see him, for she thought he died in the fire, even though his bones were never found.

With each step he takes towards her down the long empty road, a tear forms in her eyes. By the time he reaches her, barefoot in jeans and a white linen shirt, long hair damp and draggling, blue, blue eyes looking from her wheels to her feet to her legs to her eyes, they've spilled out and over and she can't stop crying.

He sinks to his knees in front of her. Lays his head in her still lap and sighs.

"I'm sorry it took me so long."

They remain that way, peaceful and quiet at the edge of the parking lot, him in dirt, her on pavement. Alice gently strokes his hair as the sun sinks and the galactic streetlights of the stars blink on. He's exhausted. Wherever he came from, it is far. She doesn't want to disturb him, nor let him go for fear he will vanish once more. This time forever.

He doesn't move until she shivers. Startled, he scrambles to his feet. Neither of them speak, and it seems neither knows where to start when there is so much to say.

"Are you cold?" he says, finally. His voice is as she remembers from her dreams: calm yet deep, warm but confident. It's a voice a loud room would quieten to hear.

"I'm okay." It's no lie. Nothing can detract from the warmth his presence brings, not even frostbite.

He laughs. Strong and hard. "It's not that cold," he says.

She laughs along with him. Stops. "Can you read my mind?"

He considers for a moment or two as goosepimples rise on her flesh. "I don't think so. Not your exact thoughts, but I do have a pretty good idea of your emotions. Can you tell what I'm feeling right now? Close your eyes and think of me."

Alice closes her eyes. Thinks of him and only him. Thinks of the strong tattooed muscles of his exposed arms, the softness of his eyes when he looks at her. She blushes.

"You want to kiss me?"

How bold she is to say it. She isn't like Jessie. Or any of her friends. Has never had a boyfriend. Not after the accident. There were boys who liked her, who asked her out, but Alice never felt quite herself in the wheelchair. Never felt beautiful or attractive or worthy of love.

But she dreamed of it. Of him.

"I've wanted to kiss you for a very long time." He keeps his distance. Head down, he watches her through his long lashes. Waits.

Alice nearly laughs again from the joy of it. All caution, all reason is thrown to the wind as she says, "Well, what are you waiting for?"

He approaches slowly, puts hands on the armrests of her chair and lowers his head.

"Wait," Alice says breathlessly. "What is your name?"

"Michael." He whispers against her lips as he kisses them ever so softly, as if he really is a dream, or a ghost. Hers part as he presses, and they sigh together as their hands find each other's faces.

There is a loud cough, and Carl says, "Get a room you two," and laughs.

Michael straightens and stumbles backwards. His face looks redder than Alice's feels. Maria stands in the doorway of reception, flicking a kitchen towel over her shoulder and waving them in.

"Come in and have some dinner."

Carl and Maria sit with them while they eat. At twenty-five, Alice certainly doesn't need a chaperone and definitely doesn't want one either. She nearly protests but shuts her mouth at a look from Maria who pauses mid-serving, wooden spoon in her hand, daring her to complain. Maria never takes nonsense from anyone, least of all a girl she nearly raised. So Alice must suffer the embarrassment of them cross-examining Michael as he eats, asking the questions parents normally would. Michael answers. Most of them.

They all know he isn't local because anyone local they already know. However, when it comes to specifying where he's from, Michael is vague—far away, no place you would know or heard of. Carl's eyebrows go up and Maria starts talking in Spanish. The only people from far away are those passing through, mostly by truck or train, not walking straight out of the desert.

"We went to the same school," Alice pipes in, giving Michael's hand a little squeeze under the table. "But his family moved away."

Which makes perfect sense. Carl and Maria choose not to comment on his lack of shoes, luggage, or even a wallet. They let it go because Michael is obviously tired, and Alice is getting agitated, and no one likes it much when Alice is agitated.

There are plenty of empty rooms in the motel. Since the diner and truck stop closed, the truckers stopped stopping, and most of the girls round the back had moved on to greener pastures. Michael is given the room next to Alice's. Maria delivers fresh towels and Carl a pair of his old sneakers for him to wear. Once they're gone, Alice invites Michael into her place.

She wheels herself next to the chrome dinette near the window and asks Michael to close the curtains. He does so but instead of sitting next to her, he examines the paintings on the wall.

"These are beautiful," he says.

"Which is your favorite?" Alice is keen to know the answer because it will tell her a lot about him and quickly.

He takes his time as he walks around the room. Their silence should be awkward but isn't. They may have only properly just met, but it seems they've known each other forever. Alice is young enough to embrace this sentiment despite being cynical enough to know life isn't a romance novel. No, it's not a storybook that makes her heart flutter and palms sweat; it's him.

He stops in front of her most recent work, the brightest in a room of troubling images. It's a painting of a long, desert landscape and at its vanishing point, a city on a hill all bright and shiny under the shade of cherry blossom trees. Above, ten moons circle and thousands of stars shine.

He's still for the longest time. She can't see his face, so wheels over to him. Looks up as he stares at the painting. Sees his tears.

"What is it?"

His breath catches as he speaks. "This, this painting. Where did you get it?"

Should she tell him? What if he hates it? Why is she suddenly filled with self-doubt?

Alice gulps and looks him straight in his teary eyes. "I painted it."

He retreats to the bed and sits on the edge with a thump. There is a fancy white bracelet on his wrist carved with thousands of bumps, lines and symbols. He presses a few buttons, and the device whirls twice around his wrist, then stills.

Alice wheels in front of him. "What is that? One of those new wrist computers?"

"Something like that." His shoulders roll, and his stomach caves.

"You look like you've just lost everything," she says.

It is the longest minute of her life before he raises his head, straightens his shoulders, takes both her hands, and looks her in the eyes. Alice blinks. She could swim in the depths of those eyes. If she knew how to swim.

"No," he says. "I've gained everything."

That makes her heart flutter even more.

He holds her hands tighter. "I want to tell you something, but I don't think you'll believe me."

"I'll believe anything you tell me." Which is probably, no, *definitely* stupid but the truth.

Their knees touch as they hold hands and for the first time in years, Alice allows herself the luxury to wish she could feel both points of contact. But wishes are fishes and there ain't no damn fish in the desert.

"I'm from another dimension. That painting. It looks exactly like my world."

His eyes never leave hers as he says it, but if he expects shock or disbelief in response, he doesn't find it.

He holds up his wrist. "This device is a transporter. It allows me to travel between dimensions, worlds, and times. The technology was crude for a long time. It's still impossible to reliably track or map coordinates, and I couldn't work on developing it for years. That's why it's taken me so long. And even this time, I didn't..."

Michael runs his hand through his thick, blonde hair. "You... you probably think I'm crazy. Do you?"

"Did you turn it off?"

He nods.

"Why?"

"Because I also used it to turn off the tracker imbedded in my skin. Now, my father can't find me and force me back to my home world. Not until I turn it on again."

"I bet he won't be happy that you did."

Michael laughs. "You're right about that."

"So, how did you get here? How did you finally find me?"

"I could sense you... since the last time—the fire—it was so frustrating, but I didn't have a transporter again until my senior year at the Cadets when I needed one to continue my research. I then tried to find you countless times, hopping from one world to the next but never succeeding. Hundreds of worlds and numerous timelines on each. Nearly got expelled…"

"The Cadets?"

"Oh… it's like a university for scientists."

He sits forward, leans towards her. Seems about to say one thing but then something else comes out.

"Strange as it may seem…"

"Strange, huh?"

"I… I don't think I find you." His long hair flops over his forehead as he examines their clasped hands. Alice resists the urge to brush it back from his face and tuck it behind his ear for all of one second before she does exactly that.

He looks up. "I don't find you; you *call* me. Anytime you're in trouble and really need help."

Alice thinks back as she fingers the diamond dangling from the chain around her neck. "The first time. The phone booth in the desert. Dakota told us about it when we were kids. I was lost and scared, cold and tired and needed help."

"Dakota?"

"My aunt, well, she's not technically my aunt but… she's my aunt. We all thought it was a fairytale—she was always telling us stories—the magic phone booth where all your dreams come true. We believed it when we were kids."

"But no longer?"

Alice shrugs. "I found it that day. In the middle of nowhere. Old and abandoned. Couldn't possibly be a functioning phone booth, right? There was a sign with a number: Dial 777 for Destiny. I reckoned it was an old gambling thing or something. Well, I dialed, and then, there you were."

"This phone booth sounds like a transporter of some sort, but 777 isn't a coordinate for my world. Where is it? Can you show me?"

"That's the problem, it vanished and never returned. I've looked. Many times." She doesn't elaborate. It's too embarrassing to admit she looked nearly every day for more than a month, then once a week, then once a month, until the fire... Doesn't tell him it's because she wanted to see him again… desperately. "Sometimes, I think I imagined everything, even now," Alice pinches her arm, then pinches his.

"Ouch," he says and rubs his arm.

"Are you real? You are real, aren't you? I'm not dreaming? I do dream about you sometimes." A lot. "This is all so unbelievable. I don't know what to think."

He touches her face, and she nearly crumbles from the rush of real in the midst of dream.

"I dream of you, too," he says. "Often."

He lets his confession hang there for a minute. Alice is afraid to break the silence. Afraid to break the spell. Afraid to wake up.

"Some say dreams are portals to other worlds, same as transporters, just harder to control," he says, finally.

Alice returns to the window. Her room overlooks the desert. It is quiet away from the road. How she wishes she could take his hand and run into the night. Turn on his transporter and hop from place to place having adventures. How she longs to stand in his arms under a full moon, coyotes singing, stars falling, and kiss him.

But none of that is ever going to happen.

"Look, things have been really hard for me lately and to be honest, I think I've finally lost my mind. It's been a long time coming, what with the fire and losing my dad, and my sister gone missing, and now my nephew, and I reckon, I've lost the plot completely. I figure I'm asleep right now. Dreaming. Sometimes, I dream I'm dreaming, and each layer of dream seems so real, like an entire lifetime lived in a few hours' sleep, and I'm always so happy because in every single one of those dreams, my legs are working. But I always return to this reality."

Alice slaps her useless thighs. They've grown so thin, what muscle remains clinging to bone for dear life.

"If I'm dreaming now, why can't I walk? Why aren't my legs working in this happy dream? Why? Why?" As she speaks, Alice's slaps turn to punches. She'll bruise but the bruises won't hurt, will they, just be ugly reminders she can't feel a thing.

"Alice. Alice, stop. Please stop."

He falls to his knees before her and takes her hands in his. Stills them. "I'm sorry. This is all my fault. I could have prevented this. Should have, but my father pulled me back before I could."

He rolls up a sleeve to reveal intricate tattoos of swirls and spirals which loop in and out of each other. Some of the lines have faded as if removed by laser surgery. She rolls up her own sleeves. She'd always thought the marks on her arms were scars from the fire.

"They're exactly like mine."

He takes one of her hands. Kisses the palm—his lips soft and dry—before bringing it to a tattoo and holding it there. Alice's fingers began to tingle, then her arm. Moisture coats her palm, and thick white smoke envelopes her hand. She jerks back but Michael's eyes meet hers. Trust me, his say. Trust me.

The tingles become tension, become something about to explode. The feeling lightning bolts through her until it reaches her legs.

"My legs." Her voice cracks in disbelief. Pain where she pummeled herself. She is not imagining it. Cramps in her calves and ankles from sitting so long. Before her eyes, her muscles flex, grow taunt, and her flesh fills out.

More of the tattoo on his arm has faded. At the same time, Alice's scars have filled in, darkened, expanded.

She looks at them. At him. "Michael, what have you done?"

He rises and holds out his hands.

"Please tell me I'm not dreaming. Please."

He smiles as he takes her trembling hands. Hope dangles before her like a carrot to a horse.

She stands. Nearly falls over from the shock of it.

He waits patiently until she feels confident to take one step. Then another. Holds her tight as she sobs against his chest. Takes her face in his hands and brushes away her tears.

"You're not dreaming," he says.

And he kisses her.

For a Good Time

Some things never go away. The need for water, the desire for sex, and the option to escape in drink and drugs when you have neither. Once, Travis had some semblance of scruples about buying and selling such things, but the world has moved on from right and wrong, from have and have not, to supply and demand.

Simpler times.

He thinks of what might have been, what could still be, but the darker his days, the longer his nights, and it seems unlikely he'll ever see dawn again.

"Boss?"

Philip, new to the ranch but not the business, stands in the open doorway of the caravan. Travis looks up from his book. The dry heat has leeched the paper brittle as beached sand dollars. In the can, he read as much as possible, and it is a habit he continues. He inserts the ten-k bill he uses as a bookmark and closes the book. Waits.

"We found her."

It hadn't taken long, only longer than he wanted. She didn't make any attempt to hide, which made it more difficult in the long run.

"Get the car."

"Sure, boss."

He drives himself as he often does, especially at night. The sky ablaze with stars and nearly bright as day. The road straight and long. The desert is dangerous, especially at night, but Travis is more dangerous still.

He sees things in his peripheral vision. He often does. Horses racing, demons laughing. Tonight, there is only a fire, somewhere in the distance.

At some point, he turns off the headlights and drives by starlight, the moon. Passes nothing but truckers with their cabs lit up all carnival ride. Their fancy horns bellow in acknowledgement of a fellow road warrior. Travis never sees them as cattle transporters, or water tankers, or whatever goods they carry. In the middle of nowhere, trucks are tickets to somewhere.

She's at a place called the Snakebite, one of many motels which mark the freeway as much as the trucks. Travelers know better than to frequent them, for they are no longer accommodation, but brothels or drug dens or last refugees before the street for the poor or migrants. Hers is easy enough to spot; the sign flashing the red fangs of a neon rattlesnake coiled and ready to strike.

The pool is empty; the lining cracked from the heat. Plastic poolside chairs are either stacked or tipped over like a drunk unable to find his feet. A dying bare bulb hisses in the one remaining lamp post over the car park. Travis parks well away from it. Even at this late hour people are awake. Watching. Waiting for trouble to find them. Hoping it won't. But Travis is neither cop nor bounty hunter. In fairness, he doesn't know what he is anymore, other than rich and alone.

He sits in the car. Watches a fat fuck tap on her door. She answers. Looks around. Sees his car. Leaves the curtains open knowing he can look in. He watches. It's not a show but a punishment, and he gets hard despite the fact. Jerks off anyway.

The next guy is different. Does not drive but is driven. He neither looks around nor knocks, just opens the door and walks right in with a leather briefcase. Privileged prick.

Travis drums his thumbs against the steering wheel as he watches her negotiate, wants to pound the condescending smirk off the bastard's face, but it isn't until he reaches into his briefcase, and Jessie closes the blinds, that Travis decides he's had enough.

He shoots the driver on the way in. Stupid fuck didn't even have the bulletproof window rolled up. The noise deafens every other sound as doors slam, curtains are drawn, and escape routes contemplated.

Jessie's door collapses with one swift kick. It isn't even locked, just closed. Travis only has eyes for the rich fuck fingering something in his briefcase. Maybe, knives. Maybe, a gun. Maybe something else. None of it good.

Jessie's eyes say she's been expecting him but nonetheless, she jumps from the side of the bed. The tools of her trade are visible: the open drawer of condoms, the towels, the plastic mattress cover poking from under the red sheet. The tools of the fat fuck scatter as Travis kicks his briefcase to the floor.

"What do you want, Travis?" She steps over the flattened door and puts her face in front of his. There are dark circles under her flat eyes, and her black slip is pock-marked with burns from cigarette ash. She looks tired but not strung out. Determined but not desperate.

The guy hasn't moved. His face is red, and his eyes wary as they dart towards the spilled contents of his briefcase.

Jessie follows his eyes. "What the fuck?"

Travis pulls out his gun and shoots the fucker straight in his red fuck face.

"Fuck, Travis. Fuck. Fuck, you fucking asshole," Jessie slaps him across the face and punches him in the chest. "You motherfucker. He hadn't paid me yet. You fuck. This was my way out."

Travis sticks the gun back under his belt in the small of his back and grabs her thrashing hands. Holds them still. Her eyes spiral from rage to panic.

"Paid you for what?" His face is as close to hers as it can be without touching. He kicks one of the blades, and it skeeters across the floor and impales itself into the skirting board with a guttering pong. "Maiming or killing you?"

The wind goes out of Jessie's sails, shoulders slumping as her chin hits her chest.

"You'd rather this than marry me?" he says.

"I'd rather fuck a cactus in every hole than marry you."

"You don't mean that."

She doesn't reply, but he can tell by her squint that yes, she means exactly that.

"I can take care of you. Of Ryan."

He stares into her eyes cause anywhere else he looks, all he sees are fat old men with beer-bellies and bad breath bearing down on her. Does she fake it? Cry out? "Come on baby. Oh. Ah." Or does she scream like she screamed at him?

Travis shudders. "What can I do to make it right?"

She dead-eyes him. Sweat-damp hair fringes her eyes, but there's no curtaining her disdain. "You can leave, Travis. Leave and leave me and mine alone."

Is she really this stubborn? Would she fuck any John but not be with him?

She catches the drift of his eyes as he stares over her shoulder at the dead bastard keeled over on his face. They've known each other long and well enough for her to follow his train of thought.

"This is my choice. That wasn't."

"I'm not the one you're punishing here."

Jessie laughs. Lights a cigarette, sits on the one plastic chair at the chipped round table next to a thin curtain, sun-bleached yellow except in the folds, which glow red from the fangs of the neon sign.

Travis kneels before her but doesn't lay a hand upon her.

"He ain't coming back, Jessie and neither is Sarah."

She slaps him. Only once, though it's obvious she wants to hit him a hundred times, hit him till he doesn't get up no more, then drag his carcass to the desert to let the vultures eat his flesh, and the sun bleach his bones.

He could make her come with him. For her own good. But Travis retains enough humanity to know that's just rape by another name. Instead, he does something even worse.

"I have Ryan." He presses down on her thighs as she struggles to rise. "I have our son, and if you ever want to see him again, you'll come with me."

Night Terrors

Her first few steps are slow. Tentative. Alice threads her arm through Michael's, fearful of a temporary cure and a tumble to the ground. They stroll up and down the sidewalk until she is confident enough to let go and walk on her own. Her walk becomes jog becomes run within minutes.

"Hah! It's like riding a bike. You never forget how even when you can't," she says and takes off.

If Michael lives for a thousand years, he will never see anything as beautiful as Alice coursing down the cracked and broken sidewalk. She runs, long, blonde hair streaking behind her. Faster and faster. Thoughts of impossibility vanish. There's no thought at all, only go. He shouts caution to her tail wind. No matter how healed, she is unused to coordinating brain with biddable legs. The sidewalk ends and dirt begins, and Alice trips on the uneven surface, and flies headfirst to the ground.

Michael is there to catch her.

He holds her in his arms as she catches her breath: laughing, crying, laughing. Near hysterics. Her face. The shudder of her laugh. How she clings to him like a buoy in an endless sea, all remind him of his first jump. He holds her without comment, only lets the gamut of emotion play across her face as she ouch-taps the raw skin of her scraped knees and says with incredulous joy:

"It hurts. Oh, Michael, it hurts."

"That's certainly something." The voice is a rude interruption. The speaker leans against a large black car; arms crossed on his chest.

"Travis." Alice hisses the name, so Michael knows he's not a friend.

Michael curses himself for not paying attention as the car pulled up and the door opened. There are plenty of kidnappings in his world, and he trained from a young age to protect himself and his family. He scrambles to his feet and puts himself between Alice and this Travis person.

Travis tips his cowboy hat back and lowers his sunglasses. "New friend, Alice? The quality of your relationships seems to have improved." He taps twice on the roof of the car. "As have mine."

The driver door opens and a tall figure in a black suit emerges. Michael's fists clench with each step the driver takes towards Travis. No shadow should stretch behind him on the dark tar, but there are layers upon layers of darkness, myriad shadows whose edges do not meet.

Michael looks quickly at Alice.

"Shadow man." The words are no more than a whisper from her taut lips.

The shadow man walks slowly over to Travis. It is impossible to see his eyes behind mirrored sunglasses, but intricate tattoos snake from his cuffs and collar.

It can't be.

Travis pats the man's shoulder. "Ain't this something else, Raymond? Girl was in a wheelchair only last night, a paraplegic for what? Ten years? Now look at her."

Raymond turns his head slightly in their direction but remains silent.

Travis straightens. "How boring life is from day to day, year to year, millennia to millennia, and then boom, everything happens all at once. Who's your new friend, Alice?" He holds out his hand.

Michael ignores the hand and does not take his eyes off Raymond.

"The quality of your relationships has deteriorated, Travis. Wonder what Sarah would have said about *your* new… friend?"

Travis takes a step forward at the mention of Sarah's name.

Alice pushes past Michael and strides straight up to him.

"Listen, you, everyone knows you're up to no good up at the ranch and ever since this…" She inclines her head towards

Raymond and spits at his feet. "This… thing has been around, there's been a permanent cloud over the desert plain."

Raymond makes no move except to find particular interest in a bracelet wrapped three times around his left wrist, which he twirls round and round. It is pale ivory and etched with thousands of miniscule symbols. Michael's stomach ties in knots.

A transporter. There are only a handful, all kept under the tightest security. How?

"El Milagro. El Milagro."

Tiny Maria swoops down the sidewalk, throws her arms around Alice and nearly succeeds in lifting her from her feet. Tears run down her face as Carl strides up, baseball cap on backwards, mouth hanging open.

Alice and Michael agreed not to tell anyone the real reason her legs started working again. It's a sure-fire way to get locked up in either a loony bin, as Alice called it, or some underground government bunker where they'd run tests and stick needles in them both until they were dead. They hadn't settled on an explanation until that moment—eyes meeting over Maria's small, dark head—yes, the miracle angle is the right way to go. If said miracle happened the day Michael walked barefoot out of the desert, that's just a coincidence.

While Alice is distracted, Michael watches the two men return to their vehicle. Raymond closes the door after Travis then studies Michael over the roof for a moment. A smile forms on his thin lips, but his teeth do not show.

As the car drives off, Michael quickly calculates his options. He has two: take Alice and leave immediately, or fight. That's it. From what he's seen of the weapons here, they're woefully inadequate, but he and Raymond are similarly disadvantaged, because only noble metals, useless in weaponry, can be transported.

Can he convince Alice to come to his world? She is ahead with her friends, everyone laughing and crying. When she looks back over her shoulder at him and holds out her hand, he hurries to take it. Fight or flee, they will decide together.

He waits till she's asleep to go find him. It's easy enough in this sparsely populated place. Michael has no detector, but he has his senses, and they all point in one direction: towards the edge of town and darkness.

Raymond is waiting for him outside the ranch compound. It's guarded by tall walls, multiple cameras and a thick metal gate.

"Bit primitive," Michael says as he approaches.

Raymond shrugs. "It does the job."

They walk away from the road, away from any sign or symptom of civilization, off into the desert. The stars are different here, and with only one moon, the night is darker than in Michael's dimension. And yet as they walk, he can make out the shadows trailing Raymond. How they writhe and claw the dry earth and tangle in the purple sage, seeking purchase. Escape.

Raymond is the first to stop. They've walked some distance at this point and are far enough from the town, no one will be able to hear them even in the still night air.

"Does she know?" Raymond says. "Does she know the price paid for her to walk again?"

Michael hesitates. If Alice knew, she would have been mortified. Refused. Hated him.

"No," is all he says.

"Will I show her?"

Michael tenses but remains silent.

"Do you? Do *you* know?"

Michael nods. "If we are from the same place and time, then yes, I know."

"Do you really?" Raymond shrugs off his blazer and unbuttons his shirt. There is a thick band of scar tissue around his neck, a collar of pale pink flesh amid countless tattooed spirals. "Have you ever seen cattle at an abattoir? They line them up in a chute. The cattle can hear, they're not deaf. Hear the cries of those before them, sense the trembling of those on either side of them. They cry. Tears. Great liquid globules. I saw them once as a child. Never thought I'd ever see anything more pathetic or terrifying. I was wrong."

Raymond throws back his shoulders and looks up at the sky. He is lean, muscular, covered in tattoos and scars.

How many…

"We console ourselves with the misguided delusion their suffering is temporary, their pain over quickly—a bolt to the brain, and it's lights out. But the time they spend in the chute? Eternal horror."

He looks at Michael then, his eyes black bores of hate.

"You know how health reserves are extracted. How could you not, considering it was your own father who developed the technology…"

Michael takes a step back. No. It's not true. It couldn't be.

"Ah, interesting. Didn't know? Did you know how your father lost one family and vowed to never lose another?"

"You don't know what you're talking about. My father would never…"

Raymond throws his head back and laughs. At the sound, the night creatures freeze and even the lightning bugs stop blinking along the plain.

Michael's voice shakes along with his hands. "I only learned what is done after I received them. Before, I had no idea." He lowers his head. "If I'd known, I'd never have allowed it. If I could give them back, I would. At the very least, I can give them to those who need them most."

Raymond's lips twist, but the hatred in his eyes does not lose its luster. "Have you ever seen a life harvested? They are lined up in a chute similar to the ones used in abattoirs. The terror and the tears. The cries for mother, father, brother, sister, for a God of either sun or both to intervene. The silent acceptance as the vice wraps round their young necks to hold them still. Their whispered prayers. Their screams. Their silence."

"But it's voluntary. No one forces them."

Raymond's laughter. As if his ghosts were given voices to protest their repurpose. The tattoos—they can't possibly be his reserves. It would mean dozens had been harvested. More. The shadows… how much reserve did he have that it's escaped the constraints of his tattoos?

"Volunteer? How do you volunteer when your entire family is held to ransom through starvation and thirst? Mothers birth many to save the few." He grabs Michael's shirt and pulls him close, holds him in a vice of hate. "Can you imagine the pain of offering one child up to the Harvester so your other children can eat?"

He could kill him. Right then and there. His strength is unnatural. Would Michael die here just when he's found her?

"Do you know how many have ever escaped from the Harvester? No? I'll tell you. One."

Raymond lets him go, and Michael stumbles back. The scar on Raymond's neck, could it be?

"I escaped. Alive but barely. Freed as many *volunteers* as I could. Killed those who manned the harvesters while I was at it. I was sixteen, only sixteen years of age. Full of fear and rage. Once, I had hopes. Ambitions. I was the youngest child of ten. Four had been harvested before me, all girls. I often asked where they had gone, what had become of them, was told they'd married, started families of their own. Why didn't they call? Visit? Why were there no pictures of them and their new families? No communication at all? It wasn't until I was in the chute myself that I knew their fate. The terror they felt. The despair. The hope, even as the collar wrapped round their neck and thousands of tiny needles imbedded themselves in their skin, that all was not lost, that someone would save them.

"I'm sure it's hard for someone from the Hill to understand this, but there were never any volunteers. Never. Only sacrifices."

Raymond pulls a golden mesh chain from the pocket of his trousers. "Did you know they developed portable harvesters? Instead of harvesting our own people, I can travel the universe and harvest others."

Michael takes an involuntary step back. "What have you done?"

Raymond advances, chain held out in rigid hand. "Want to try it on? See?" He traces the tattoos on his own torso tenderly as one would the skin of a lover, "Join them?"

"No..."

"There are disposable people on every plane. It's easy to harvest here. So many dark souls willing to assist me. For a price. As in most dimensions, the wealthy are the worst. Limitless wealth means insatiable thirst. The women at the ranch? Their babies are sold to those who can afford them. Some to rear, some to rape. The women to me. When the wealthy are done playing with their young toys, I also take their life force.

"Your reserves are nearly depleted. If I wanted to kill you, I could. I might and will. Just not yet. I want you to feel hope. To feel love. Watch as I strip it all from you and everyone in this wretched place. But your parents first. Your siblings next. Go now, return, and I will take your "miracle" woman. I will destroy every world you call home."

He's bluffing. Father's security is the best in most dimensions. He'll be safe. So will the family. Alice has no such protection. He's bluffing but for how long? Should he return home? Would he find his way back again? Take Alice with him?

"I bet you're desperately wondering how you'll be able to save everyone, but you're asking the wrong question. You should be asking how I found you."

"How?" The word escapes. How had Raymond tracked him when he tried so hard and failed to find Alice… until… now. Now, he can pinpoint her exact location, find her anywhere. Ever since he gave her nearly half his reserves… Michael gasps. His hand involuntarily goes to the tattoos on his arm.

It can't be…

Raymond fingers the scar around his neck as he looms. They are of similar height, but he seems taller, broader and is undeniably stronger. The more controlled the anger, the more potent it is, Michael's father once told him. Not even a muscle twitches on Raymond's face.

"They extracted some of my life force before I escaped. It is in you now and your miracle friend too."

Raymond buttons his shirt and shrugs his blazer back on. Rolls the gold chain round and round in his hands. "Choices. Choices. Choices. Nice to have them, isn't it? Yours are limited now. You must choose who you will save and who you will sacrifice and, in the end, know you are powerless to do anything other than be harvested."

The chain is returned to his pocket, but the threat remains. No, not a threat, a promise. He stares out over the desert. Not a creature stirs, and the night is stuffed with silence.

"They play music when you're in the chute. A futile attempt to keep everyone calm because they can't dose you. It contaminates the transfer." The amusement leaves Raymond's face. "Do you know what song they played for me? No? Well you should."

and he sings...

And though it takes a thousand years
Though I shed a million tears
Though we live and die and live again
I will find you...

At the End of the Day, All Roads Lead Home

Ryan stares at Raphael. Raphael stares at Ryan.

"Why are you looking for my mom?"

"Your mom? Jessie Williams? About yea tall?" Raphael gestures to his shoulders. "Long blonde hair?"

Ryan holds out his phone and there, on the home screen, smiling big and looking pretty is Jessie.

"Wait…what? How old are you, kid?"

Ryan debates answering. Even though Raphael rescued them, he's learning quickly there aren't too many people on this earth who can be trusted. Still, what's the harm in telling him his age?

"I'm ten."

"Ten, huh?" Raphael drums his thumbs on the steering wheel and stares out the front window as if thinking deeply about something. "Ten." He starts the engine and reverses the pickup.

Ryan grabs the steering wheel. "Wait a minute. Hold up."

Raphael brakes and whips his head to Ryan. "First off, kid, don't ever pull a wheel when someone's driving not unless you plan on dying. Got it?"

Ryan gulps and nods as his hand slides from the wheel.

"Second of all, what is it?"

Ryan bites his lip. He isn't afraid of Raphael. How could he be? But there's a set to his eyes that says he's reached the end of his rope and isn't playing, certainly not with a ten-year-old.

"Where are we going?" Ryan asks. Estella is quiet, curled up in a ball on the back seat, but her eyes are huge.

"First, we're going to bury Daniel, then I need to get you two someplace safe and then I'll go find your mom."

"I'm going with you!" Ryan tries not to raise his voice, but it comes out in a girlish screech.

Raphael's eyes roll back to the top of his head. "Listen, kid and listen good. As you may have noticed, there are really bad people out there," He gestures to the vast emptiness below them. "And they're looking for you and this girl, and I've a gun and one box of ammo, courtesy of Frank, but I can't keep you two safe and find your mother at the same time. Do you understand?"

Ryan opens his mouth to argue.

"Do you understand?

Ryan nods.

"Now, all I have to figure out is where I can take you both where you'll be safe."

There is silence as they bite their lips and stare out the front window.

"Dakota!" they both say at the same time.

Burying Daniel takes longer than Raphael would like, but he doesn't rush it. The spot Frank leads them to is sheltered by a small rock formation deep in the hills and off the beaten track. Raphael would never be able to find it again even with a tracker and a pack of sniffing dogs. Hopefully, no one else will either.

Raphael and Frank do the digging while Ryan holds Estella's hand. There are no more tears, only prayers. Frank fashions a marker with a couple of sticks and Estella ties a bow around it with a ribbon from her hair.

Frank leads them back to a main road where they toot their horns in goodbye. There's a sense of urgency now, even the kids are tense. Raphael thinks about hitting the highway to make time, but it's not worth the risk. He sticks to back roads until there are no more back roads to be found. Every time they pass a vehicle, Ryan scoots down on the back seat. Awake or dreaming, Estella doesn't get up and doesn't stop whimpering the entire time, and Raphael finally turns the radio on low to drown her out, though all that accomplishes is providing her accompaniment.

Somehow, they make it safely to Dakota's place.

"Stay in the truck, kid," Raphael says as he unfastens his seatbelt and slides from the cab, gun cocked and ready.

Of course, Ryan does no such thing.

"Stay here," he tells Estella, then follows Raphael.

Ryan steps on the gravel path and nearly has his head blown off when Raphael whips around.

"I told you to stay in the truck. Fuck me, Jesus. Fuck, my heart."

Ryan would laugh but he's choking on his own spit. Raphael sighs deeply. "Kid, you're going to be the death of me."

Ryan shadows Raphael, but Dakota's place is deserted and looks like it has been for a few days.

"Any idea where she could be?"

Ryan thinks to not say, mostly cause Aunt Dakota is probably gone for a very good reason, but also because Raphael refuses to tell him how he knows his mom, other than they are "old friends".

"Look, if you don't know where she is, it's back to your Aunt Alice."

"She's probably at the observatory."

It's a five-minute drive up the main road, then another ten down a rural lane before they come to the turn-off for the observatory. From afar, the dome is big but up close, it's huge.

"How the hell are we ever going to find her in this?" Raphael pulls to a stop next to another truck and waves his hands around the compound of buildings, the observatory dome a giant fly's eye in the middle.

A door opens right in front of them and there, smiling bright as candles on a birthday cake, is Dakota.

There isn't much talk as they sit to eat the meal waiting for them and as soon as they are finished, Ryan and Estella are bundled off to sleep in separate rooms. Much as he knows he needs to rest, Ryan doesn't. He listens at the door to the adults talking.

There's a balcony to his room, and Ryan goes out there to think about what he heard, what he needs to do and how he's going to do it. He doesn't remember ever being so tired. No time for sleep though, he's got figuring to do.

In the distance, there is the sound of thunder. The sky is dark and getting darker until there is only the nimbus of the rising moon leaking through gathering clouds. He won't find solutions in the approaching storm, only more danger.

It's unexpected, but not unwelcome when his bedroom door opens, and Estella pads across the room to stand next to him on the balcony

He's been lonely since his mother left. Lonelier still once her calls stopped coming. He hopes she isn't dead but figures he would know. Somehow, he would feel it if their bond was broken. Something inside him would scream and scream and scream. There is only silence. How must Estella feel? Not only knowing her father and brother are dead but having watched them die?

He doesn't look at her. Doesn't say a thing, only holds out his hand as she stands by his side, eyes dry but her heart crying.

And she takes it.

Not long after, they see the lights. Blinking and twinkling, carousel spinning, Ferris wheel turning and the sound of music crisp and clear as a bell. Calling them. He's been warned all his life about the carnival but maybe, just maybe, it will be worth the risk. Maybe there's something there to save his mom, and Estella to find some peace.

Maybe, there's even magic.

Time to Talk

"Did you find her? Oh, for fuck's sake, shut your mouth and answer me. Jessie? Did you find Jessie?"

The only one who isn't surprised to see Alice standing on her own two feet is Dakota.

"Close your damn mouth, Raphael and answer me."

It takes a few seconds, but he finally gets words out: "I thought… What? How?"

Alice growls and clenches her fists. "My sister. Did you find her? And where is Ryan? What have you done with him?"

Dakota wraps her arm around Alice's shoulders and leads her to a weathered sofa mostly used by Hyun-Ki to read.

"Calm down, Alice. Ryan's here. Sleeping and safe."

Alice lets out a huge sigh of relief. "Thank fuck for that. Where is he?"

"Let him sleep, he's had a long few days," Raphael says.

"And who are you to tell me what to do about my nephew?"

Raphael takes a step back. Who is he, indeed?

Dakota pulls back from Alice and gives her a hard look backed by a stern talking to: "You mind your mouth now. If it wasn't for Raphael, your nephew would probably be dead right now. Or worse."

It's at that point, Alice remembers how Ryan went missing on her watch, and she shuts her trap.

"Aren't you going to introduce us?" Dakota says, looking at Michael who hasn't moved from the doorway.

*

They sit around the communal table under bright fluorescent light, the harsh glare of indecision and the impending darkness of reality bearing down on each of them. Surprisingly, it is Hyun-Ki who struggles the most with the idea that Michael is from another dimension. This skepticism stems from being on the cusp of having his life's questions answered. At least some of them. When faced with Michael's claim, he demands more proof than anyone so his heart will not be broken.

"It is human nature to be myopic," Michael says. He is uncomfortable lecturing someone over twice his age because although their technologies are discrepant, Hyun-Ki is still an elder. "Despite evidence to the contrary, I always expect any plane I visit to be terrestrially similar to my own, just at a different evolutionary stage. However, arriving in the middle of an underwater metropolis of arthropods and nearly drowning from shock quickly set me straight. There are places… things out there, we cannot imagine."

"So, this…" Hyun-Ki examines Michael's ivory bracelet with its thousands of etchings over the rim of his glasses. His finger hoovers like a lover over the fine detail, but he doesn't dare touch it. "This transporter can take you to infinite dimensions across time and space?" His eyes are wide, his hand trembling.

"Yes, but the technology is still relatively new and continuously being developed. There is no reliable mapping system, so each trip is random. I'm making progress on a geo-plotter, but the task is daunting. At this point, the only coordinates we know with certainty are those on our world." He pauses. Considers. "The coordinates for my home are 93-681-27, in case anyone ever needs them."

"Why would we ever need them?" Alice says.

It is Hyun-Ki who answers when Michael won't. "In case something happens to him, and we need to return him to his world. Or, if we need to escape this one."

Michael has everyone repeat the coordinates three times and save them to their phones. He demonstrates five times which knobs to twist to enter the numbers but doesn't press the send button.

"Technically, anyone in physical contact with someone wearing a transporter can transport simultaneously, but it's not been tested thoroughly. I believe the phone booth Alice told me about may also be a transporting device."

"The phone booth?" Dakota nods as if in confirmation of something long suspected.

"This is all fascinating," Hyun-Ki says, "but how do we know this bracelet is nothing more than a gorgeous piece of craftsmanship from one of the market stalls in Santa Fe?"

Alice shakes her head. Since he healed her legs, his tentative sense of her has solidified. A threshold must have been crossed. He will be able to find her now. Anywhere. Any when. Will Raymond as well? No, it's too risky. There will be no demonstration.

"He healed my legs and as far as I know we don't have the technology to do that anywhere on this planet?"

Hyun-Ki nods. He wants to believe, that much is plain. Dakota puts a calm hand on his trembling one.

"Unfortunately, my healing capability comes from a less than reputable source."

Michael lowers his head. It would be good to unburden his soul. If she knows, will Alice still look at him as she does now? Eyes glittering and lips smiling. There is more than gratitude in her shine. There is love. Michael has never loved any other woman, and the thought of losing her is unbearable. It occurs to him to lie, to obfuscate, but love based on deception is not love at all, only another form of harvesting.

So, he tells them. Watches as they look away, draw their elbows from the table and fold them into crossed arms. Tells them how he didn't know until recently that the tattoos conferred upon his body were the life force of murdered souls. As he speaks, he realizes there is no excuse, no explanation. *There are no volunteers, only sacrifices.*

He rolls up his sleeve. Lines and swirls and circles remain on his left bicep but there are also scars. How many lives they represent, he can't possibly guess.

"I was young. I didn't understand what was being done, not completely. Once I learned, I couldn't undo it. All I can do is try to disseminate my health reserves to those in real need. Like Alice."

He stares at his twisting hands the entire time he makes his confession but finally gathers the courage to look up at Alice. Her mouth is agape, and her eyes wide with dread and horror.

"Alice..."

He reaches for her, but she draws back.

"No. This isn't true. It can't be." She rises and backs away from him. Slaps her legs over and over as Dakota rushes to stop her. "Take it away from me. Take it. Why? Why? Why would you do that? What have you done to me?"

"Alice... please. Please forgive me."

There is no rebuke, only a curse before she storms out of the room. "Never. Go back to where you came from and never return."

Dakota grabs Michael's arm to keep him from following.

"Give her time," she says. "it's a lot to process. I believe you, but your innocence doesn't mitigate the burden of your gift."

Michael returns reluctantly to his chair and turns his gaze to the others who look no less horrified.

"Raymond is also from my world. He escaped harvesting and has a vendetta against my father, who invented the technology. Michael pauses. He doesn't share his suspicion that some of his reserves were harvested from Raymond. How this enabled Raymond to track him to their world. Nor does he mention the implications for Alice. After a deep breath, he shares what he knows with certainty, and only what they need to know without frightening them too much.

"What this means is my family and anyone close to me, including Alice and all of you, are in danger. I only just discovered that Raymond has a portable device and is harvesting lives here. The women at the ranch, children, anyone. So many lives."

It must be hundreds, more.

"He cannot be killed; his reserves are immeasurable. He will heal and heal and heal again. I don't know how yet, but I believe I'm the only one who can stop him. If he's left here unchecked, there is no knowing how many he will kill. How strong he will become."

"What the actual fuck is going on?" Raphael finally speaks up. Exhausted, he was nodding off up to the point Alice started screaming.

Dakota leads Raphael to the kitchen. Makes him a coffee with two tablespoons of instant and three sugars.

"You wake up, now. Jessie is in danger."

Raphael holds the cup to his lips without drinking. "I've been trying to find her. Wait, do you know where she is? Where?"

"She's up at the ranch with Travis and that monster."

"Travis?" The word is a whisper of disbelief.

Dakota clucks her tongue. "Travis is no longer the boy you knew. Maybe he never was. There's a darkness in him... you think this Raymond is the one to worry about? Travis..."

Dakota is never one to hesitate. Always straight, always sure. But something holds her tongue and trips her words.

"Travis what, Dakota? Travis what?"

She sits next to him at the table. He runs both hands through his hair and shakes his head. If anyone needs rescuing, it's Raphael, but there's no time for that.

"Dakota?"

"I know you've been having a hard time lately..."

"You don't know the half of it."

She leans forward. Takes both his fumbling hands in her own and stills them.

"Maybe, maybe not. But there's no time for a pity party, darling. Your Jessie is in a heap of trouble, and you need to get her out of it."

"I'll do anything for Jessie. Anything. I've missed her so much..."

"She's not the same girl you knew either. There's been a lot of growing between you two, none of it closer and not much of it good."

"If you only knew..."

Dakota doesn't know, but she has a pretty good idea. "You're not the only one on the edge of despair and once that line's crossed, it's almost impossible to return. Jessie is up there with Travis because she reckons her options have run out. Now he has her, he'll never let her go."

Raphael sits up. "Has her? What does that mean?"

Should she tell him? Handsome fucker or not, Raphael needs to start using that brain of his instead of his heart. His hands instead of his pecker. She always thought he was Ryan's father until she overheard Travis talking to the boy; saw him take the hair from his head. Put two and two together. No way Jessie would have lain with Travis willingly. Travis has a hold over her, and that hold is Ryan.

"Travis killed the abortionist who took Sarah's life. I suspect he also killed his brother Cal, his parents and set the fire that killed Jessie's Pa."

The blood drains from Raphael's face. "What?"

"You been gone too long. Travis got a ten-year bid at Eyman, where, if truth be told, he got lean and mean. He always blamed Jessie for Sarah's death. Always had it in for her, and now she's up at the ranch."

Raphael jumps up and nearly stumbles over his chair. "I'm going up there."

"Hold on a minute. The ranch isn't what you remember. It's more like a prison these days, tall fences, cameras everywhere. Armed guards. Pregnant women are going in but only their babies are coming out. The mamas are never seen again."

Raphael freezes. "Travis? Trafficking? I can't believe… my best friend."

"He used to be your best friend."

"No, this can't be right. He was an asshole when I saw him the other night, but I don't believe it."

Dakota purses her lips. Once again, Raphael is going to have to learn something the hard way. As she watches him stride through the door, she only hopes this time, he survives the lesson.

*

Despite being full of questions, Hyun-Ki is silent as Michael paces up and down the narrow corridor of his office, blinded by consequences instead of focusing on solutions.

"She's never going to forgive me."

Hyun-Ki is no expert in relationships and has no acquaintance with betrayal. Yet sometimes, those with the least experience can see the most clearly.

"She might. If you don't force her."

Michael stops his pacing. "You're right. Thank you, you're right."

Hyun-Ki gestures to a chair which Michael stares at for some seconds. It's obvious he wants to rush to Alice, but he sits.

"I have so many questions, I don't know where to begin," Hyun-Ki says.

Michael stares at the closed door as if willing Alice to walk through it. Where is she? Outside… is she leaving? No, she's standing still.

"Is it true? That you are from another dimension?"

"Yes." Michael rubs at his tattoos.

"How do you travel?"

"On our world, the technology may be nascent but compared to this world… the math is quite complex. I don't know if I have the means to explain it in terms you can comprehend. Not quickly." Michael twirls the ivory bracelet round and round his wrist. "I spent years developing a geo-plotting device, but it's still impossible to target a specific world with accuracy. I came across hundreds of versions of Alice in different timelines before I found the right one."

"The right one?"

"Same as there are infinite worlds, there are also infinite variations of each. That's the theory, anyway. It may turn out there is a finite variation, we just haven't been able to prove it yet. But there's only one Alice for me and she's here."

"How can you be certain? What is the science?"

Michael smiles as if at a young child taking his first steps. "There is no science, there is only my heart."

*

Dakota finds Alice outside, staring at the sky. The clouds have cleared and the full moon bathes the desert in an ethereal light. Though the clock says one thing, the light says neither day nor night but sometime in between. A time between knowledge and action, contemplation and decision. A time when promises are made and broken.

Dakota remains silent as she scans the sky. She doesn't need to watch the news to know this world is about to end, or at least their place in it.

"You think we can see his home from here?" Alice shrugs. "Probably not."

She looks at Dakota then. Drying tears coat her eyes. "Do you believe in fate?"

"I do."

"Can you please tell me—cause I really need to know—why is fate such a bastard?"

Dakota says nothing, for there is nothing to be said.

"I thought he was my soul mate…"

"I can't comment one way or another, but my understanding is that our soul mates aren't perfect people, they're just perfect people for us."

All the stuffing seems to go out of Alice. Alice who only ever wanted to be loved. "I don't know what to do. I don't think I can ever forgive him."

Dakota puts a hand on Alice's slumped shoulders. "I can't tell you what to do or what to feel, honey. All I can say is that when the time comes, and you got to choose one way or another, don't choose cause you're lonely, choose cause you're sure."

Alice nods. Straightens. "Where is everyone?"

"Raphael's gone to get Jessie. Hyun-Ki is talking to Michael, and the kids are probably conked out." Dakota hugs her tight as she can before fate takes her away, then says, "Let's check on them. Don't think the dream catchers I put up are going to stop all their nightmares, not after everything they've been through."

But when they get to their rooms, both the children are gone.

Negotiating a Future

The big fat man tips back his tall black top hat and looks around. His eyes finally settle upon Ryan and Estella.

"Sorry, no unaccompanied minors."

Ryan scrunches his lips. He knows his way around rules, and most can be bent if not broken. Estella's small hand is cold in his own. They're wearing pajamas and sneakers without socks on their feet. She seems as exhausted as he feels. They should be sleeping, but this may be their only chance.

"Please, mister. We need help, and I heard we might find it here."

The Showman's eyes narrow as his smile grows. "Well, we're in the entertainment business here, not Search and Rescue, and performers must be paid so let's see the shine of the coin in your pockets."

Ryan fishes around in the one pocket of his pajama pants. Nothing, not even lint.

The Showman purses his lips and waves his cane. "Off with you both. It's a very busy night. We're the best show in twenty-five galaxies and always in demand. Time's a-wasting." He lowers his top hat, taps his cane on the hard ground three times, then vanishes in a puff of smoke. A thick metal gate crashes down from nowhere, blocking their entrance.

What now? Estella stares down instead of up, a sweep of long brown hair half-covering her face. She's ephemeral as a sleepy ghost in her white nightgown, which is three sizes too big. He must save her. But how? How would he feel if he lost his entire family and in such a horrible way? Probably want to die too. Who cares about tomorrow when the people you love aren't going to be there, and the only way you might see them again is by dying too?

He understands as much as he's able. He hasn't seen his mom in months and far as he knows, she could be dead. He gives himself a shake. No, don't think that. Just don't. Figure out how to save everyone.

He gently brushes the hair back from Estella's face. "I know you're tired and sad but hold on. Okay? I'll find a way in, and we'll get some help."

Ryan examines the gate. The bars are thick and high, and there's no foothold to climb. Not to mention the enormous lion which has appeared on the other side and is pacing up and down. He leads Estella away quickly and quietly. There's got to be another way in.

The carnival is bigger than it appears and after ten minutes of skirting the perimeter, Ryan has failed to find a way in which isn't barred or guarded in some manner. They pass a twirl-a-whirl, the human cannonball, and the carousel. Above everything, the Ferris wheel spins, and with each turn of the massive wheel, a new song tinkles music magic over the entire place.

Finally, he spots their chance. One of the spikes has come out from a tent and a bit of the fabric is loose. Loose enough they might be able to crawl under it. The only question is, who should go first? The desert is dark and quiet. Too quiet. It's the silence of being watched. Danger ahead. Danger behind.

"You go first, Estella." He holds the loose tent flap up for her. "Be careful and don't go anywhere, just wait for me, I'll be right behind you." He squeezes her hand one last time for good luck, and she crawls under.

Immediately after her feet disappear, a dog begins to bark. Not one dog by the sound of it, but a pack. Why did he send her first? Why? She'll be eaten alive. Ryan scrambles under the tent, rough stones scraping his knees through thin cotton, heart a-panic. He can't lose her too.

When he jumps to his feet, it's to find Estella standing before a dog that towers over her, its chest parallel with her face and both its two heads barking globules of drool all over her. Estella isn't afraid though. She reaches out with a sure hand and pets the broad chest, murmuring quiet words in Spanish.

Ryan's eyes widen, not at the fearsome creature, but the way it immediately stops barking, closes its two mouths and lays at her feet. The minute both heads begin to snore, he puts a finger to his lips and leads her away.

They nearly make it to the far side of the tent, but a chair rolls out from the shadows and blocks their path. Upon it sits a beautiful young woman with long hair which is black as the dogs. Her smile seems genuine, not the fake smile of the Showman, as if she's welcoming an old, or soon to be new, friend.

"I see my dogs like you," she says to Estella. "In all my years under all the stars, I've never seen them fall asleep so quickly or soundly before. Usually, they each take an end of any unannounced visitor and pull."

Ryan looks back over his shoulder and shudders.

"You two are very welcome," the woman says. "it's been so long since I've had any interesting visitors, and you two are special indeed. Now, tell me. Who are you?"

Ryan is unsure how much information to divulge because according to Aunt Dakota, information is valuable, and knowledge is power. He reckons their names are enough to be polite without giving too much away.

He extends his hand. "I'm Ryan, and this is my friend, Estella."

The woman takes his hand, holds it firmly and shakes it once. Something inside him clicks, and the world goes hazy for a moment.

"Nice to meet you, Ryan. My name is Lily."

Estella does not offer her hand. Her eyes are big and dark as she stares at something on a stand next to Lily's desk. Lily follows her eyes and gently lifts a small wooden box. It's plain and unadorned, but she holds it gently as one would something of immense value.

"This music box belonged to my assistant, Bartholemew. He went mad when it broke. Stormed off into the desert to find the song again, and I haven't seen him since."

Estella holds out her hand, not for a handshake but for the music box. Lily looks her up and down. Satisfied by what she finds, she smiles and hands it to her.

Estella opens the box, and there is music.

"Ahhh…" Lily sighs and begins to sing:

You say tomorrow never comes
But it's near, my dear, it's near.
We say we'll never say goodbye
But here we are, tonight we're here

Ryan begins to sway. He forgets about the dogs, death, fear, and horror and thinks only of early morning sunshine, ice cream before it melts and his mom's fierce hugs.

Tonight, we will set the world alight.
Tonight, the world is ours
For tomorrow comes too soon.
And tomorrow, tomorrow, is yours.

A spell. He is under a spell. Ryan slaps himself across the face and snaps out of it. He runs over to Estella and closes the lid. The music stops playing, and Lily stops singing. She takes the box gently from Estella, places it back on the stand, and dusts off her hands.

"You two seem lost, so it's good you've found me. Others in this place are not nearly as friendly or as good at directions."

Lily claps her hands and a bright green neon sign blinks on:

FISH FOR A WISH

Under the sign, an old-fashioned well appears, with a roped bucket and all. Ryan takes a step towards it.

"Does it make your wish come true?" he says.

Lily nods. "But we all have so many wishes, don't we? There's no way of telling which wish you will catch. It's said that if you clear your mind of any but your most fervent desire, it will come true. But that's a challenge for the best of them, and you are both just children…"

"Can we fish for anything or only the possible?" Ryan says.

"Anything. Who knows, you might catch time itself."

"Can I try? Please, can I try?" Ryan has only has one wish: to find his mother. But, what if he finds her, and she's hurt or worse, dead? That's not a good wish.

Lily smiles. "You see what I mean."

He'll wish for everyone in his family to be safe and happy. That will cover all the bases. He will think of nothing else as he lowers the bucket into the well. Then Estella can have her turn.

"Can I do it? Please?"

"Of course, however, we must first discuss payment."

Ryan's shoulders slump. Neither of them has any money or anything of any value.

"Are you certain of that?"

Can she read his mind, or do his eyes give that much away?

Lily seems to grow taller as she circles three times around the well, running a finger along the rough stone lip as she goes. "I've grown quite bored since Bartholomew left. Despite the infinite variety of eons, time passes so similarly from day to day. Is it boredom or loneliness? I can't say, but my fee will compensate for either. One of you can fish for a wish, the other must stay with me and become my apprentice."

Ryan freezes. He can't possibly stay here. He can't leave Estella either. Doesn't she deserve the wish as much as he does? Even more so?

"Thank you for your offer, Lily but the price is too high for either of us to pay." He takes Estella's hand. "Come on, let's go. We'll find some other way. "

Estella shakes her hand free. "No, Ryan. I will stay." Her voice is calm, committed. "There is nothing for me out there anymore. I will stay with Lily and the dogs."

"But you could wish for your father and brother to come back. To rewind time so none of this ever happened."

Estella frowns. She is around his age but seems ancient as she looks at him with well-water eyes. "I love mi papa and hermano, but they are gone now onto their next life. Who am I to make them come back to mine?"

Lily steadies the bucket as Ryan turns the lever to lower it into the well. He does not think of how white Lily's skin is as it glows in the neon of the sign, does not think of the sadness in Estella's eyes as she moves from him to sit in Lily's desk chair, he only thinks of his family healthy and happy and found.

The bucket hits the water with a splashing thunk.

Lily claps again. "You've caught something. Now draw the bucket back up in order for your wish to come true."

It's harder to wind the rope up. Harder, as in nearly impossible. At one point, Ryan's feet lift from the strain of it, and he's nearly pulled into the well along with the bucket. He grits his teeth, and with each groaning breath gains an inch. Finally, near exhaustion and about to give up, the bucket breaches the surface of the well.

"Ah," Lily sighs as she looks into it.

"Goodbye, Ryan," Estella says from the chair. "And gracias."

"Estella..." Ryan reaches for her, but it's too late to undo what's been done. She does not seem unhappy anymore, only sad and even that sadness has left her mouth and is lifting from her eyes.

The bucket begins to glow. The warm light, a beacon, a comfort, a hope. The light grows. Bigger and bigger till it fills the room. Till Ryan sees nothing but the light. Till it blinds him. Arms raised against it, he stumbles back, and he's falling.

Falling.

Falling...

*

Ryan opens his eyes to dawn cracking the horizon. He is alone. The carnival is gone and, in its place, there's one of those old-fashioned telephone booths. It looks as though it hasn't been used in a hundred years. He walks around it a few times, looking for any booby traps. Stares in through the open accordion door at the phone. It's on the hook and above it there's a sign:

DIAL 777
for
DESTINY

The phone booth where all your dreams come true? Ryan picks up the receiver. Miracle of all miracles, there is a dial tone. Wait. What number should he call? This one or the other? He shuffles his feet. Stubs his toe against a cracked bit of cement. Closes his eyes.

Dials.

"Hello?"

The phone nearly drops from his hand. "Mom? Mom, is it you?"

"Ryan! Where are you? Are you okay?"

"Mom. Yes, it's me. I'm okay. I don't know. I'm in a phone booth in the middle of the desert. Where are you?"

He can hear the fast panting of her breath, then a rattle of static crackles over the phone. "Baby… up… go… love you."

"Mom. Please, you need to listen to me. Go with Raphael. Find this phone booth and call this number, 93-681-27, and you will find me. Mom? Did you hear me, 93-681-27."

The line goes dead.

"Mom?" Did she hear him? "Mom? Mom?"

He bangs the phone back on the hook. Picks it up. Pushes his luck. Dials again.

And someplace,

somewhere,

someone answers.

And the wind begins to howl.

Darkest Before Dawn

There's cold and there's coldness. The difference not in degree but solidity, and the first time she meets Raymond's eyes, Jessie knows he wouldn't melt in hell, even if he was there for eternity.

He fastens a chain around the neck of the woman who kneels before him, looks over her head at Jessie who sits with Travis at the long dining room table. Holds her gaze while an ecstasy comes over him as the woman caves in upon herself slowly, disintegrating until all that remains is a heap of smoking clothes and some skin

Jessie tries to hide her horror as she turns to Travis. Fails miserably.

"Travis..."

There is no corresponding horror in Travis' eyes. He has obviously witnessed this before. "I told you Ryan is somewhere safe. Stay with me and you can see him soon, but I would suggest not attempting to leave again or speaking to any of the other women." He looks at the charred clothing on the white marbled floor. "It won't end well for them."

She leaves as quickly as she can and retreats to her assigned room and its bed. There she lies, staring at the ceiling as if some solution to her present dilemma will reveal itself. She didn't believe that woman *Emily, Emily Taylor is... was her name* when she approached Jessie in the corridor and whispered conspiratorially about what happened to the mothers once their babies were adopted.

"I saw... oh God, he killed her. I tried to warn the others... they wouldn't listen. They think I'm crazy. Please tell my family to come get me. Please, I beg you."

And while Jessie didn't believe her—how could she? —she also firmly believed no woman should be held against her will.

Jessie closes her eyes. It's her fault the woman *Emily, Emily Taylor* was murdered. All her fault. She should have believed her, been more careful, not marched to the front gate and demanded it be opened for them both.

"Please help me. I'm so sorry. I never should have given up my baby." Those were Emily's last words.

Jessie sits up, clutches the duvet and considers ripping it to shreds. Ryan. Where is he? Where is her son? She's looked everywhere she can access. It's how she found the maternity ward. Travis keeps promising to produce him, but she's been at the ranch a week and still no Ryan. Is he being held captive somewhere in the compound? Still with Alice? Did Travis do something to him? Raymond? No, she can't think that, refuses to even contemplate it. She's seen the women, but she's also seen the men with their thick lips and thicker bellies loitering in the lounge. The babies being 'adopted', the young kids. Was Ryan one of them? No, Travis wouldn't do that to his own son.

Travis. She didn't think she could hate him more than she already did, but she does. He holds Ryan over her whether he actually has him or not. If Jessie stays at the ranch, has dinner with him every night—dresses up, dolls up her face, nothing else, only dinner—she can see her son.

Eventually.

Maybe she'll take one of those steak knives with their ivory handles and shove it in his cold, black heart. But the dining table is long, the distance between them too great, she'd be stopped by the goons in their black suits who masquerade as staff.

She sits with him every night. He makes small talk—how was your day? *How the fuck do you think my day was? I'm a prisoner here. I watched soap operas, the sun rise, the sun set and thought of another ten ways to kill you.*

"Where's Ryan? Where's my son?" is the only answer she ever gives.

To which he replies, "*Our* son."

There's a knock on her door. She doesn't bother to answer. There's no lock. Whoever it is, they will let themselves in.

It's Travis.

"I'm sorry you had to see that," he says.

She hates him with all her heart, but Jessie sits up and says what she must in order to live with herself another day.

"Travis, talk to me. Please. This is not who you are. A child-trafficker, a murderer."

A rapist.

Stop kidding yourself, Jessie; it's exactly who he is. He's a beat dog who yearns for affection but will bite any hand held out to him. He runs a hand through his hair. It's thinner now. Same as his temper. He looks about to say one thing. Says something else.

"Things might have been different if Sarah hadn't been murdered. Everything would have been different."

Guilt softens her. "I miss her too. I miss her every day but Travis, what would she say if she saw you like this? Knew what you are capable of?" *But she already knew, didn't she? Vet school was an excuse; Travis was the real reason Sarah aborted their baby*. "What you've done? Stop this now. Let me see my son. Let us both go. Free these women and get away from that demon."

Travis sinks to the chair next to the bed. "I… I don't know how, Jessie. Not anymore. Please…"

The door slams open, and there is Raphael, looking very much the worse for wear but alive and relieved to find her.

He is not alone.

*

Travis has Jessie and Travis has guns. Raphael also has a gun, but more importantly, he finally has a reason. There is nothing more dangerous than a man with a reason who doesn't care if he lives or dies.

Jessie's eyes widen as he enters the room. He wants to run to her: hold her, kiss her, rewind ten years and never leave in the first place. How would that have turned out? Pointless to wonder. All he holds of her is memory, hope, and a letter scrawled in a bible.

He takes a step forward. Points his gun at Travis with one hand. Holds out the other. "Jessie."

She blinks. "You're too late, Raphael."

She does not meet his eyes as she says it; she's looking over his shoulder. Filled with the same dread he felt in the grove, Raphael realizes who is behind him but doesn't yet truly understand *what*. He flashes back to the young girl prone on stone, the look in that maniac's eyes as he fastened the chain. The knife. He can't let the same happen to Jessie.

"You're too late, Raphael," Jessie repeats. She rises and moves but not towards him. She threads her arm through Travis'. Both men's eyes widen, but Raphael is the one who feels the knife in his heart. "I'm with Travis now."

"I don't believe you." She's lying now like she lied before to protect him.

Jessie deadeyes him. "Doesn't matter what you believe, it's the truth. We have a child together."

That's a fucking gut punch. He knows she has a kid but not whose. Had hoped it was his; thought maybe, it was. Her eyes soften. Goddamn you, Jessie. Don't feel bad for slicing and dicing my heart.

"I know. I met him. Fine young man."

Her mouth opens. Closes as the shadow man moves to his side.

Jessie says nothing even though her eyes plead: Tell me! Please, tell me. Where is my son?

"I'm not leaving without you," he says.

At that, the shadow man knocks the gun from Raphael's limp hand and punches him in the kidneys. As Raphael folds, he snaps a gold mesh chain around his neck. Raphael struggles. Paws at the chain, but it's impossible to dislodge as thousands of tiny needles embed in his skin. He falls to the ground, strength evaporating as every atom in his body reverberates. He's dying. Motherfucker, not like this...

"No," Jessie screams, then quickly whispers something into Travis' ear.

Travis jerks his head at the shadow man, and the chain is removed. Raphael collapses, praying to a God he doesn't believe in to take him to the next life any way other than that way—pulled apart and sucked into the black hole of that monster's cadaverous soul.

Two security men enter, lift Raphael under his arms and drag him to the door. Travis wraps his arm around Jessie's shoulders and tenderly strokes her neck.

"Get him out of here."

They drag him to a room in the barn and toss him in. Bind him so tight, he ain't leaving except in a box. The walls are tall and windowless. One bare bulb hangs from the middle of the ceiling. There's nowhere to go and no way to get there. He can only wait for whatever fate Travis decides to bring to the door.

When Hell Freezes Over

Jessie's eyes shine. Not with love or tears but commitment. She's not thinking of Travis when she knocks on the door to his room. Doesn't see him as she takes his sweating hand and leads him to his bed, sits him on the edge and kneels in front of him. Doesn't feel him as she eases off first his cowboy boots, then his socks.

His feet stink, not of sweat but of fear. Good.

"Jessie?"

She looks up at him. Sees Raphael. "Isn't this what you want?" She massages one foot, then the other.

He sighs. His hands hover hesitantly over her head before they grab the bedspread instead. Who does he see as she unzips his pants and eases them off. Sarah? So be it.

She takes her time. Strips him naked, leans him back gently and undresses herself slowly. His cock is rock hard and twitching. For the first time, she thinks she might puke. Instead, she swallows her stomach's protest and kneels next to him. His hands clench as she takes him in her mouth.

He takes her then as she knew he would. Pulls her down and rolls himself over her. Face inches from hers.

"Do you want this?" he says urgently.

"And if I say no? Would you do it anyway?"

He draws back. "No. No, Jessie, I wouldn't."

She almost feels sorry for him in that moment. He knows what she's doing and why but can't stop himself from wanting it. Was his guilt the last link to what remained of his humanity? Would her permission assuage it?

She reaches up and touches his face. Takes his hand and puts it on her breast.

He squeezes. Can she kiss him? Can she close her eyes and pretend his clean-shaven face is rough-stubbled like Raphael's? His thin lips, thick and full?

She can.

"I want you, Travis. I do." The words come out without hesitation, though she nearly trips over his name.

He believes her because he wants to. Needs to. Must.

The hardest part is when it's over and they're lying limbs and sheets entangled, her head in the crook of his shoulder, his arm around her. She wants to ask him but knows it will defeat her purpose. Fucking him once is not enough to build his trust; she'll have to do it many times. Both her reasons are worth more than the price she will pay.

He looks down at her, eyes gentle and needy as he strokes the sweaty hair back from her face. Her smile is as fake as her orgasm.

"Do you want to see our son?" he says.

Jessie nods, not trusting herself to speak.

Travis reaches for his phone. It lays next to his gun on the nightstand.

"Raymond," he says, "bring the boy to me, please. Take all the men with you."

Jessie stiffens.

"Make sure nothing happens to him." When she stiffens again and looks up at him with pleading eyes, he adds, "or anyone else." He puts the phone down. "Don't worry, he won't hurt anyone."

He examines her face. Sees the fear in her eyes.

"It's going to be okay. It's all going to be okay; I promise." He kisses her once on the forehead, then holds her tight. Tight as the lie that binds them.

*

Jessie waits till he's asleep, snoring gently. She eases off the bed, careful not to wake him. Briefly considers slipping out the door. Reconsiders.

She's shot a gun before but never at someone. Pa always said, you aim, you best be fixing to kill. She picks up Travis' gun. It's heavy. Loaded. She takes the safety off.

Can she do it? Does she want to? Yes and yes. She's far enough away that he can't grab it if he wakes, close enough to bash his brains in the second he opens his eyes.

His eyes open.

Jessie doesn't hesitate. She smashes the gun into the side of his head. There is a sickening crunch and a howl of pain, before his eyes close again. Has she killed him? She leans over him, an executioner sharpening her axe. A trickle of blood pools at his temple, drips down the side of his face.

She should get out of there and fast, but she spots the safe in the corner of the room. There will be money in there, jewelry, more guns. All things she needs and desperately.

She tries the obvious combinations first: Sarah's birthday, his. Sarah's death day and funeral. Hope and desperation rise and fall with each attempt.

Nothing.

What else could it be? No, he wouldn't. Not even Travis is that fucked in the head. She tries it anyway—the date he raped her.

The safe opens.

There's nothing inside except an envelope. She pulls it out. Reads the enclosed paper. Freezes. Teeters between wanting to finish Travis off but slowly over a period of a week, or at the very least, blow his pecker off.

"Fuck you, Travis."

She shoves the paper in her back pocket and goes to find Raphael.

She finds the women first. They're all in one long room like a semi-private hospital ward. Or a college dorm. All heavily pregnant. Most sleeping.

"Ladies, you need to get out of here and get out of here now."

A tall, thin woman with an enormous belly rises and approaches. Looks her up and down. In the eye. There's life in this one yet. "And go where?" the woman says.

"Anywhere, just get the fuck out of here," Jessie urges but no one's moving. "Do you know what will happen to your baby? To you?"

Another woman approaches. Not as pregnant nor as thin. Beautiful. "We can't. We signed contracts. We were paid handsomely. These babies..." She touches her belly and a fond smile forms, "aren't ours."

A third waddles over. Small with milk-full tits and wearing a robe, she looks about to drop any minute. "We were promised they'd go to good homes. We've all met our adopting parents. They're good people. I'd trust my family with my life."

By then, the rest have formed a circle around Jessie. Why do they see her as threat and not savior? Fuck it. Jessie turns to leave. Pauses. She's already got enough on her conscience; she doesn't need this too. She'll make one last attempt.

"Those loving parents are mostly fronts. Your babies will be sex-trafficked, and you will be murdered. Like Emily was."

Gasps. Jessie has seen the look before. One of the stops on her road was a motel down by an evangelical mega church. They came from miles around, human locusts in their campers and mini vans. The men with their families, the godliness in their words but not their eyes. Those were trained on the motel which they'd visit after their God talk and BBQs. While their women took care of their broods, they went to spread Jesus to the whores. Once, one of the wives came looking. Opened the door as her husband eased himself into Jessie. Stood there slack-jawed, eyes wide, as he pounded away. Murder in her eyes as they met Jessie's. Then a curtain dropped. She said nothing. Did nothing. Just backed the fuck out and closed the door behind her.

They suspect, want confirmation, but once they have it, must deny what they see with their own eyes, and know in the pits of their shuttered hearts. But, just like Jessie flashes back to driving across the desert in Raphael's truck, listening to tunes and smoking while warm air blows through open windows, hair whipping, eyes stinging, and hearts singing while some woman's husband sticks his wick inside her, everyone must make compromises with their own realities.

Jessie backs towards the door. Looks over her shoulder and all around. "There's the door, ladies. You decide." Fuck em. She has to find Raphael.

The rest of the building is deserted. All the guards must have gone with Raymond. Where? Where did they go? Where is Ryan? Raphael has seen him. He'll know. Damn it, where is Raphael?

The barn. He must be in the barn.

It's across a wide courtyard, draped by branches from heavy trees, wooden walls constricted by the heat and caving in. Raphael is there, locked in a room, much as she suspected he would be. The key dangles from a hook by the door so she won't have to shoot it. What if she's too late? What if he's already dead, his clothes a puddle on the ground.

"Raphael?" she whisper-hisses against the thick-wood door.

"Jessie?"

She hears him. Barely. The key slides into the lock, and she throws open the door. He's hog-tied and bruised but not chained, head lolling on shoulder, moaning and groaning as a bruise supernovas across his temple.

"Raphael!"

More groans. Fuck, she'll never get him out of here. Jessie tries to undo the knots, but they were tied by someone who knew their way around a rodeo.

"Wake up. We're getting out of here."

His one good eye opens. "Jessie?"

"Hold tight."

Her nails splinter as she tries to get a purchase. Fails. She rummages through a nearby bench for a knife and finds a hacksaw. It will have to do. Panic and need locomote her arm back and forth, and she's through the rope in no time. Raphael crumbles into her arms.

Jessie's tall and strong from all the years at the diner and motel, not to mention those months jerking off gummy grandpas and closet cases trying to fuck themselves straight, but a slumped Raphael is too big for her to budge. Jessie chooses violence and slaps him across the face.

"Get the fuck up, Raphael, or you're gonna die."

He groans.

"Get up, or I'm going to be the one who kills you. Ryan is in danger, and we have to go save him."

Raphael raises his head. Tries to open his swollen eye. "Ryan?"

"Yes, Ryan." Jessie pulls the DNA results from Travis' safe out of her back pocket. "Our son."

Knowing the Future

Dakota knows what's coming but there's nothing she can do to stop it. She's been wrong before, well, not exactly wrong, just fuzzy on the details, but when she knows, she knows.

And she knows.

Therefore, it is no surprise when the intercom buzzes and the video display reveals Jessie and Raphael. Dakota knows Jessie will immediately storm out again once told her son is gone. Dakota will have just one moment to intercept her before she flies back down the stairs screaming Ryan's name as she races out into the night and deep into the desert to find him. And in that moment, Dakota takes Jessie into her arms and whispers in her ear.

"Believe, my darling. When all else fails, believe."

Dakota knows she can't stop him following, but she grabs Raphael by the forearm.

"Wait."

Hyun-Ki keeps a gun to scare off coyotes when he goes out at night. Dakota holds it out to Raphael, but before he can take it, a figure fills the open doorway. A figure of shadows.

There are no polite introductions, no idle chit chat. Without hesitation, Dakota shoots the shadow man three times: in the chest, the leg, and the head. Raymond goes down, gaping holes in his forehead and chest, perforated femoral artery pumping blood to the floor. He shouldn't get up again, but Dakota knows he will. Any of the three shots should have killed him, none of them do.

Lines of tattoos which curl around his fingers and snake up his sleeve, crawl to his wounds in an inky smoke.

Move, woman, move. Get everyone out while you still can. But Dakota's legs are rooted like cacti in a hundred year drought, grown down, down, down searching for water and finally finding some a hundred feet below. Nothing or nobody is going to uproot them.

Raymond shakes his head, pushes himself to his feet and cracks his neck. He scans the room. Advances on Dakota and Raphael.

"Where is the boy?"

"Carl, no!" Dakota screams.

Carl emerges from the stairwell and enters the room. He clenches a tire iron in one fist and swings it at the back of Raymond's head.

Raymond easily intercepts the blow. He grasps Carl's wrist and snaps it backwards with a sickening crack. Holds him upright by the scruff of his neck as he pulls a gold chain from his pocket and snaps it around Carl's neck.

Carl's eyes go wide, then wild. Dakota shoots him again and again, but Raymond does not go down, only grows bigger and stronger as Carl withers to a husk. It is over quickly but seems forever. The light in his eyes is the last thing to leave as Carl meets Dakota's horrified gaze. Raymond removes the chain and tosses Carl's deflated carcass to the floor, looks at Dakota and her empty gun.

The gunshots bring Alice and Michael running from rooms on opposite sides of the large open plan living area with Hyun-Ki trailing behind. Michael reaches Alice before Raymond does. Steps in front of her and roars, "Run. All of you, run!"

Nobody moves except Raymond who grabs him by the neck with one hand while holding the gold chain in the other. Michael tries to fight him off—kicks, punches, thrashes, even tries to bite the hand that holds him fast—but it's impossible to fight the strength of dozens in one man.

"Stop trying to resist," Raymond says. "You knew this time would come. I will take back my life as well as yours. Then the life of your woman and everyone you know and love."

Michael pries at the vice-like fingers around his neck. Anything. Anything but being harvested by this demon. It's no use. "I love you, Alice. Run!" he says, as the chain swoops down.

Raymond stops. Considers the squirming Michael in his grasp. "No, not here. I will make you watch as I suck the life from your brothers, sisters, parents. You."

He reaches for his transporter.

"Motherfucker!"

Alice screams and jumps on Raymond's back. She wraps her legs around his waist and grabs his head. Rakes her nails across his eyes and gouges one out. Goes for the other.

He roars and releases both Michael and the gold chain which skitters across the floor. Teeters backwards as he attempts to shake her off, but Alice clings to him.

"Alice!"

Michael picks up the chain. Would he? To save Alice, yes. Raymond eyeballs the chain and for the first time there is fear in his eyes. In the two steps it takes Michael to reach them, he has flipped Alice over his shoulder and placed his hands on either side of her head. One twist… and her neck will be snapped.

Michael freezes. "Alice…" His voice is barely a whisper.

Raymond straightens, breathing hard. The gouged eye dangles from an empty socket which boils with smoke. In slow motion, it retracts. Raymond blinks and looks at Michael with both eyes. There is malevolence in them and a smile on his lips. "Which is worse? To lose all hope?" His hands tighten on Alice's head, and her eyes begin to bulge. "Or to have fruitless hope forever?"

He drags Alice to her feet. "You will never find her."

Raymond activates his transporter and in a flash of light, they are gone.

Eternity

They tumble. Twist and spin, then spin some more. Through worlds and times and dimensions, bathed in brilliant strobing light. It would be beautiful if Alice wasn't intent on clinging for dear life to this monster, while simultaneously trying to kill him.

93-681-27. If only she can get the transporter from his wrist she can escape to Michael's world. Hopeless, when all she can do is hurtle through space and time. Her breath is ragged, her throat constricted. She should be dead but isn't. Finally, she manages to get him face-to-face, noses slipping off each other, her legs wrapped once again around his waist.

"Die, you bastard," she hisses in his ear before biting down and ripping half of it off with her teeth.

He laughs. "You cannot kill me," he says, "only die."

She bites off half of his other ear.

He reaches his transporter before she can do anything to prevent him. They stop spinning and land with a thud.

Thrown free on landing, Alice tries to scramble to her feet and falls flat on her face. The world they have landed on is a desert but not like home. Sand. There is only sand and dunes of sand as far as the eye can see. Above, there are two suns. Sweat pours out of her and within seconds, she's bone dry. She won't last long here wherever here is. So, it's with some relief when Raymond's shadow looms over her. She looks up. There has never been hate in her heart but there is now, and she's taken aback by the feral fearsomeness of it. It masks her despair at seeing him healed. All her efforts were wasted.

"Fucking kill me, already," she says through sand-gritted teeth, eyes still darting in every direction, searching for a rock to bash his brains in. Something. Anything. But there's nothing, only sand. Burning hot sand.

Raymond smiles. "I don't think so."

He holds her by the neck and stares into her eyes. His are black glaze over a molten core. Alice is afraid then, afraid of being sucked into that inferno. But he has no gold chain, only intent in his eyes.

"No!" Alice screams as she feels the same tingling sensation as when Michael healed her legs. "No, don't."

"Ah, but I will," Raymond's face is inches from her own, his eyes so close she can't see them anymore, only feel their darkness boring into her, pouring into her veins. Finally, he releases her, and she falls back into the sand. The skin on her arms prickles as new tattoos form. Spread.

"That will keep you alive until I return. And now that you have enough of my reserves, I will be able to find you, no matter where or when you are."

"Fuck you." Alice gathers herself up. She's strong now. Maybe as strong as he is. She rises. Launches herself at him.

But with one quick twist of his transporter, Raymond is gone.

"Fuck!!!"

She wanders. Wanders and wanders. Time passes slowly in this world. The suns never seem to budge from their position of roasting everything alive. Spasms of cell death and regeneration wrack her body as she trudges through the dunes. Sun and light and heat and dust. She can't escape even when she closes her eyes. There's got to be someone, something, someplace, somewhere on this piece of shit world.

Finally, a specter of shade. A hollow in the middle of a dune. A cave. What could be waiting? Does she really give a shit? Whatever it is, maybe it will kill her and quick. Alice runs the last few feet, trips over a rock at the entrance and goes flying into beautiful, cool darkness.

It isn't long before there's movement from the back. A frantic scurrying as something makes its way towards her. Good. Fucking finish the job already. She won't be used as a pawn against Michael or anyone else she loves.

Love. I love him. Damn it, I do.

The figure reaches her, crouches and brushes back the hair from her face. "Aunt Alice?"

"Ryan?"

Before the End but Only Just

"I can find her." Michael fiddles with his ivory bracelet and vanishes.

"Well?" Dakota says to a stunned Raphael. "Get a move on."

He doesn't need to be told twice.

"Find Jessie, find the phone booth."

"The phone booth?"

"You need to believe now, Raphael. Find it quick before the moon is high overhead."

He stops at the door. "Why? What's going to happen?

"Mind me now… and hurry."

Dakota and Hyun-Ki are left to stare at the pile of Carl's clothes.

"He was a good man," Dakota says after some few minutes. Not prone to tears, she can't stop the ones that fall.

"Well, well, well. Looks like I missed the party."

Travis enters the room. He's followed by a half-a-dozen, black-suited security guards, Joshua Thomas, and two other officers of the law.

"Looks like you didn't miss the truck that hit you," Dakota says.

Travis smiles. "That hurts my feelings, Dakota. Especially since I was assaulted by your niece and her partner." He steps aside and the officers move in. "The law is here to take them into custody."

"Are they now? From what I hear, my niece was imprisoned up there at the ranch along with a good few women whose babies you sell to bad men who do heinous things, and Raphael went to liberate her."

Dakota approaches Travis and raises her hand as the men raise their guns. She points a finger in his face. "I once thought there was hope for you. Every time you did something more despicable than the time before, I still hoped one day you'd turn yourself around."

Travis blinks. For a second there's a specter of something gray as regret. Then it's gone.

"Where are they?"

"Where's who?"

Travis smirks. Signals to the guards and the law, and they spread out. Dakota doesn't protest. Neither does Hyun-Ki. Far as they're concerned, they can take as much time as they want to search, it will only give Jessie and Raphael more time to get away.

They trash the place, wrecking as much as they can while searching for people long gone. Hyun-Ki grimaces when his telescope case is opened and the contents dumped, lenses skittering across the tile floor, but he keeps his mouth shut. After about ten minutes, they give up.

"Be seeing you, Dakota," Travis says.

"Oh, I very much doubt that."

She sees it one last time before he vanishes through the door. Regret. She thinks to encourage it, draw it out. Doesn't. What will be will be.

She picks up two long and narrow wooden sticks from the carnage on the floor. "It's time," she says to Hyun-Ki, once they're gone.

He nods and leads her to the balcony.

Forever and Always

Michael senses Alice's trail but it's obscured by shadow. It doesn't make sense; what has happened? He whizzes through worlds and dimensions. It could go on forever and ever and ever, but Alice might not have forever or even much time at all.

He returns home to ask his father for advice and that's where he finds him, sitting comfortably on their long sofa, arms across the back, mother on one side of him, father on the other. No sign of his siblings. Or Alice.

"Took you long enough," Raymond says.

"Get out of here, son," his father shouts and is rewarded with a punch in the face.

Michael bristles but remains still. "Leave them alone, they have nothing to do with this."

Raymond throws his head back and laughs. Loudly. Wildly. Entire tattooed chest rippling and convulsing with an absurd transgression of amusement.

"They have everything to do with it." Raymond moves his hands to each of Michael's parents' necks. His mother's shoulders are straight. Her head high. Father's eyes dart for something, anything to use in defense. Spies the trophy Michael won in school for his paper on geo-plotting. Looks up at Michael, over to his wife.

"She doesn't have much time, you know," Raymond says. "Who will you try to save? Your loving parents or your lover? You'll fail twice, but it will be amusing to watch you try."

At that, his father lunges for the trophy and smashes it down on Raymond's knee. Michael leaps, shouting at his parents to get clear. He lands hard, battering Raymond in the crotch. Michael straddles him as he crumbles in pain, puts him in a stranglehold, presses his transporter, and they're gone.

They spin through darkness and strobing light. It's nearly impossible for Michael to hold him, shadow-slippery and determined as he is to get away, but if he doesn't, he will lose everyone dear to him. Raymond will gather them all and make Michael watch the slaughter. He knows this now, and this knowledge is enough. If Alice can be brave and ruthless, so can he. He buries his face in Raymond's neck and bites as hard as he can, ripping his carotid artery.

Blood splashes across his face and into deep space. Before Raymond can heal, Michael uses his reserves to heal both ends of the severed artery so they cannot be reconnected.

"Heal that, asshole," he says as he pulls the transporter from Raymond's wrist and instantly teleports away.

*

Michael. Help us. Michael, please.

He can hear her now. The shadow has dissipated, and he can once again pinpoint himself within her. She is in the last place he ever would have looked, deep in the desert of his own world. He lands at the cave entrance, and she runs out into his arms.

"I knew you would come."

Michael takes Raymond's portable harvester from his pocket and throws it as far as he can into the sand before teleporting them all away.

His parents are waiting when he returns with them. They coo and coddle Ryan, feed him cold dirun and hot pame. His mother leads Alice away, draws her a bath and leaves her to soak. When Alice finally emerges in a pair of his mother's trousers and a button-down sweater, an exhausted Ryan is curled up on the sofa, although he is not asleep.

"My mom." He sits up and crosses his legs. "She's not here. She hasn't come. I need to go back."

Alice scoops Ryan into her arms and kisses the top of his head. She meets Michael's eyes, but any answer he has is not one they'll want to hear.

"I can't find our way back to your world because Alice is no longer there. She was my only anchor point."

Tears pool in Ryan's eyes at this news.

"But…" Michael continues before the tears can spill, "the telephone booth is a transporter, and they know the coordinates to get here. If they can find it, they will come."

Ryan leans forward. "I told mom. She knows."

Alice kisses his head again and holds his hand tight. He has a scar now upon his finger in the shape of a crescent moon. Same as hers. Same as the others. She lays him back on the sofa. "She'll come," she says.

"Promise?"

"I promise. Now time for sleep."

Hope a much stronger sedative than anxiety and despair, Ryan is soon asleep, and in his sleep, his lips mutter and eyes dart in dream. Sleep, however, is the furthest thing from Michael's mind and judging by the questions in Alice's eyes, she feels the same. He puts one of his winter coats over her shoulders and leads her to the garden.

Alice tilts her head back, eyes wide at the strange sky. After some long minutes, she says, "It's really real, isn't it?" and shivers.

He wants to put an arm around her. Hold her close and never let her go.

"I'm sorry," they both say at the same time, turning to each other as the world turns towards daylight.

She reaches up, cups the side of his face with a cold hand. He takes it in his to warm it.

"Do you forgive me for bringing you here? I might not ever be able to return you to your world. I don't know if this world is any better, but I don't want to live in any world without you."

She says nothing and just when he thinks she might not answer at all, Alice nods once as if to herself, and says…

Last Chance

Jessie runs. She neither knows where she's going or where she's been, only that she must find her son. Screams of his name have become hoarse croaks, then pained silence and internal pleading with whatever god is padding across the desert floor or flying through the sky. Please, let me find my son, I beg you. Please let me find him alive and well.

Jessie knows about giving up and letting capitulation umbrella her against hope. Not this time. This time, she will not admit defeat. This time, she won't run away but will protect her son. She summons bile-tainted saliva into her mouth, throws her head back and screams one last time.

"Ryan, where are you?"

And in the night, a light blinks on and a phone begins to ring.

Jessie runs.

She has seen the phone booth only once before, but from a distance. It's old and old-fashioned. Some of the lettering is sand-blasted clear. The light bulb is bare and fizzling. She throws herself inside and picks up the ringing phone.

"Hello?"

"Mom? Mom, is it you?"

"Ryan!" His name comes out in grateful prayer. Thank you, gods of the desert, the sky, the stars. "Where are you? Are you okay?"

"Mom. Yes, it's me. I'm okay. I don't know. I'm in a phone booth in the middle of the desert. Where are you?" His voice comes in and out as he speaks as if travelling a great distance over disconnected phone lines.

A phone booth in the middle of the desert? It can't be. Jessie looks around but she's completely alone.

"Baby, hang up the phone and go to Aunt Dakota. I'll come get you. I love you."

"Mom… listen. Go with Raphael." Raphael? "Find phone booth… call this number, 93-681-27… find me… Mom… hear me… 93-681-27…" His voice becomes more warble than speech. Static crackles the line, and it goes dead.

"Ryan?" Silence but she can't hang up. Jessie depresses the receiver again and again. "Ryan!"

Did she hear him right? 93-681-27. Hard to tell through the static. Jessie's heart races and sweat blossoms from every pore. Light catches the corner or her eye. Gunfire. The hum of drones overhead catches her ear. A figure runs towards her.

Raphael…

"Call this number..."

Jessie puts the phone down.

When Your Time Comes

Travis hears it before he sees it. A roaring in his ears like the roaring of his brain and the beating of his heart. Fucking Dakota. Fucking Dakota drawing water from a stone. Not a drop but a deluge. Fine spray falls like rain, foreshadowing the torrent about to descend on him and his men, and as the flood reaches them, he thinks not of what is, but what could have been. Sees Sarah's smiling face in the dusty, moon-glowed foam, and opens his arms to receive her.

3.14159 26535 89793 23846 26433 83279 50288 41971 69399 37510 58209 74944 59230 78164 06286 20899 86280 34825 34211 7067…seconds before the end

I love you.
Oh, how I love you.

A Beginning

Dakota and Hyun-Ki stand on the observation deck. The water won't last long. Already the lungs of the desert are breathing it in like amniotic fluid. It will be gone by morning. There will be new life or old life returned to life. For a week or so. Then sage and cacti and dust. Again. For resurrection is fleeting, and the desert always returns to its inherent form.

"They're okay," Dakota says without prompt or premonition, only knowledge.

Hyun-Ki stares over the water as the sun breaches the horizon. Stares and wonders what died in the deluge, for all that now springs to life.

"I wouldn't have minded exploring the universe," he says with a sigh for there is nothing more soul-crushing than a missed opportunity to experience the impossible.

Dakota wipes her wet hands down the front of her pants and roots around in her deep pockets.

"Then I guess it's a good thing Michael gave me one of these."

To the ordinary eye, the wristband she holds out could be mistaken for a watch or an ivory bracelet or anything other than what it is: a transporter.

"How?" he says.

"I don't know much about physics. Less about quantum mechanics and almost nothing about time and space, but Michael went forward before he came back and left it."

"When?"

"Only this morning. Not too soon but not too late."

"Except for Carl."

"Carl Tucker Mason was the only one I told."

The transporter is light but grows heavy in Dakota's hand. She slides it onto Hyun-Ki's wrist and takes his hand.

"Everyone else is safe, and we're welcome to visit any time. We have the code to their world and can explore infinite others."

She looks up, and they stare into each other's universes.

"Are you ready?" she says.

He kisses her gently and squeezes her hand. "I've been ready my whole life."

Acknowledgments

Publication of my debut novel has been a journey, and I'm grateful to many people and organizations for helping me along the way.

I would like to thank Jennifer McMahon for her support, editorial feedback and encouragement. Her steadfast belief in this novel meant the world to me.

Many thanks to Ashling Dennehy and Davena O'Neill for listening to my feverish plotting and character development ideas and for always being in my corner. Additional thanks to Ashling for her brilliant work on the cover design.

And to the coolest publisher there is, Adam Van Winkle and Cowboy Jamboree Press, thanks for believing in me and this book and helping make my dream come true. You are the best.

A very special thank you to the enormously talented photographer, Keith Bernstein for use of the cover image. Nothing could be more perfect.

Thanks to my fellow writers and friends in my writing group, Thursday Night Writers Tralee: Rich Anthony, Eadbhard McGowan, Gordon Pinckheard, Deirdre Sheehan, and Anna Zacharias for all their feedback and support over the years, including on this book.

Thanks also to those who very generously read In the Desert and wrote brilliant blurbs: Melissa Flores Anderson, Stephanie Austin, Andrew K. Clark, Jonathan Danielson, Claire Hennessey, Rónán Hession, Sabrina Hicks, Charleen Hurtubise, Jennifer McMahon, Noel O'Regan, and Casey Stegman.

Many thanks to everyone who has supported me on my writing journey through the years, including the Irish Arts Council, the Irish Writers Centre, and Kerry County Arts. Also, Noelle Campbell-Sharpe and Mary O'Connor for many amazing sojourns at Cill Rialaig, June Caldwell and Susan Tomaselli, and all my friends and family. Thanks also to my High School Honors English teacher, Mrs. Reshenk who drilled writing mechanics into me; your lessons have endured all these years.

Thanks to my colleagues at Kerry County Council who gave encouragement and guarded my peace in the cafeteria during break times while I furiously scrawled in my notebooks and edited nine drafts.

Thanks also to my parents and siblings for always believing this day would come.

As much as they drove me mad for petting and walks, thanks to my dogs, Dusty and Eddie and rabbit, Lexi for keeping me company on the long nights spent writing and editing and not grumbling too much when I said, "in a minute!"

And to Alvin Case who rang me out of the blue one bright and sunny day and took me on the road trip of a lifetime. Without that trip, this book might not have ever existed.

Finally, but most of all, I'd like to thank my beloved sons, Ronan and Liam, for their patience, support and love. Everything is always for you. And remember, anything is possible if you believe!

About the Author

Barbara Byar is a working-class American writer living in Ireland for over 25 years. Her critically acclaimed, collection of stories: *Some Days Are Better Than Ours* (Reflex Press) was short-listed for the Saboteur Awards. Her short fiction has been published and prize-listed widely. She was shortlisted for the Irish Book Awards Irish Short Story of the Year in 2023 and longlisted in 2021. A recipient of an Irish Arts Council Literature Bursary and an Agility Award, she is editor of *MOTEL* (Cowboy Jamboree Press). *In the Desert* is her debut novel.

Find her at:
barbarabyar.wordpress.com or substack.com/@barbarabyar

Printed in Dunstable, United Kingdom

80355189R00163